Praise for An Act of Treachery

'She writes powerfully about complex moral difficulties'
The Times

'With this book Widdecombe enters the select ranks of those whose second novel is as polished as their first. A tale of illicit love, hate, and loss in Occupied France . . . this book is both a morality tale and a romance, confirming the MP for Maidstone and The Weald as an eloquent story-teller'   *Glasgow Herald*

'An ambitious novel . . . stuffed full of interesting moral themes'   Caroline Moore, *Sunday Telegraph*

'A gripping read'   *Sunday Express*

'The novel is very well structured . . . Catherine is an interesting creation . . . Widdecombe is to be applauded for the range of her ambition within this book: the admirably large cast of characters is well handled; their dilemmas are believable and the narrative makes for compulsive reading. What is more, *An Act of Treachery* seems fuelled by a genuine passion for an understanding across nations and borders'
Bel Mooney, *The Times* Play

'Widdecombe's point is a powerful one: that everyone is compromised in war and that only love commands real loyalty'
Wendy Holden, *Daily Mail*

'An intriguing story, which seems destined to end in disaster until the unexpected twist in the final pages'
Good Housekeeping

Ann Widdecombe is best known as a Member of Parliament and for her broadcasting and journalism, but has long had ambitions to write novels. She was born in 1947 and grew up moving around the country and abroad with her parents, as her father served in the Admiralty. She was educated at the Universities of Birmingham and Oxford and now lives in south London. She is the author of three other novels, *The Clematis Tree*, *Father Figure* and *An Act of Peace*. She writes her novels on long train journeys and in Singapore, where she visits her Chinese nanny.

By Ann Widdecombe

The Clematis Tree
An Act of Treachery
Father Figure
An Act of Peace

An Act of Treachery

ANN WIDDECOMBE

PHOENIX

A PHOENIX PAPERBACK

First published in Great Britain in 2002
by Weidenfeld & Nicolson
This paperback edition published in 2014
by Phoenix,
an imprint of Orion Books Ltd,
Orion House, 5 Upper St Martin's Lane,
London WC2H 9EA

An Hachette UK company

1 3 5 7 9 10 8 6 4 2

A CIP catalogue record for this book
is available from the British Library.
ISBN 978-1-7802-2682-8

Printed and bound in Great Britain by
Clays Ltd, St Ives plc

The Orion Publishing Group's policy is to use papers that
are natural, renewable and recyclable products and
made from wood grown in sustainable forests. The logging
and manufacturing processes are expected to conform to
the environmental regulations of the country of origin.

www.orionbooks.co.uk

For my Godchildren,
Clemmie, Jack and Billy
in the hope that they grow up
in a more peaceful world

Acknowledgements

I was born in 1947 in England whereas the events in this book take place principally between 1940 and 1944 in wartime France. I have therefore had to rely on the expertise of others. I am grateful to Mrs Colette Farrell, Mrs Jeanne Hunt and Mrs Françoise Bratt for sharing with me their memories of life as teenagers in occupied France and for reading the final manuscript. Ian Ousby's Occupation: The Ordeal of France 1940–1944 was an invaluable companion, and Hervé Le Boterf's La Vie Parisienne Sous L'Occupation tested my schoolgirl French, but was again a useful source of reference.

I am much indebted to Julian Lewis, Keith Simpson, Julian Brazier and Martin Windrow for their advice on military matters. I must also thank the German experts at the City of London Freemen's School.

I am particularly grateful to Mark Coote who painstakingly assisted in the research and the interviewing and then, well beyond the call of duty, sorted out my rebellious computer!

However, this is a work of fiction and any errors of fact or any anachronisms are my own.

Ann Widdecombe
February 2002

Berlin 1961

All day we have watched them building that great, cold, cruel wall; stone by stone, coil of barbed wire by coil of barbed wire and as it has grown, so has our despair. We menace them with our hatred, our eyes boring into their distant forms, but, inexorably, they build, build, build a wall not to keep their enemies out but to keep their own citizens in, a wall to imprison free men and women.

Kurt got out in the last wave of refugees, carried in a blanket by two young women, strangers whom he had not seen before nor since, who took pity on him as he crawled on his hands and the half of the one leg the war had left him. When we can leave Berlin he will come to stay with us for a while until he has traced his sister who preceded him to the West.

We are sitting in a small, overcrowded, dingy café, drinking ghastly coffee and watching, mesmerised, although there is a chill now in the air and soon it will be too uncomfortable to stay. We are hungry but somehow it seems indecent to eat, callous to go, an act of desertion to turn our backs on that determined, deadly activity.

Germany now appears completely divided, families cut off from each other. For how long? For ever? Will the West act? America, Britain? When I suggest it, Kurt mentions Poland and Hungary and predicts that the West will express outrage but do nothing. Unhappy, morose, helpless, he orders more coffee which none of us will enjoy and none wants.

The sound of a brief protest reaches us, a minor disturbance, ineffectual, angry, token, heartfelt. Willi stands up and stretches, reluctant to stay and reluctant to go. He takes the handles of Kurt's ramshackle wheelchair, which he bullied, bribed and cajoled to obtain and I stand too, gathering up my handbag and blue lace gloves which Mutti gave me for Lotte's wedding.

As we prepare to leave the café I look back, not at the table we have left nor the wall they are building, nor the small knots of angry, weeping people but at the two girls.

They too have been watching all day, from a room on the second floor of a house near the café. Sometimes they have looked out together, leaning over the window ledge for a better view, a more certain angle, and sometimes one has looked and described the scene to the other. They must be about thirteen and fifteen and as they have watched the building of the wall and the goings-on in the streets so I have watched them.

One has long fair hair and the other a modish permanent wave and I know exactly the mixture of fear, excitement and wonder they feel. I know that one moment they are filled with dread and the next with the excitement of witnessing a major event in history, that they are fascinated as well as repelled, that they want to play a role in the drama unfolding before them even as they yearn for the stability and security of a childhood in which the grown-ups were always in control, capable of meeting any challenge. I know that they want to crush the oppressor and receive the thanks of grateful compatriots, that they imagine themselves heroines of a resistance movement.

They hate the oppressor; want to shoot him, humiliate him, hear him beg for mercy, see him wet himself. And they are fascinated by him, want to know him, like him, love him, share victory with him.

I know because, twenty-one years ago, I too was fifteen, with long fair hair, and I leaned out of a window with my sister and watched a conquering army from another Germany in another age, as the Nazis marched into Paris.

one

A Cry in the Dark

They had entered Paris, arrogant, triumphant, condescending, the previous Friday, but we had as yet seen no Germans though we spent hardly a minute away from the window. Our parents had confined us to the house and I was growing every minute less afraid and more resentful, for I should have been roller-skating with Bette by the Eiffel Tower and looking forward to a visit to the cinema, not sitting here with my elder sister, Annette, watching an empty street.

I was going through one of those awkward phases in which I both drew closer to my siblings and quarrelled with them more and especially with Annette who thought her seventeen years gave her the right to patronise me although, at fifteen, I was now an inch taller than she was and still growing.

Martin was twenty and had already gone off to join the then embryonic Free French in England. We had argued furiously one day over my friendship with Bette and when I had cooled down and was seeking him out to make peace, my father told me he had gone to fight and I was wretched with a guilt which still occasionally nagged in spite of the happy letters I had since received.

Annette was the next eldest. She was formidably bright and destined for the Sorbonne but I did not resent that because I was academically idle and happy to be so – to the despair of my father – and, more importantly, I knew myself to be beautiful, with the longest, thickest, fairest hair in all Paris. It was therefore frustrating that I had not the faintest idea how to capitalise on my

3

looks as I was painfully shy. I spent hours in front of my mirror imagining myself to be Viviane Romance but I was certain that other girls knew more about being women than I did and the thought took away my confidence.

My younger sister, Jeanne, was eleven and my baby brother Edouard was just walking. A few months before I had overheard a conversation between my grandparents in which Edouard was described as a mistake. These days I thought I knew what that meant and felt rather grown up in the knowledge.

My grandparents lived with us and occupied the top floor of our house near the Avenue Charles Floquet. I adored my grandfather and confided in him but Grand-mère was strict and scornful of my laziness at school. I visited upstairs only when certain that my grandmother was helping out in the kitchen below me.

My father, Pierre Dessin, was a professor of English at the Sorbonne and found my poor marks embarrassing, but he tried hard not to favour Annette. In this he was assisted by his unfeigned admiration of my long yellow hair which was a genetic freak in a family of dark-haired, sallow-faced, not particularly well-favoured beings. My grandmother remembered an aunt with identical hair and peaches and cream skin. Nevertheless my father was demanding and persistent in his quest for high standards, often subduing our spirits just by being there when we wanted to be frivolous or silly. He was rarely aggressive but I was vastly more relaxed with my grandfather.

The nuns who taught me in the Convent School in the Rue de Varenne were much less impressed by my looks than they were despairing of my attitude to work, frequently making unfavour-able comparisons between Annette's prowess and my own. I was separated from Bette in class because we would both giggle helplessly when obliged to practise English phonetics in front of hand-held mirrors to ensure our lips were forming the words correctly. I hated English, with its impossibly inconsistent spelling and the grammar I could never master despite everyone's insistence that it was simple compared to our own language. Even my father's persistent coaching could not save me from ignominy.

Martin had tried to interest me in maths but I was a dunce with algebra and could not follow a geometrical proof to save my life. He had given up in despair.

I had little concentration, being easily distracted in lessons, dreaming through Mass on Sundays, wearied and inefficient during chores at home. I did not want to remain much longer at school but the only attraction of getting a job was the prospect of some money.

Suddenly I was concentrating fiercely, for Germans had entered the street. Annette abused them profanely, but softly because she was frightened. I looked at them in disappointment, having vaguely expected the sort of strutting formations which now paraded daily down the Champs-Elysées, not a handful of six or so soldiers looking curiously about them in relaxed fashion. I wondered where the Germans would stay and suffered a frisson of excitement and unease at the thought that one might be billeted with us.

Annette, having discharged her patriotic duty by cursing the oppressors of France, began to assess those now before her with the critical eye of a seventeen-year-old. She decided that a tall, stentorian-voiced man of about thirty was too arrogant but that a younger, stouter one was too feeble. I picked out a laughing, fair-haired youth who looked scarcely out of school and Annette was predictably scornful. Boys might be all right for me, she declared, but she preferred men.

We both moved sharply away from the window as the object of her scorn saw us and waved. A few moments later Annette cautiously peered round the curtain again only to find him still watching and laughing. Quickly she moved back. The same sequence followed several times before I realised that she and he were playing a game.

'Annette,' I whispered, shocked, 'you are flirting with the enemy.'

'Nonsense,' retorted my sister furiously, 'I was playing infantile games with a kid who probably misses his mother.'

Sulkily she moved away from the window and I was faintly conscious that I had destroyed her fun by moralising at the wrong moment. I had been going to tease her about Emile, our nineteen-year-old second cousin, the object of her latest crush, and ask her what he would have thought but now I desisted. Annette had a fearsome temper and I avoided provoking her whenever I was perceptive enough to read the signs of an impending storm because she could be both cruel and spiteful and I still cried rather too easily. It was a habit which exasperated my parents, who made unflattering comparisons with Edouard. Frequently after such quarrels I found consolation in admiring the reflection of my wonderful hair, tossing my head, glorying in the movement of my thick mane.

Still irritated, Annette began to berate me about my friendship with Bette. I had heard it all before from her, from Martin, from other girls in my class. Bette had what they called 'a reputation'. She behaved inappropriately for a young lady of her age. Well-brought-up girls did not act like that. Because her unusual name sounded like the French for beast, *bête*, the most common adjective applied to her by the disapproving was 'wild.' Oddly she seemed to like this, apparently feeling flattered by it.

I heard Annette in silence, not feeling compelled to defend Bette, who never bothered to defend herself and who shrugged off the censure of others as at best amusing and at worst irrelevant. I would have given much for just a fraction of her insouciance and mammoth self-confidence.

Eventually Annette wearied of her tirade and turned back to the window. 'They've gone,' she said and I was not sure if she were relieved or disappointed.

'We'll be able to go back to school soon.'

'Yes.'

She did not sound enthusiastic and I looked at her in surprise.

'I wonder what it will be like?' she mused and I knew she was not talking about school but about life under the Germans.

A few minutes later my sister Jeanne came to find us. Usually she came to show off about her schoolwork, which was brilliant but, when she wanted praise, she invariably pretended to need help instead and just as invariably she sought it from Annette rather than from me, producing some horribly difficult algebra or translation so that Annette would marvel at how she was doing such complicated work at so young an age. My elder sister always obliged.

My comfort lay in knowing that Edouard loved me enormously and that he would always come to me before any of the others, toddling precariously, steadying his balance by clutching my skirt, looking up trustingly as he tried to communicate. I hoped he would grow up to be less clever than the others – or at least less enthusiastic about being clever – and I knew I should be ashamed of the hope for he was a boy and I had been taught that it was important for boys to be clever and grow up to be successful and keep their families well.

Today, however, Jeanne was unaccompanied by any tedious textbook. She too was preoccupied with the conqueror and for a while the three of us stared out of the window, hoping for another glimpse of enemy activity, but we watched in vain. Wherever else the Germans had business that day it was not in the vicinity of the Avenue Charles Floquet. In the evening some of my mother's relatives came to visit, among them our two second cousins Emile and Robert.

Rumour was rife and contradictory. The Germans were oppressive: we would live under a regime of curfews, starvation rations, hostage taking and torture. We might be shot if we forgot to acknowledge an officer, all the remaining men would be rounded up and sent to some unspecified destination and no woman would be safe from the appetites of the conqueror's rank and file.

The Germans were very correct and courteous. They wished to woo not oppress. They wanted us to believe that life under them would be better than life before they had come. We would be able to go about our daily lives unmolested and the officers would shoot their own soldiers if they stepped out of line.

Nobody in our small family gathering was prepared to accept either version unconditionally. 'We shall just have to wait and see,' observed my mother, predictably but accurately, and no one contradicted her.

My father raged against our native leaders rather than against the enemy. Gamelin or Weygand, Daladier or Reynaud, they were all as bad as each other, generals and politicians alike. They had no will but Hitler had and that was why he was successful. My father retained this view throughout the war, being one of a minority who did not condemn Britain for shelling the French navy at Mers-el-Kebir and he never mentioned Pétain's name without a snort of derision.

Pierre Dessin was clear-headed and far-sighted. That was why we had not joined the Exodus, when so many had fled Paris to escape the German invasion – the population of the city had fallen below a million – thus keeping our family and home intact. Often I would read the adverts for lost children in the coming months and think how it could have been Edouard or Jeanne. Early in the war, when food was less scarce, we had stocked our house with sugar, flour, yeast, dried fruits and even obtained a hen which Jeanne christened Catherine, presumably to annoy me. I thought the name suited her and soon we all called the creature Catherine the Second.

We had what for Paris was a comparative rarity, a small back garden which we dug over to grow vegetables. Long after others had begun to feel the severity of shortages we had the means of producing eggs, bread and greens. Of course we suffered too in the end but it took longer and we stayed healthier than many.

An unfortunate consequence of my father's tendency to be right was that he had scant time for any opposition to his wishes and my mother had long ago given up any attempt to impose her own will, almost invariably falling in with him. He loved his family enormously and would have given his very life for any of us but it was, I later realised, the love of a benevolent despot.

So we listened to my father's views with respect but when my grandparents began recalling the previous war the young people moved to the dining room where my cousins pushed the table against a wall and Annette and I rolled up the carpet. Soon we were dancing to music emanating from my absent brother's gramophone. As Annette danced with Emile I had to make do with Robert who smelled of strong and unnecessary aftershave and paid me stilted compliments on my tumbling yellow hair.

We danced decorously and formally. I had a feeling that Bette might have behaved very differently had she been there. I wondered why Bette always seemed to find it necessary to draw so close to her dancing partners, to retain her hold on the hand of whatever boy helped her up when she fell while skating, to smile at perfect strangers when good-looking men passed us in the street. Tonight I was faintly perturbed by a vague but insistent notion that, had they been alone, Annette might have behaved towards Emile as Bette did towards so many. I at once deplored such conduct and wanted to copy it, to understand it, to search for its undefined, elusive magic.

'I'm in love,' Annette whispered to me when we had put out the bedroom light.

I sat up and peered through the darkness in the direction of her bed.

'With Emile?'

'Isn't he wonderful?'

As there was no way of answering that truthfully at such a moment, I remarked that she would keep the same name if she married our cousin.

Annette snorted in disbelief. 'I'm not talking about marriage. I am talking about being in love, wildly, beautifully, madly, hopelessly in love. Emile, my darling Emile.'

Long after she slept, I lay awake puzzling. What would life be like now the Germans had come? Would we have to learn German at school? Could I persuade my father that it might be better for me not to attempt baccalauréat at all than to fail humiliatingly and could I face a job day after day without the prospect of school holidays?

Above all, did not love and marriage always go together? What was Annette talking about?

Just as I began to doze a scream sounded in the night air, faint but still unmistakably a scream, a woman's scream, a sound of terror as she faced some hazard in the darkness while I lay warm and safe. It did not recur but I had never before heard a cry of fear in our road where by day children pedalled on tricycles and called to each other as they played. At dusk the lights went on in the houses where mothers prepared to welcome home the older children from school and the men from their work.

With no reason for such certainty I was sure the Germans were responsible for that scream, that whoever cried out was not being robbed or subjected to something which I always vaguely described as worse by a Frenchman. The Germans had come, they had been in our road that day and now someone screamed. The word *Juden* floated into my mind and I cowered under the bedclothes, wondering if I should wake my father, taking refuge in the absence of further cries as my reason not to do so, guilty at my inaction, grateful for my own cosy safety, worried that new dangers stalked my life, envious of my sister's sleeping calm.

In the morning no one else could remember hearing any scream, although Jeanne rebuked me for not calling the police. I thought her indignation more likely to stem from pique at having been deprived of a drama than from concern for the unknown woman.

To my disappointment I found that life had quite suddenly returned to normal and that we were to go back to school. My only consolation was the prospect of exchanging news about the Germans with Bette, though I had the wisdom not to confide this to Annette or Jeanne as we walked to the Convent.

We did not walk together for long because we were regularly joined by other girls along the way and divided naturally into age groups. I walked with Cécile, Françoise and for the last hundred metres or so with Bernadette as well. Annette referred to us dismissively as 'the ankle sock brigade'.

It annoyed her that I did not mind the insult because I genuinely hated stockings which I wore, protesting, only when I had to look particularly well dressed. Socks did not ladder and were quick to put on in the mornings when Annette seemed to spend an inordinate amount of time adjusting her seams. I simply could not understand the attraction of the nasty brown things which Annette wore with such pride now that she was in the top class and allowed to, a privilege that others of my own age group appeared to regard with unaccountable longing.

Bette hated ankle socks with the same passion I brought to bear on being obliged to confine my hair in thick plaits. On arriving home Bette rushed to discard her socks and I my hair ribbons. When I visited her home, a large apartment a few streets away, we played with her secretly acquired lipstick and powder and giggled as we bashed each other with her large brown teddy bear, Alphonse. Recently we had giggled less because Bette had enlarged her supply of make-up and took it more seriously and she seemed to prefer twisting my hair into a series of impossible styles to playing with Alphonse. Illogically I felt sorry for Alphonse and regretted our lost fun. Dimly I understood that Bette and I were beginning to enjoy different things and that this might weaken a long friendship, but whenever this thought surfaced I repelled it firmly.

On this occasion I missed Françoise whose family had left Paris in the Exodus. Indeed it was a very depleted assembly at school which Sister Benedicte lectured on doing our duty under the Occupation. Disappointingly this duty turned out to be paying even closer attention to our studies, carrying on as normal and allowing the Germans as little chance to disturb our routine as possible.

Times might become very hard. The world was at war and we could expect increasing shortages and restrictions on our activity. It was each girl's duty to bear such privations with fortitude and to show more concern for others than for herself. Such charity did not of course extend to the Germans who were the undisputed enemy of our country and of all things Christian and decent. We must be patriotic and pray daily for liberation, but we must not engage in silly token acts and provoke the enemy, thereby inviting retribution and worrying our parents who would have plenty of other things to be anxious about. Resistance should be left to the grown-ups.

We listened and then, subdued and faintly excited, we split up into our classes for the first lessons of the day. Next to maths my biggest dread was Latin. Not only did the language defeat me with its precise construction and seemingly endless rules, but the nun who taught us had little patience with stupidity and none at all with laziness, regularly humiliating me with her sharp tongue and setting extra tasks which I carried out as lamentably as the original ones.

Today, however, as we struggled with the second book of the *Aeneid*, I felt an unusual interest and I sensed the same in Cécile who was wont to yawn whenever she was obliged to face the misery of translating Virgil even though her efforts invariably drew praise and but for whose whispered help my own would have attracted even more derision.

The flame and fury of the sack of Troy were missing from the invasion of Paris: there had been no bloody slaughter, no din of battle, no portents erupting from the Heavens, yet in my imagination I walked with Aeneas. When he and Creusa became separated in flight they were my parents, fleeing the Germans and whatever dark force had prompted that cry in the night. Anchises suddenly became my grandfather; Iulus, who trotted beside his father with unequal steps, was Edouard.

Caelum ruit, Troia fuit. I felt tears stinging my eyes and dreaded making a fool of myself before realising that the class was as intent on the story as I and Sister Aloysius unusually gentle. Heaven falls. Troy is no more. Could it be that Paris might one day disappear as completely as Troy, its Eiffel Tower a mere legend which future historians would be unable to verify? Could Notre Dame be reduced to rubble? Would archaeologists a hundred years hence dig up fragments of the pictures which filled the Louvre?

'No,' said Bette firmly when I proposed this scenario during break. 'These days nothing will ever be lost entirely because there are so many books across the world, so many photographs. People will always be very sure that Paris existed and where and when. But that doesn't make us any safer. The Germans could still raze Paris to the ground.'

Cécile argued that would be the last thing they would do. Paris was no good razed if what Hitler wanted was an empire. Instead the Germans would set up an administration like the empire makers of old in Africa and places like that. Bette disagreed, pointing out that this piece of empire making was being resisted, that a war was raging and that actual battles might be fought in Paris between the English and the Germans.

The debate was inconclusive and the uncertainty left me feeling not so much afraid as resentful. I wanted merely to be left alone to live the sort of teenage life I had been expecting to live without this unwarranted intrusion into my daily routine. I had formed a definite but unspecific notion of privations yet to come and I felt unreasonably cheated. At that moment the Germans seemed less a menace than an irritation which I wanted to brush off as an insect from a sleeve.

The feeling persisted when Father Jean told us we must pray for our enemies. I did not share the outrage of some of my classmates or the saintly compliance of others. I would forgive the Germans when they had gone and left us to get on with our lives, and only then would I pray for them, not now because they were just too much of a nuisance. My feelings were reminiscent of my attitude to Edouard when he was being tiresome and persisting in some naughtiness. The enemy should go back home to Mother; his behaviour was simply too bad for him to be welcome.

Yet at night I was afraid again and tried to sleep early to avoid hearing any cry which might ring through the darkness.

two

By *the window of*
Le Printemps

As I approached my sixteenth birthday in the September of 1940 I realised that the celebrations would be different that year. Rationing meant that the usual large family dinner would lack meat and there would doubtless be an over-emphasis on vegetables and fruit, then still readily available. Martin would not be there to tease me and tell me I would soon be a big girl, and my choice of presents would be restricted. The curfew was still eleven o'clock, there being then no resistance to produce the reprisals of early-evening confinement, so at least I could hold a party that evening or go to the cinema with other young people. It was the first birthday in the family since the Germans had arrived and only Edouard seemed oblivious to the changes.

I was still young enough for birthdays to be important and I grumbled to Annette that I hated the war, the war, the bloody war. Not even my father swore, at any rate within earshot of his daughters, and I expected a satisfyingly shocked reaction but Annette was too preoccupied with her own woes. Emile was showing an interest elsewhere, having been observed holding an umbrella over Françoise Desgranges while getting wet through himself. The lady in question was a year older than my sister, strikingly beautiful and much mooned over by the young men. Martin had also admired her and sought any excuse to find himself in her company.

Meanwhile at school we were all in a ferment over an impending visit from the Bishop. I cannot recall now which Bishop it was – certainly it was not Suhard, the Cardinal

Archbishop. It might have been a diocesan Bishop or one with special responsibilities for the Order or a Papal representative, but whoever he was his impending arrival was causing the most immense upheaval. We had to relearn our catechism and I spent hours parroting lines I had forgotten soon after my First Communion eight years earlier.

Annette and I used to question each other morning and night as we dressed and undressed.

'What is a Sacrament?'

'A Sacrament is an outward sign of an inward grace . . .'

We rehearsed the definition of every Sacrament from Baptism to Extreme Unction, occasionally correcting each other or arguing. I did the same with Bette and Cécile on the way to school or during break. One moment I felt fraught with anxiety and the next consumed with boredom.

The nuns did nothing to reduce the tension. A programme of spring-cleaning was set up and we all had to help, dismantling and reassembling any object that might have hidden recesses in which dust could lurk. 'As if the Bishop cares,' scoffed Bette as she passed down a pile of exercise books from one of the higher shelves in the stock cupboard and solemnly dusted the place it had occupied. I passed up the books and she replaced them.

We had to rehearse what felt like all the Gospels and practise hymns till I was hoarse.

'You would think the Pope was coming,' snorted Cécile as we stood in line to practise a procession in honour of Our Lady of Lourdes. Unfortunately Sister Benedicte overheard and handed out a penal essay on respect for the Church.

Annette complained that all the fuss was getting in the way of her preparations for baccalauréat while I thought only of my birthday and the Christmas holidays despite the latter being three months away. Jeanne complained of stomach-ache and she and my mother whispered a great deal so that I guessed what was happening, but did not dare enquire in case I mentioned something my little sister was not supposed to know.

I guessed I was being sent away so that Jeanne and my mother could be conveniently alone when I was asked to go and find

Edouard who was being unnaturally quiet. I located him upstairs with my grandparents.

'How's the catechism?' asked my grandfather with a wink.

'Horrible. I'm word-perfect one day, then my mind goes completely blank the next. I hate it. I just pray the Bishop doesn't ask me anything.'

'He's not God, you know,' pointed out Grand-père. 'He too has had to take exams and worry about them. He was once a small boy who cried for his mother just like Edouard. Remember that. Especially remember it if he frightens you.'

I knew the advice to be good as usual but I still wanted the visit to be over and consigned to the past.

'What would you like for your birthday?' Grand-mère tried to distract me from thoughts of the Bishop and Edouard looked up, as if excited at the mention of birthdays though the concept could not yet mean anything to him.

'An end to this silly war.'

'And have you by any chance a second choice?'

'An end to the Occupation, to rations, to curfews, to all their interference.'

'Amen,' said my grandmother. 'But you may have to settle for the usual soap instead.'

I could hardly believe my ears. From the age of twelve I had loved all things scented: powder, soap, dried flowers, the sheets after washday. My birthday was always sweetly perfumed but I had assumed this year that would not happen. We were not yet resorting to the terrible Savon de Marseilles which made such a misery and a mockery of washing in the second half of the Occupation, but soap was becoming harder to get and luxury soaps were well nigh unobtainable by the ordinary Parisian.

'I have a little store,' smiled Grand-mère, 'saved up over time, but quite fresh and fragrant.'

I flew to her and hugged her, my life transformed, my hopes soaring. I would have scented soap for my birthday after all.

The problem of the white dresses was less easy to solve. The nuns had decided that for the procession, on the occasion of the Bishop's visit, we must all wear white dresses and white mantillas. Few of us possessed such items, never having needed them since our First Communions, and although there were still clothes in the shops at the end of 1940, many smaller outlets had not reopened after the Exodus and shortages had begun. No sane family faced with clothing four children for winter would have given priority to white dresses and mantillas.

My mother and grandmother relished the challenge. The Germans should not stop their children obeying the orders of the Holy Church. Three white dresses and three white mantillas must be produced. At school we swapped stories of desperate remedies. One girl tried to bleach her mother's black mantilla but succeeded only in ruining it altogether as well as wasting the bleach. Another sat up all night turning a black mantilla to white with the aid of a crayon from her infant sister's collection. She had worn the crayon down to a tiny piece of wood and her mantilla was now grey but she knew of another white crayon . . . Others used sheets, net curtains, old blouses. One girl made dresses for two from her mother's wedding dress, which had been faithfully preserved for years through an early widowhood.

In our own household we cut up white sheets and trimmed the results with lace from the best napkins. None, not even the poorest, would concede defeat. Annette's mantilla was cut from my grandmother's tablecloth, which covered a small, round table in her sitting room.

Through it all we tested each other on the catechism, the miracles, the parables, the beatitudes, the apostles, the main saints' days.

The Bishop was to say Mass and a priest would visit the school the day before to hear our confessions. Meanwhile we continued ploughing our way through the sack of Troy.

'*Infelix simulacrum!*' Creusa's ghost conjured up a vision of a wraith clad in white and I pictured her in a mixture of sheets and tablecloths. The resulting fit of infectious giggles earned four of us a detention during break.

To escape the wrath of Cécile, who was among those punished, I went off with Bette after school. My birthday fell on 3 October, the Bishop's visit the day before. Thoughts of both had dominated the weeks since the return from the summer holidays and I was glad when Bette suggested walking to her apartment by means of a detour past the main shops.

Each time a German passed us Bette gave a *sotto voce* curse. If the enemy heard he did not react but I wondered what it must be like to live in a strange city and be hated and reviled. With insight I realised that this part of it must be worse for the soldiers I saw around me than would be the fear of being stabbed in a futile gesture on the part of an outraged patriot, not that there was much resistance at that stage. I repressed the thought angrily; it smacked of sympathising with the enemy.

Yet why should I not sympathise? Is that not exactly what Christ's teaching bade me do? Pray for thine enemy. Do good to them that persecute you. Forgive. All I knew was that I did not want to sympathise. I wanted to hate with all my heart and all my soul and if that were mortal sin so be it.

As we drew close to Le Printemps I saw a magnificent dress in the window and turned to Bette excitedly but she had lingered in front of another shop so I stood on my own, staring longingly at a garment designed for someone older, richer and decidedly more chic than I. A matching handbag was placed beside it.

I knew that even were I able to afford such a dress it could have no practical use because it was not young enough in fashion and I had no occasion on which to wear such a creation but I enjoyed it as an aspiration. In five years, maybe ten, I would want something like that in my wardrobe. I went on gazing in adoration, wondering who might buy it and when Bette came up to join me I asked her if she thought either of our mothers would look good in it.

Bette shrugged. 'I don't suppose it matters. Soon the only ones who will be able to buy that sort of thing will be Germans.'

'German soldiers don't wear dresses.'

'Their mistresses do.'

As if on cue a woman ran up to the window followed by a laughing German officer. Bette turned away in disgust but I lingered, unable to take my eyes off the dress. I heard the German tell the Frenchwoman that it would take him a year's pay to buy the suit she was admiring. His French was very bad and it irritated me, causing me to wonder if my even more inadequate English had the same effect on my teachers.

Suddenly the woman spotted the dress and moved to stand beside me in order to get a better look. The soldier moved too and, feeling crowded by them, I turned reluctantly away. The German muttered an apology and I looked at him, meeting his eyes for the first time.

Until then I had not got particularly close to the enemy. The signs of the Occupation were everywhere: the swastikas at the top of the Eiffel Tower, hanging from official buildings, fairly covering the Palais-Bourbon; the official signs in Gothic letters; the posters reminding us to be in order and, above all, the conqueror himself, walking, shopping, eating, sightseeing, ever in our midst. Yet, unlike others who had been confronted with Germans asking the way or for some other innocuous piece of information, I had not once, in the three months since they arrived, had any conversation with the invaders.

I did not do so now, acknowledging the apology with a small smile but no words, yet the encounter shocked me. The German was quite young, perhaps twenty-five or so, open faced and happily smiling. He might have been any one of a number of young Frenchmen I knew of that age who had begun to disappear from Paris. He looked happy, boyish, kind. It was not at all how I expected the enemy to look and I rejoined Bette in ill-defined confusion. I had instinctively liked the man I had just looked at and I should not have done so.

I did not confide in Bette, who had a deep hatred of Germans, from fear that she might treat me with the contempt she showed them, but my unease remained. I found I had lost interest in the window-shopping expedition and, like a lost or unhappy child, I wanted to go home. If Bette found my change of mind surprising she did not say so and we made our way to her apartment without her uttering any protest or enquiry.

As usual we were the only ones there for a couple of hours as both her parents worked, her father as a doctor and her mother as a secretary. I used to wonder if she was lonely when nobody came home with her and secretly rejoiced in my own large family where my mother and grandparents were ever present in the house, which was always warm, lit, welcoming and full of Edouard's incomprehensible chatter.

We sat on her bed and Bette rolled down her navy blue knee socks which in the autumn term replaced the white ankle socks we wore in summer. We all wore ankle socks now, even proud Annette, for stockings had been among the earliest casualties of rationing. She rubbed her hand up and down her legs, her lips pursed as she made her assessment.

'Hmmnn,' she muttered, 'time for a shave. What about you?'

I stared, baffled. 'What?'

'Your legs. Are they hairy?'

I supposed they were. It was not something I had ever thought about and in any case I was fair and the growth on my legs was not unsightly.

'It isn't just looks,' pronounced Bette, 'it's feel. Do they feel rough?'

Still bemused I copied Bette and began to run my hand along my shins. I remembered now that Annette had a lot of dark hair on her legs but my mother did not. Clearly Bette was about to initiate me into some rite of adulthood. I began to giggle.

'You see, men don't like it. They like women to have smooth legs so that when you sit on their laps they can stroke them.'

My giggles turned to immoderate laughter. I could not imagine any circumstances in which a grown-up would sit on someone's lap. Offended, Bette led the way to the bathroom and ran cold water into the handbasin.

'It's better with hot water,' she assured me.

Most things were better with hot water, but the means to heat our homes were declining so we stoically tried to work up lather with cold water and Bette's father's shaving soap.

'Is it rationed?' I asked as we spread it over our legs. Bette shrugged nonchalantly.

Inevitably, I cut myself, not once but half a dozen times. I yelled and giggled and pressed cotton wool to my wounds where it stuck and hurt to retrieve. Bette kept assuring me it was only a matter of practice until she suddenly cut herself and swore and we both collapsed in uncontrollable mirth.

We tidied up, removing the evidence of our activity with a

degree of diligence which suggested that Bette was not quite so casual as she had seemed and I knew then that either razor blades or shaving soaps were rationed or perhaps both. Unlike Bette I felt guilty, but could not concentrate on the feeling for long because I was too preoccupied with the niggling pain of my cuts.

'Let's have a drink,' said Bette.

I followed her along the hall, expecting her to turn into the kitchen to make coffee and wondered whether I should say no to that too because it was in very short supply even then. Instead she ushered me into the lounge and took a bottle and two glasses from a cupboard.

'What is it?' I asked.

'Pernod.'

'No. We can't. Isn't there some wine?'

'Oh, give it a try. Just a little drop.'

'Your parents will notice.'

'No. This bottle has been here for years. It is good to have a drink after work.'

'Bette, we aren't at work. We're at school.'

I would not be persuaded. I had a history of getting into scrapes with Bette. At twelve she had persuaded me to try a cigarette and I had been miserably sick. At fourteen she had induced me to stay out until ten o'clock one evening and I had been gated for a fortnight. Now my legs were in shreds as a result of her bright idea of shaving. I was not going to get drunk as well.

Bette gave in gracefully but pulled a face as she put the bottle away. I pointed out that she could still pour herself a drink, but she told me with a straight face that only drunkards raised their glasses alone. Instead she switched on the wireless, very low, and motioned me to put my ear to the set, promising that we should be able to 'pick up the BBC'. We failed and Bette finally settled for dance music and careered round the room swooning in the arms of an imaginary man.

I grinned. 'What's he like?'

'Tall, dark, just divine.'

Things divine reminded me of my neglected catechism and the impending Episcopal visit. I knew I should go home and do some revision but the prospect was too dreary. As Bette danced,

21

occasionally closing her eyes for too long and bumping into the furniture, I found my thoughts straying to the German officer I had seen by the window of Le Printemps, to his utter normality, to his open cheerfulness, to that engaging smile. I could not hate him.

'Bette, what would you do if a German asked you to dance?'

I expected her to say she would turn on her heel, slap his face even, but she replied that she would accept and then spend the entire dance stamping on his toes. I smiled, but I did not believe I wanted to stamp on the toes of the officer I had seen. I had no desire to hurt him at all, rather I wanted him to keep smiling. It was a thought I kept to myself.

Eventually I forced myself to get up out of the chair and go home, where I showed Annette the damage to my legs.

'Fool!' she scoffed. 'Don't you know it makes the hair grow thicker? Bette, of course! Who else would lead you into such nonsense?'

Deprived of sympathy, I ignored her until bedtime. That night was the first since the Occupation when I fell towards sleep without half expecting to hear a scream in the dark. I had seen the enemy and he was just an ordinary chap.

'Bless me, Father, for I have sinned. I copied Cécile's Latin homework when she wasn't looking, I stole – by using – shaving soap and a razor blade from my friend's father, I have uncharitable thoughts towards my older sister and I keep thinking about a German officer I saw in the street.'

Thus did I set out my misdeeds for the assessment of Father Tessier when he came to hear confessions prior to the Bishop's visit. As it happened he was my usual confessor and the priest of the parish where I worshipped.

Usually he told me to pray for Annette and say three Hail Marys so I was surprised when he asked in what way I thought of the German officer.

'I liked his smile.'

'Why do you feel that is sin, my child?'

Even more puzzled, I stammered that he was the enemy and I was not being loyal to France because I would actually like him for a friend.

I sensed a relief in the priest, the cause of which I could not identify, as he prescribed the usual three Hail Marys and told me to go in peace.

I felt anything but peaceful when the Bishop came. I was sure he would ask me a question which I would not be able to answer and then the nuns would berate me for letting them down. I tried to get a glimpse of him as he celebrated the Mass but saw only his back.

After Mass we processed around the hall, singing hymns in honour of Our Lord's Mother, in a strictly rehearsed order. In each class the girls with proper dresses went first while those of us with improvised ones followed. We each held a candle and sang the words from memory, vigorously conducted by the music teacher, Sister Thérèse, who stood on the right of the stage while the Bishop sat in the centre. As we passed him we curtsied and I stole a glance at his face, expecting grave approval of our efforts, but he looked merely wistful and when we were once more standing in rows I saw him smile at the smallest children who were bringing up the rear of the procession and only then passing in front of him.

I realised my grandfather was right. The Bishop was human. He was a man about ten years younger than Grand-père with very grey hair and a large nose. I feared him no more.

I did, however, fear my lack of knowledge. After the procession the Bishop visited each class in turn. When he came to ours I tried to make myself invisible but to no effect. With a sinking heart I saw him look straight at me and heard him ask my name.

'From what race did Our Lord come?' he asked me. It was not what I had expected.

'He was an Israelite,' I said and waited, somehow conscious that I was expected to find that significant.

'Yes. In other words, He was a Jew. I want you all to remember that. There may be some very difficult times ahead and I want you to remember that.'

The Bishop paused and we looked at him with faces of solemn obedience and at each other with a hint of puzzlement. Of course we knew that Jews faced persecution in Germany and, inattentive to anything as serious as the news on the wireless, I had a vague idea that it had something to do with the sort of shop you were allowed to own. So far, however, we were unaware of any problem in Paris. Also, having remembered that Christ was a Jew, what exactly were we supposed to do about it? My mind wandered off into a fantasy in which I hid Yvette Levin in a secret room cunningly concealed by my wardrobe.

Indeed we were all now looking covertly and with embarrassment at Yvette, who was pretending not to notice. She was as Catholic as the rest of us but her father was Jewish. I knew this only because she was awesomely clever and studied Hebrew privately, frequently referring to it when the class was studying the Old Testament. Her older brother, Adam, had rebelled against their mother's Catholicism and embraced his father's faith, but there were three smaller children in various classes in the junior school whom I often saw at church. One was particularly charming and I hoped Edouard would be like that in a few years' time.

I was brought out of my musing by Cécile's standing up to answer a question I had not heard.

'Love thy neighbour as thyself.'

The Bishop nodded, satisfied, and began a gentle exposition, which I guessed would have led to the conclusion that we must love the Jews as ourselves, but he had not reached this point when Bette's hand shot up.

'Do I have to love the Germans?'

For once I was concentrating fully, my interest awakened, for was this not the very issue with which I had wrestled myself?

'Yes,' said the Bishop quietly, 'as individuals. But that does not mean you have to love what they stand for. You must hate that.'

We stared. I had rarely heard such plain talk since the beginning of the Occupation, for France was still pretty ambivalent and our elders protective, anxious to guard us from dangerous reactions. Instinctively, I believed my parents would have agreed with him.

'But you cannot fight what they stand for in the middle of a war,' persisted Bette. 'You have to fight *them* and that means killing thy neighbour.'

Bette's tone was not rude but it was uncompromising, offering battle, and as such contradicted everything we had ever been taught about respect for priests let alone bishops. There were a few gasps and Sister Céline intervened sharply, bidding Bette mind her manners. I had a fleeting impression that the Bishop would not have reacted in this way, that he might have been willing to explore Bette's views and guide them, but he would not oppose a nun in front of her class.

In a few more minutes he departed for another class, leaving Bette to the ire of Sister Céline who told her to write an apology. The exchange between Bette and the Bishop took up a great deal of conversation over the next few days, convincing some that indeed she was bold and wilful and others that she had unexpected courage but I could think only of the Bishop, of his expression as the youngest children paraded before him, of his gentle questions, of his unexpected denunciation of National Socialism, above all of my own fear and panicky revision before his visit.

By the window of Le Printemps the conqueror had seemed but a harmless boy and now the Bishop himself had seemed but a gentle, harmless old man. Nobody except Bette, the reliable rebel, played the roles I expected. The German officer and the man who wore the mitre were disconcertingly human. Somehow the discovery was not reassuring but threatening. I turned from it and clutched stubbornly at my fleeing childhood.

The day after the Episcopal visit the Vichy Government issued its first Proclamation against the Jews. I was too busy with my birthday to notice.

three

Robert

I had always loved autumn when I crunched carefree through the leaves, delighting in new exercise books at school and the first fires in the grates at home, which always made me glad that I did not live in an apartment where such a luxury was unknown. As the air chilled with the onset of winter, I thought of Christmas with its merry cosiness and positively rejoiced in the shortening days. In this at sixteen I differed little from when I had been eight.

This autumn was different. One of the first things the Germans had done was to align French time with German time so the mornings were depressingly dark. Paris was moving from the limitations imposed by Occupation towards actual privation and the prudent were already anticipating a great deal worse to come. Catherine the Second was now housed indoors overnight in case she were stolen. My mother lamented the necessity but I was secretly pleased, being sure the poor bird would be much more comfortable.

We had no new exercise books at school but were told to fill up old ones first and indeed to write on the covers too. As for fires in the grates, we had instead to wear ever more layers of clothes and, as if these physical woes were not enough, my father now began to make increasingly stringent demands of me in respect of my schoolwork.

I must understand that everyone had to grow up some time and realise that qualifications were for one's own sake, not trophies to be sought as a result of pressure from others. I had been lazy long enough and I should begin to think of my future, also of my duty to God who had given me a brain and to my fellow men on whose behalf I must learn to exert it. At the moment all I seemed intent on doing was limiting my own future. Thus ran his strictures evening after evening.

My mother supported him, saying I must do something to earn my keep until I married, otherwise I would end up as a shop girl, bored and poorly waged. Even Annette joined in the grumbling because she had been pressed into helping me with my reluctant studies and naturally preferred other ways of spending her time.

I resisted with inactivity and irritable complaint. My long, beautiful hair was less of a consolation than usual because washing it, with too little shampoo and no fire to dry it, had become a mammoth chore. Then, to complete my misery, my parents decided that my cousins and their parents should be invited for Christmas until New Year. That way we could pool our resources and ration card allowances and reduce expense by having one home to heat and light instead of two.

The thought of any intrusion into our family over Christmas was bad enough but the idea of spending the holiday with Emile and Robert was well nigh unbearable. Annette would be jealously possessive of Emile, Robert would be tiresome and my parents would spend all their time with the older relatives instead of with us.

To my surprise Annette was equally unenthusiastic. Emile was forever flirting with some girl or other, she no longer liked him and she certainly did not want to spend Christmas with him. I could have his company all the time if I wished. I did not wish. Her love of tidiness and order was offended by the thought of Jeanne moving in with us to allow our cousins to sleep in her room. It would all be chaos.

Meanwhile the clouds of Occupation were darkening. In early October there had been mass arrests of communists and in November Paris roused itself for its first public demonstration against the occupiers. Yet there was still an air of uncertainty. The enemy behaved correctly and Pétain continued to urge collaboration, but two days before Christmas there was an execution.

A week earlier I had escaped the inevitable recriminations produced by the termly review of my academic performance by passing the evening upstairs with my grandfather while my grandmother assisted the Christmas preparations downstairs.

'I hate school, I hate exams, I hate work and I hate all these rows,' I said without heat. 'Why can't you all accept that? Annette is clever, so is Jeanne. Why can't I be different?'

My grandfather appeared to weigh this up carefully. 'What do you want from your life?'

'To marry, have children, live happily, and until then to be left alone and not harried about maths and French and long-dead kings and other countries' climates. I do not care whether two triangles are congruent or not, nor how many colonies there are, nor how hot it is on the Nile.'

The old man smiled in genuine amusement. I should never have dared speak in such a way to either of my parents. An image of the Bishop suddenly rose in my mind and I believed he would have understood my rebellion as well as he had understood Bette's when she spoke to him from her heart.

'I do not think that would matter if you were enthusiastic about something, anything. You talk about marrying, but you hate cooking and housework. You never read anything but trivia unless schoolwork obliges you to. You don't like music, sport or art. You have no idea what sort of job you would like to do. You are very beautiful, Catherine, but no man worth having is going to be attracted by ignorance and idleness.'

It was the kind of lecture I was hearing daily, but my grandfather alone could deliver it without provoking me, largely because, having had his say, he would not insist on a response or embark upon repetition of what, even from him, was tediously unwelcome advice. I resolved that after the Christmas break I would spend more time at Bette's home where there was so little parental interference.

My grandfather began to talk of the war and predicted a difficult year ahead but my thoughts were on Christmas and the prospect of sharing the festive season with Emile and Robert.

They arrived on Christmas Eve bearing gifts and encountered a sulky Annette, who had decided to punish Emile by flirting with Robert, who was unreceptive, much to his brother's amusement. At Midnight Mass, held an hour earlier than usual in observance of the midnight curfew, Robert positioned himself between Jeanne and me, and I realised what a good voice he had as he sang the responses. Immediately he seemed less irritating and more interesting, and I was friendlier than usual as we walked home.

His own interest appeared to lie largely in keeping Edouard amused and he spent hours kneeling on the floor building towers of toy bricks which Edouard promptly knocked down. Absorbed in the toddler's reactions, he ignored the rest of us unless we spoke to him directly and sometimes even then did not seem to hear. When Edouard's tiredness at the end of each day led to tantrums, Robert would haul the child upon his back and trot upstairs imitating the neighing of a horse.

I began to resent this monopoly of my brother, who had always shown a strong partiality for me rather than my sisters. The visit was nearly over before I began to realise that what I resented was not the time Edouard gave to Robert, but that which my cousin gave to the child. With me my cousin was awkward and uncertain, with my small brother he was confident and in control. Unaware of the interest I was taking he acted naturally, relaxed and at ease with himself.

On the morning of my cousins' departure I woke at five with an overpowering thirst and crept down to the kitchen in search of water. It was dark and very cold as I picked my way downstairs, with only a weak moon shining through the high landing window to guide me. Shivering, I drew my dressing gown round me more tightly and pushed open the kitchen door. Catherine the Second gave a lazy, quizzical cluck. Then from somewhere came a small warning cough, unmistakably male.

I jumped in fright at the same time as Robert said, 'It's only me. Who is that?'

'Catherine.' I peered into the gloom and saw him stand up from somewhere near the stove and come towards me. 'What are you doing here?'

'Emile snores like an animal at the zoo.'

'Wouldn't you be more comfortable in the lounge?'

'Here is warmer. I have brought most of my bedding down.'

We stood in front of the window in the moonlight and I was glad it was not brighter, conscious of how odd I must look with my hair in tangled disorder and my ancient dressing gown, with its fraying cord and childish motif on the pocket, drawn over warm, unglamorous pyjamas. My slippers were old ones that Martin had grown out of and I wore them with a mixture of guilt and sentiment.

I found a glass and drew some water from the tap. My gulps sounded loud in the night air and I had a notion they made me seem gauche and unsophisticated. I was glad when Catherine the Second began to rustle about.

Eventually my thirst was satisfied and I placed the glass back on the draining board, but I went on standing by the window, not wanting to leave Robert, not knowing what to say to justify staying. As we stood there, friendly and awkward, we heard the patrol.

Stamp, stamp, stamp. The sound of two men walking in step drew nearer. It was the only sound from without, the only disturbance of the dark silence. Robert and I turned our heads towards the sound, two dark silhouettes waiting for two dark silhouettes who would presently pass by the window, their footsteps growing louder and then receding. Stamp, stamp, stamp. The sound of Occupation.

The men were unaware of us as we watched their dark outlines pass. We waited until the sound of their oppressive tread had died to the faintest echo, then Robert whispered, 'Damn the Germans.'

'Amen,' I said quietly.

For a brief moment, united by resentment and perhaps fear, we had lost our shyness, but now it returned and after a few seconds' silence I said I must go back to bed. He kissed me quickly, a cousinly peck on the cheek. It was a kiss such as I received from him each time our families met but I sensed this was different. His words confirmed it for as I made my way to the stairs I heard him sigh.

'You are beautiful, Catherine,' he whispered and I scampered upstairs certain that I was in love, warmly excited by it, longing to tell Annette in the morning, even wondering if I should wake her now. I had suddenly become of greater consequence, I was a woman, possibly a *femme fatale*, on a par with worldly Bette and with my pouting sister who knew all about men.

I was horribly disconcerted later in the morning to find that there was nothing different in Robert's attitude towards me. He did not give me a small, secret smile when nobody else was looking. His eyes did not meet mine in meaningful glances. He did not give me anything more than the usual brief hug when they all left.

I had spent hours on my appearance and was rewarded with nothing more than a rebuke from my mother for being late and keeping everyone waiting. Feeling rebuffed and puzzled I discovered an unlikely source of consolation in thank you letters. I found some pale blue paper, with a flower motif, left over from a gift of two years before, and wrote a longer letter to Robert than the others who had to be content with plain white paper.

Bearing in mind my grandfather's strictures about men disliking ignorance, I threw in some comments about Molière. Robert duly wrote and, in a letter which filled barely half a page, thanked me nicely for the socks and said he preferred chemistry to Molière.

Nevertheless I returned for the Easter term more kindly disposed to academic work than hitherto, but my enthusiasm did not survive the examination of the reforms introduced by Henri IV's great minister, Sully, which occupied the last lesson of the morning. I knew that no chemical equation was going to rekindle it.

On our way home I told Bette about Robert. At least I told her of our meeting in the kitchen but spared myself the humiliation of recounting his seeming indifference thereafter.

Bette was full of congratulations. 'Do you feel powerful?' she asked.

I stared at her. 'Powerful?'

'Yes. Don't you feel he would do anything for you? That he's enslaved by your very smile? That he would fight dragons for you? That when he is not with you he is pining away?'

'Er . . . no, not exactly, I haven't thought about that.'

'Oh,' said Bette and her disappointed tone told me I had failed the test. I was not, it seemed, in love after all.

Annette was even less encouraging when I told her Robert had sighed, 'You are beautiful, Catherine.'

'He probably meant the hen.'

As the weeks passed and I heard no more from Robert I began to share my sister's opinion and to discover that it was my pride which ached more than my heart. I thought of him occasionally and also of the German officer at Le Printemps and of the Bishop but mainly I thought of my rapidly growing height and the spots which now and then broke out to ruin my complexion and confidence.

Shortly after we returned for the summer term my Aunt Sophie was taken ill. Always mildly eccentric, she had for some time been showing signs of the onset of dementia and now she was suffering from bronchitis and needed temporary care. It was not the first time and usually my mother or grandmother went to stay in her large apartment in the heart of Paris until the crisis had passed.

This time neither could oblige. My grandmother was herself ill with a heavy cold and did not feel up to the prospect of moving, organising and caring. My mother was preoccupied with Edouard who had chickenpox and Jeanne who had a harsher version of my grandmother's cold. Only Annette and I were well and able to help, but whereas my sister was working hard for exams, I could hardly contain my glee at having a reason to miss school.

My parents groaned about Aunt Sophie's unreasonableness in refusing to leave her apartment and stay with other family members but they decided to send me nonetheless. There was an indefinable suggestion that I might not be up to the job, although nobody actually said so, and I packed a small case with a light heart. I would invite Bette to come round after school. Unfortunately my parents anticipated exactly that and forbade me to have any friends in at all. Aunt Sophie was ill and needed peace and quiet, I should concentrate on looking after her and use any spare time to catch up on study.

I was undaunted because I knew that once my friends realised why I was away they would call anyway and I could truthfully claim that I had not invited them and was just being polite, particularly if I could persuade them to carry out the occasional small errand for the invalid. Selfishly I hoped Aunt Sophie would not recover too soon.

I found her feverish, weak, irritable and wanting to be left alone so I began to explore the apartment with the excuse of needing to know where things were but in reality to look for books, the wireless and other sources of entertainment.

Aunt Sophie had always hoarded, not in expectation of a war but out of habit. Much of it was irrational – heaps of newspapers, yellow and curling, empty boxes in every shape and size, a drawerful of nails, moth-eaten cardigans. The items were all neatly stacked in cupboards and drawers and around them the shelves and floors were clean and shiny, my aunt combining the collection of rubbish with fastidious standards of cleanliness.

It was the bathroom that held my attention with its large cupboard containing row upon row of shampoos, soaps, tooth-pastes and talcum powder. There had to be enough here for more than a year. I knew it would be no use asking if I could take some home: Aunt Sophie's meanness was legendary in the family. I knew also that I would not simply help myself, even though I was certain she would not miss any of it. The war had not then blurred the moral code. Parisians were not yet eating their neighbours' pet cats nor braining pigeons in the parks and I had no notion of stealing shampoo.

Still, I saw no reason to stint myself while I was there dancing attendance on the owner of all this luxury and two weeks of scented bathroom bliss followed, marred only by the scarcity of hot water.

When she was awake, Aunt Sophie was demanding, irritable and critical, frequently calling me Annette or Margot my mother's name, but for most of the first week she slept, waking only to eat or use the lavatory. Bette, Cécile and Bernadette began to visit and we giggled over anti-spot remedies and the tales they brought me of school, but only Bernadette stayed for long. The others were too serious about revision.

In the middle of the second week my mother appeared to find Aunt Sophie lying unwashed in bed, a pile of dirty dishes from the previous evening in the sink and me with my face made up from cosmetics I had found neatly hoarded in one of the spare bedrooms. My schoolbooks were too obviously still in the case in which I had carried them, but an unsuitable novel was lying open by the easiest of the chairs in the lounge. All Paris must have heard the row which followed.

From then on a member of the family called each day.

'Have you washed up, infant?' asked Annette wearily as she arrived on the Thursday. Her tone was not unfriendly and I felt guiltier than after my mother's tirade. On Saturday Aunt Sophie demanded to know what I was doing there, as if aware of my presence for the first time. When I explained she said she had never heard such rubbish, that she had not been ill since she was a girl and that if she were she would not be troubling anyone to look after her. The next day Robert arrived to help me take my things home.

My heart fluttered when I saw him, but he did not appear affected by the meeting. As we turned into the road on which I lived I stole a glance at his profile and thought how weak his face was. I decided he was stupid, gawky and far too young for me. It was quite incomprehensible how I could have fallen in love with him. Yet when he kissed me on both cheeks as he left, I was conscious of a sense of loss.

There followed a period of relative calm. My mother did not return to the subject of my derelictions when I had been supposedly looking after Aunt Sophie, my father gave up his campaign to persuade me to apply myself to my work and, in order to give Annette peace in which to revise, I began to spend a great deal of my time playing with Edouard or climbing the stairs to visit my grandfather. I felt suspended in time, waiting for Annette, Bette and Cécile to return from what seemed like some strange planet, which must happen once the exams were over and the summer break began. I knew my own performance would be desperate and felt surprisingly resigned.

Released from the pressures of work, Bette and Cécile became irresponsible, trying to find ways of evading parental rules, revelling in unaccustomed idleness, on one occasion actually waltzing in the street and cannoning into an older German officer. I should have known there was trouble brewing but their fun was infectious and I could not get enough of their company and nor could Bernadette.

It was the Germans who dampened their high spirits, imposing an early curfew in response to some outbreak of protest. In that summer of 1941 evening hardly began before we were closing our windows and wondering how to while away the hours. Recklessly Cécile and Bernadette began to wonder how they might defy the restrictions. Bette was scornful, but her insistence that it could not be done only provoked the others to plot wildly.

It all came to a head when a group of us met to celebrate Bernadette's seventeenth birthday. Unusually she lived on the ground floor in a large apartment next to the concierge's. A party had long been planned and to prevent disappointment several of us were spending the night at her apartment while others were staying with some neighbours in the same block. It enabled us to have our fun post-curfew and there were makeshift beds and mattresses everywhere. I had spent hours washing my hair in egg and vinegar and longingly recalled the shampoos at Aunt Sophie's.

Bernadette's mother had made a large cake but even so it produced only the thinnest slice each. We wound up the gramophone, danced and laughed. Presently the doorbell rang and two Germans appeared carrying a bottle and seeking to join the party. When Bernadette's father had persuaded them to leave he insisted we reduce the noise and at intervals thereafter interrupted the revelry to enforce the order. Cécile looked mutinous.

When the party was over and guests had left for neighbouring apartments, I found myself lying on cushions in the lounge with a blanket pulled over me as six of us tried to sleep in similarly makeshift conditions. Excitement made it difficult and soon we abandoned the effort and sat up to whisper to each other in the dark.

Bernadette, who had given up her bed to someone else, was there as was Yvette Levin, Cécile, Bette and Sylvie.

Sylvie. I scarcely knew her. She was younger than us but in our class because of the Exodus. I do not even know the basis on which she had been invited to the party and I am certain that I would have forgotten her altogether but for that night. As it is I can recall her very clearly: the slight flat-chested figure, the somewhat greasy curls, the snub nose, the reedy voice.

Sylvie. But for her I would now be the mother of a French family, probably still in Paris, visiting my siblings and their families, watching my parents age, taking my children to French schools, welcoming my husband home to some Paris apartment. I might even now be walking by the Seine or sitting outside a café on a Parisian boulevard or watching the tourists by the Eiffel Tower. I would have been *Klausless*.

I had always believed that when something happened which altered your life it would be dramatic, immediately recognisable; that the world would suddenly pause as you entered that moment of time; that in the background some imaginary music would strike a loud chord. Instead the words which altered my life were uttered by little Sylvie something or other in a thin, squeaky, usually unheeded voice.

Bernadette and Cécile had returned to their theme of defying the curfew, of engaging in some small act of defiance which would restore our self-respect. Their proposals were wild. Cécile believed that we could creep out on the streets, avoid detection by the patrols and take coffee in the centre of Paris on the grounds that the women who consorted with the Germans must be out after curfew and who was to know that we were not of the same mind?

Bette crushed that with a description of Paris after curfew which I suspect indicated first-hand knowledge. Women did not, she insisted, wander around after curfew any more than men and, even if they did, was that how we wanted to brand ourselves?

Bernadette was only fractionally more reasonable. We could listen for the patrols and then, when they were likely to be out of sight, we could rush out and put a large notice on the pavement saying six loyal Frenchwomen had made fools of the Germans. We could sign the notice with false names.

'Six?' queried Bette and we all looked at Yvette Levin.

'Six,' said Yvette equably. 'But we don't need to do anything so harebrained. All we need is the satisfaction of having been out when we should be in. We can do that by being out for just a few seconds. We are on the ground floor so we can quietly open a window and climb out. We don't have to alert the concierge by using the front door. Then we get straight back in again. We will still have broken the curfew.'

We chewed this over with relief and disappointment. It was too tame a proposal for Cécile and Bernadette but Bette and I agreed.

'We must go somewhere,' insisted Bernadette.

Then Sylvie spoke. 'I know what we can do. Let's go to Henriette's.'

four

An Act of Defiance

We all looked appreciatively at Sylvie. Henriette lived two blocks away, also on the ground floor, but it was not necessary to go by the street. At the back of the blocks ran a narrow alley and we need walk along it only for two minutes or so before arriving at Henriette's. It was risky but, apart from Yvette's suggestion of a very token defiance, it was the only feasible plan before us. The block where Henriette lived was bounded on one side by a large shrubbery in which we could hide. It was ideal for our purposes.

Bette alone resisted, the most impetuous, frequently irresponsible girl among us suddenly cautious. When she saw it was hopeless she tried to insist that Yvette should not go but should remain in case our absence were discovered, causing Bernadette's parents to panic.

It was obvious why she was trying to keep Yvette safely indoors. We would all be in serious trouble, danger even, if caught but she alone was Jewish and facing some vaguely understood retribution. Drancy, the transit centre which was to become the first port of call for Parisian Jews en route for the concentration camps, was to be set up later that summer, but then all we knew was that Jews who disappeared did not return.

Yvette, however, would not be talked out of going with us and in the end we left a note in a prominent place for Bernadette's parents. I looked at it miserably as I propped it up on the mantelpiece, hoping that in a couple of hours I would be looking at it again, that it would still be unread and that we would all be safely there to witness its destruction.

We decided to go without coats or jackets. The night was warm and we could not risk retrieving our outer garments from the hall pegs in case we disturbed Bernadette's parents. Anyway it felt good to be going in our party garb, as if the clothing of merriment were another act of defiance, a statement that Occupation or no Occupation we were going to enjoy ourselves. Cécile and Bette had already changed into pyjamas and were now changing back.

When we were ready we suddenly hesitated, reluctant even to open the window let alone climb through. The curfew demanded that all windows be kept shut. We stood, holding our breath, listening for any distant sound of a patrol. In my imagination I heard it: stamp, stamp, stamp. In reality I did not and there were no more excuses. Cautiously Bernadette first unfastened and then opened the window. She peered out and then climbed on to the sill. Stamp, stamp, stamp. My ears strained as she jumped but still I could not hear the sound we dreaded. One by one we joined Bernadette who closed the window as best she could.

Then we ran. Sense demanded we creep but we ran headlong, giggling, fearful, exulting in the adventure, longing for its end. Caution abandoned, only one end was possible. As we approached the point where we must turn out of the alley and alongside the block where Henriette lived, two helmeted figures loomed at the far end of the passage. One shouted and we scattered in confusion.

Yvette, Sylvie and Cécile ran forward and turned out of the alley. Bernadette, Bette and I ran back the way we had come. A shot rang out and Bernadette whimpered but she continued pelting down the alley while Bette and I stood still before turning to face the soldiers whose hands were already reaching out to seize us.

For a moment the four of us stood looking at each other. There is little I can look back on with pride from those terrible years but it gives me pleasure still to remember that in the midst of peril I thought not of myself but of Yvette, praying that she had reached Henriette's, had roused her and been safely admitted.

The Germans looked at us, startled. I do not suppose that two girls in party dress were the type of curfew breaker they had expected. They glanced at each other and shrugged. One covered us half-heartedly with his gun while the other searched the alley and some of its byways. I began to realise that the temperature had dropped and I shivered with cold and fear, but there were no more shouts or shots and I felt certain that Bernadette at least must now be safely at home while the others must have found refuge at Henriette's or in the shrubbery outside.

Bette and I were arrested and taken to the Kommandantur. Fear gave way to disbelief as I wondered how on earth I had allowed myself to be embroiled in what now looked more like an act of undiluted madness than of patriotic defiance. I imagined our parents being woken, dressing hurriedly and arrested too. In my misery the impending mortification of their incredulous wrath or anxiety seemed suddenly worse than anything the Germans could do. I could picture Annette's supercilious sneer.

We were taken along a corridor and then left sitting on hard chairs which had been placed in a row beside the wall of an outer office. There were three chairs between us and we were forbidden to talk. I looked at Bette expecting the comfort of a comradely grin but she was staring straight ahead, her face expressionless. Abandoned, I assumed a casually interested expression and began to look round the office and to watch its activity as if I were just killing a few idle moments.

Two men were at work. One had his back to me and kept his head bent over his desk, his shoulders hunched. I never did see his face but for a while I stared at his hand which was writing furiously, focusing on the glimpse of watch beneath the cuff. Once he yawned and stretched and the cuff fell back revealing the dull pewterish metal. He moved some papers away from him and I watched the hand again, the smooth, hairless skin, the short, very clean nails. I wondered what his wife was like and if she pressed his cuffs, before recollecting that she must be miles away in Germany if she existed at all.

I realised the other man must be of higher rank not just from the insignia on his jacket, but from the way he handed work to his colleague, conversed confidently with telephone callers and twice entered the inner office without knocking. I dimly wondered at so much activity in the middle of the night.

When I met his eyes I had the distinct impression that he wanted to wink. He was youngish, fair-haired and reassuring, reminding me briefly of the officer I had seen by the window of Le Printemps. I risked a smile and he shook his head in gentle reproof.

Soon I realised that I was tired, that my greatest need was for sleep, that everything else could be postponed until I was once more ready to face it. I yearned for my own bed, aching to be safe at home, listening to Annette's breathing from the other bed with a whole night's sleep ahead of me.

'Mademoiselle!'

I woke with a start to find the German looking down at me. Bette was already standing and we were taken into the inner office and up to the desk of what was obviously a very senior officer, a man a few years younger than my father with thick dark hair which had gone a striking iron grey at the temples and over the ears. He surveyed us from very blue eyes before speaking in faultless French.

As I stared at him, absorbing the blue medal with gold engraving at his throat and the Iron Cross on his tunic together with the insignia of rank on his shoulders, the younger man gave him our names and addresses and then added a few sentences in German. I wondered if Bette could translate it.

'You are aware of the curfew?'

With momentary panic I wanted to deny it, to say our clock had stopped, to say Bernadette's mother had suffered a heart attack and we were running for the doctor, to say we had seen a mouse and jumped out of the window with fright. Then the moment passed and I reacted much as I did on those comfortless occasions when I was summoned to Sister Benedicte, whose unheeded words on leaving resistance to our elders now rang in my head.

I simply nodded. He looked at Bette who did the same.

'And of the penalties for defying it?'

'Being shot by one of your strutting fools.'

I gasped and stared stupidly at Bette, wondering what on earth possessed her to utter such words, particularly as there had been little anger or contempt in her tone. She had not spoken as one moved by emotion but rather as one stating a wearying but widely acknowledged fact. I half expected our interrogator to spring up and shoot her on the spot and briefly closed my eyes in case he did.

He raised his eyebrows, but his tone when he spoke was mild, even though the words were menacing.

'I am Colonel Klaus von Ströbel,' he announced, 'of the Army. Mademoiselle is fortunate I am not of the Gestapo.'

It was both a promise of mercy and a hint of the retribution he had in his power. Bette did not wilt but went on looking him in the eyes, making no response.

Unprovoked he turned to me. A suspicion formed in my mind that he was amused not irritated, that all Bette's courage was wasted, that he considered it mere bravado, that he regarded us as two remarkably silly girls. Indeed, seeing us through his eyes, I knew he was right and I prayed that Bette would utter no more insults, not because I was afraid for her but because I did not want her to make a fool of herself.

The realisation that we looked fools made me feel quite grown up, for once superior to Bette in knowledge.

'Why did you go out after curfew?'

I began to answer in what I thought was a mature and measured tone, the sort of tone grown-ups used when resolving a minor difference. I wanted to laugh indulgently at my own folly and seek to dismiss it as unworthy of any further time on his part or ours. Instead I heard my tone grow petulant and peevish.

'It's a classmate's birthday and before you came we could have gone out and enjoyed it. Even if it was just a normal curfew we could have gone out to each other's houses but instead we have been cooped up all evening. Well, we don't see why we have to put up with it all. We are sixteen.'

We are sixteen. I might as well have admitted to being six. He turned from me back to Bette and I no longer felt grown up but like a child who has spoiled a party with a tantrum.

'How many of you were out after curfew?'

'Six,' said Bette at once with no apparent consciousness of treachery and after a moment's shock I realised that he probably knew that already. Our captors would have seen the others sprinting off.

'And where did the other four go?'

'One went home and three ran on to a friend's.'

'And you think they are safe?'

It was not the question I had expected but Bette did not seem surprised. For perhaps three seconds they looked steadily at each other and with a cold jolt I realised they were trying to share their minds. Then Bette said slowly, with the first hesitation I had heard from her since we jumped from the window, 'There is one I am not sure about.'

At once I knew what she intended and gave a strangled, urgent 'No.' Neither so much as looked at me.

'Yvette Levin.'

'Levin,' repeated von Ströbel. 'Jewish?'

Again I sensed hesitation, but Bette nodded before giving Henriette's address and describing the shrubbery outside it. The German wrote down the information and summoned the fair-haired officer, issuing orders in an incomprehensible flood of his own language. The officer clicked his heels and departed with urgency.

'Idiots!' It was the first time he had displayed any anger at all.

It seemed a fair summary and he did not enlarge on it. Instead he rose and retrieved a hat from a stand in the corner and gestured to us to follow him. At the door he turned, muttered something morose and gave another order. The fair-haired soldier went to a cupboard and came back with two officers' overcoats which he handed to us. Colonel von Ströbel watched as we put them round our shoulders, I miserably, Bette matter-of-factly.

It was pointless to argue. The night would now be colder and we could not walk through Paris in party frocks. In the end we did not walk at all but were peremptorily ordered into a car, our captor sitting in front by the driver.

The shame of that drive through the city! I imagined Parisians looking out of their windows and thinking we were collaborators, the girlfriends of German officers, being taken home after a night out. In reality most people would be asleep and those who were not would stay away from their windows after curfew, but I could not get the thought out of my head, any more than I could suppress the realisation of a greater humiliation to come: in a few moments I would be facing my parents who would be summoned from their bed to hear of my folly.

Bette was dropped off first, her father coming drowsily and fearfully to the door. I could not hear what was said and the Colonel's face was a mask when he returned to the car. Bette gave me a reassuring wave before the door of the block shut and I was left in lonely misery for the rest of the journey.

It took what seemed an age to rouse anyone in the household and I shivered wretchedly beneath the ludicrously draped coat until I saw my grandfather looking nervously from an upstairs window and heard my father's steps as he came downstairs. Absurdly I wanted to run.

By the time the German had finished his explanation my mother had also come downstairs. In his fluent, easy French Klaus von Ströbel spared me nothing. He told how six of us had gone out after curfew, how we had been shot at, that there was a Jewish girl among our number, that we had been rude at Headquarters, that we did not appear to understand the extent of our misconduct. On this occasion he would take the matter no further but should there be a next time he would react very differently – or the Gestapo would.

My father was forced to thank him though I could see he hated doing so, but when the door had closed behind his unwelcome guest it was my mother who began to rebuke me. My father interrupted her by saying, 'Bed. We can talk about this in the morning.'

I woke early, gazing at the sun filtering through my curtains, longing to be free of worry, to know that the others were safe, that Yvette Levin stood in no danger. I wanted to be able to rejoice in the sunny day, to spend it in idle amusement, to gloat over the weeks which must yet pass before I returned to school. Irrationally I found myself hating Sylvie. If only she had never had the idea of going to Henriette's we would now still be at Bernadette's home, sleeping peacefully, untroubled by fear and self-recrimination.

Edouard came in and jumped on my bed, chattering merrily. Today he irritated rather than soothed me with his babble and happily expectant face, but I could not have found the heart to push him away. Instead I disappeared under the bedclothes hoping he would take the hint to go or at least to keep quiet.

'Germans! Bang! Bang!' giggled Edouard.

I stayed resolutely beneath the blankets until I really did fall asleep, to dream that Edouard was out after curfew and shouting, 'Bang! Bang!' to two helmeted figures who advanced towards him along a dark alley. Waking, I felt the relief flood through me and rejoiced in the sunshine after all.

I did not get up until I had heard the door shut behind my father as he went to work and the whine of the vacuum told me that the household was established in its normal routine. Even then I delayed my arrival in the kitchen to face the inevitable recriminations until I had bathed, dressed and made my bed, taking longer over each than was necessary, postponing the confrontation I was sure must follow.

Ersatz coffee added to my misery but Catherine the Second had obliged with fresh eggs and my mother was surprisingly restrained about my escapade of the night before, reminding me that war was not a game and that the bullets which had been fired at us were real, but not demanding any explanation of my folly or dwelling on the matter for long.

'Let it be a lesson to you,' she concluded grimly, and that I found to have been the attitude of most of our parents, the unlikely exceptions being Bette's.

By unspoken agreement we reassembled at Bernadette's apartment where the rest of the party had long since risen and dispersed. Over cups of coffee we exchanged stories of the previous night. Bernadette herself had been the first to be chased as she sped along the alley, but the Germans had spent a few precious seconds with Bette and me before one of them went after her and she had reached her window before she heard the pursuing feet.

Here however she encountered an unforeseen difficulty, the window-sill being higher than she realised. In desperation she tried to haul herself up but could not get the necessary purchase and she was resigning herself to being caught when three of the other girls looked out with scared faces and handed her a wooden stool. She had barely shut the window when her pursuer turned out of the alley.

The four girls cowered on the floor, knowing the stool below the window was a giveaway, expecting a peremptory rap on the glass, the ring of the doorbell, even a shot through the pane.

When none of these things happened, they sat shaking on the bed while Bernadette told them what had occurred and they debated whether or not to rouse her parents. At first they decided not to, reasoning that there was nothing anyone could do. Then someone remembered that Yvette Levin was Jewish and they were panicked into action.

There was no telephone in Henriette's flat so Bernadette's father rang a grumbling concierge who reluctantly agreed to see if she could rouse anyone. This took some time and one of the girls began to cry with tension before Monsieur Bastide returned from the call with a grim expression. Cécile and Sylvie were safe, he told them, but no one knew where Yvette was. For a certainty she could not be at home which was in a different part of Paris. There was nothing for it but to watch and wait for morning and the end of curfew.

It was now Yvette's turn to describe what had happened and she told us that Cécile and Sylvie had outrun her but before they could rouse Henriette they heard pursuing steps and all three flung themselves into the shrubbery, Yvette still some way behind the others. She only just reached cover as her pursuer turned on to the path. At first the soldier ran past but soon returned and made a cursory search of the bushes before going back to where his companion was guarding us. After what seemed like an age first Cécile and then Sylvie tried once more to awaken Henriette, this time by throwing clods of earth from the comparative safety of the shrubs.

When these efforts were no more successful than previous attempts Cécile walked up to the window, banged loudly and dived back into the shrubbery. Still Henriette slept but her younger sister woke, peered fearfully out from behind the window and then jumped back as Cécile emerged from the bushes. Then Henriette was leaning out and helping Cécile in and seconds later Sylvie followed.

Yvette stayed put. She saw the other two look out cautiously and even fancied she heard Cécile call her name but she remained hidden. She was further from the window than the others had been and they could not be certain if she was still behind them when they reached the sanctuary of the bushes. When she heard the window shut she felt frightened and lonely but could not yet bring herself to leave the bushes and be exposed, however briefly, to the view of whatever malevolent eyes might be watching.

At first she feared Germans and then, illogically but compellingly, wild animals: a lion escaped from the zoo perhaps, a jungle python rustling through the pretty Parisian shrubs. The wild animals became ghosts, which knew where she hid and trembled, enfilading towards her through the night. Reasoning would not dispel them but eventually the temperature did and Yvette was aware of nothing other than the physical discomfort of cramp and cold and the paralysis of fear.

Several times Yvette steeled herself to make a quick dash to Henriette's window, yearning for warmth and safety, in her mind vaulting the sill and falling into a homely, untroubled world where capture cast no shadow. Once she thought she saw Cécile peering from behind the glass, once a light was switched on bathing the grass with welcoming light. Then the beam was gone and only the pale light of the moon remained. Shivering, terrified, miserable, Yvette wept, afraid that even the small, sad gasps she made would betray her.

She knew she must move or freeze when a greater trial presented itself as the weight in her bladder commanded her attention with a growing, unignorable urgency. Once more she looked at the window and calculated the distance to safety. Cautiously she began to move, now as much conscious of impending ignominy as of discovery. Yvette was in the very act of crawling out of the bushes when she heard the distant footfalls.

Cowering back, her physical needs forgotten, she held her breath. The sounds grew louder, the tread now accompanied by voices, as the soldiers turned with purpose out of the alley and began methodically to search the bushes. When they found her she made no sound but the cramp left her unable to walk immediately and she was half dragged to the alley and then to a waiting car.

Yvette closed her eyes, trying to block out visions of the Gestapo, distraught parents and disappearing never to return, but she no longer wept. It was a matter of honour now not to cry in front of the enemy, a pathetic, futile gesture, a minute rag of pointless pride in which to wrap a shrinking spirit.

Eventually she drew herself from a slump to an upright sitting posture and made herself look at her surroundings, aware now of the hammering of hope against her ribs. Surely they were taking her home for she knew of no official building in this direction. Then she thought suddenly that they were going to pick up her parents too and a low groan escaped her.

'We are nearly there, Mademoiselle,' said one of the men in heavily accented French. Yet he spoke kindly and Yvette could not prevent a return of hope.

Sitting in the kitchen, after her captors had gone, shivering, blurting out the sad tale of lunatic defiance, Yvette had wondered for the first time how the Germans knew her address.

'Bette told them,' I said and the others looked at me in astonishment as I explained the scene in von Ströbel's office.

When I had finished my story they all spoke at once, exclaiming that Bette was a fool and Yvette could even now have been dead or enduring some terrible fate, but I disagreed. I knew that Bette had been given some insight which I had not shared, that she had sized up the situation accurately and had known that she was helping rather than betraying Yvette. Flighty, irresponsible Bette had somehow saved the day.

Yvette herself had nothing worse than a bad cold and bad memories to show for her adventures. Cécile had been quietly admonished by her parents and loudly berated by her older sister. Bernadette had been told there would be no more parties until she learned to behave more responsibly. Only Bette received immediate punishment, being confined to home for a whole week.

I have no idea what happened to Sylvie. I cannot remember her being one of our crowd again, although I suppose I must have spoken to her at school. I do not know how she spent the rest of the war, what she did either at school or after she had left. Her intervention in my life had been made; the consequences had yet to manifest themselves.

Bette's parents allowed her friends to visit after two days and we crowded into her bedroom to ask what had made her trust von whatshisname. I bounced Alphonse up and down on my knee, the ageing teddy bear comforting me with its memories of childhood, security and innocence.

'There were photos on his desk. One was of a girl about your Jeanne's age. He saw me looking at it and when I met his eyes I knew he wasn't going to hand us over to the torturers or whatever. He just saw us as daughters.'

'Still, it was an awful risk,' demurred Bernadette.

'Nothing compared to the risk Yvette had already taken. We must have been mad.'

'We must not be mad again, at least not like that. We could have put our parents through hell.'

It was Cécile who had spoken and none argued. Sister Benedicte had been right: acts of defiance were best left to those who would put them to better use than walking about Paris in party frocks. For the first time in a year I remembered the scream in the night which I had heard when the Germans first arrived and a chill of fear passed through me.

Youth, however, is resilient and soon we were making the most of the school holidays as if nothing had happened. Occasionally we talked about the escapade, especially to admiring non-participants, but with decreasing frequency.

Once I told Bette that I thought the young German in the outer office was good-looking but she could not recall him. She did, however, comment on the Colonel as having a striking head of hair and remarkable eyes and she did remember his name.

Von Ströbel, she reminded me, Klaus von Ströbel.

five

An Insect and a Rose

When I next saw him I could not immediately remember his name.

His own memory was more reliable.

'Mademoiselle Dessin,' he greeted me, as we met by chance near the Quai d'Orsay, and I noticed the way the crow's feet at the corners of his eyes crinkled when he smiled.

I felt at a disadvantage because I had to fumble in my memory for his name, because I did not want to be seen talking to Germans, because I felt under some obligation to him which I was uncertain how to acknowledge but, for some reason which I did not fully understand, principally because I was dressed in my school uniform which I was beginning to resent as shapeless, unappealing and drab. When I had last encountered him I had been embarrassed by my inappropriate glad rags; now I was shamed by what I was sure was my only too appropriate school uniform.

'Colonel von Ströbel,' I remembered.

He clicked his heels and bowed. 'And Mademoiselle Bette? How is she?'

I pulled a face. 'She likes school and exams and is working flat out for baccalauréat this year.'

Von Ströbel looked amused. 'And you?'

'I hate it and I shall be seventeen next week but I have to stay until I have at least tried the bac.'

'And Mademoiselle Levy?'

'Levin. She is very well and we are all very grateful to you.'

My words seemed stilted and fulsome, my manner at once embarrassed and too effusive. Feeling myself blush I glanced covertly and frantically around me, hoping to be able to hail someone I knew but my eyes met only those of a briefly curious, middle-aged woman. Preoccupied with my own dilemma I failed to wonder at his ability to remember all our names, to attach any significance to it.

'Will you permit me to buy you a coffee, Mademoiselle Dessin?'

I wanted to refuse graciously but firmly, to make him understand that he was still the enemy even if a kind one. I wanted to turn and run away, far away, from a situation to which I was not equal. I longed for home and security, but he was old enough to be my father and had saved Yvette Levin from some vaguely understood doom. Had he been younger and less authoritative or had I felt no debt of gratitude needing to be repaid then I might have extricated myself from so unwelcome a position. Instead I stammered an acceptance and we walked together in the direction he indicated.

People glanced at me with concern or scorn and I looked at the pavement, yearning for the walk to be over, relief flooding through me when we arrived at the café only to be replaced by guilty enjoyment when I tasted the coffee and discovered it to be real.

By the time I summoned up the confidence to look around me I had a pretty fair idea of what I would see: Germans accompanied by the occasional Frenchwoman. Coffee like that would not be served to the invaded, only to the invader.

I tried to think of something to say to Klaus von Ströbel. Before I succeeded he said he hoped I had not got into too much trouble after my little escapade with the curfew. I responded that only Bette's parents had been angry enough to impose sanctions and he smiled, commenting that doubtless our families were too relieved that we were safe to think of much else.

I assented and said I liked the coffee so he ordered another cup and asked me what I wanted to do when I left school. As there was no way I could answer both truthfully and impressively I shrugged and muttered that I was still deciding.

He asked me why I hated school so much and I said it was not school I hated but the relentless studying of things that bored me. Tonight I should have to complete an essay on the Fronde which had been hanging over me for a week and I found the whole subject too miserably complex to have a chance of producing anything remotely competent.

He smiled again, then frowned slightly in concentration. Presently the furrows disappeared from his brow and he began to unravel the manoeuvres of the various factions in an explanation of the Fronde which left me not only enlightened but entertained. It was as though he were telling me a longish anecdote rather than providing a lecture on French history.

I listened with an attention I would have found difficult to accord Sister Bernard Thérèse who had taught us history throughout my time at the Convent. I listened and I understood but I was not filled with any desire to know more; I had all I needed for my essay. I also had the material I needed for the present conversation and asked him if he was an historian and where he had learned such good French.

He had, he told me, studied English history at Oxford between the two wars, that he was particularly interested in Scottish history, that he had a natural liking for languages and spoke English, French and Italian fluently. I tried to remember what I knew of Scotland and recalled its being a cold and mountainous country stuck on the top of England. The men there wore kilts. Principally, however, I thought of dancing. Madame Paschale, who took games and maths, ran Scottish dancing on wet days when we could not go outside at break.

I wondered whether he had made friends at Oxford and what he would do if he met one of them in a battle. Laughing, he replied that he had many friends across Europe, in England and Italy especially, but that war appeared to be an occupational hazard of being male and that he would cross its bridges when he arrived at them. It was a surprising answer and I was by no means certain of its orthodoxy although he had said nothing to indicate that the current war was either unnecessary or unjust.

Eventually I became aware of the sinking sun and the passage of time. I had long since finished my coffee. I jumped up in haste, thanking him, guilty that I had enjoyed myself so much in the presence of the enemy, refusing his offer to see me home, wondering how I should explain my lateness. He looked mildly disappointed but otherwise he appeared more cheerful and relaxed than when we had met near the Quai d'Orsay. I was not at all sure that I should be making life happier for the enemy, but I was obscurely flattered that he had enjoyed himself in my company.

I was also conscious of pleasure when, after walking a few metres, I turned to wave and found him still looking in my direction. He too waved and I hoped he would come safely through the war and return unharmed to the wife and three children about whom he had talked so fondly.

I suppose some of that warmth must have been evident when I described the meeting to my parents, even though I was at pains to chronicle my confusion at the chance encounter. Colonel von Ströbel had undeniably been kind to us and I felt I was obliged to be friendly in return. At any rate it had seemed churlish to refuse a cup of coffee. My parents received such sentiments without enthusiasm but offered no criticism beyond advice that I had now done my duty and should refuse any further acts of friendship from the oppressors of France. My being seen in such company could be misconstrued.

I sensed an ill-defined fear behind their words and sought to reassure them by telling how the German had unravelled the complexities of the Fronde, feeling certain that such academic prowess would be welcomed even if stimulated by the enemy. To my surprise my father looked hurt.

'You could have asked me about that.'

Startled, I tried to imagine asking my father about anything academic. I could hardly tell him that he was the last person I would ever consult, that I was diminished by the air of suppressed exasperation which had always seemed to lie just below the surface of his answers, that I sensed ridicule in him and in most of my teachers, that I knew I was a great disappointment and did not wish to remind him by asking questions which seemed sensible to me but daft to him.

It had never occurred to me that my father might have found my withdrawal distressing. If I had thought about it at all I would have assumed that his reaction would have been one of relief at being spared regular proof of my stupidity.

I was surprised too at the real pleasure with which Sister Bernard Thérèse praised my von Ströbel-inspired essay. Here at last, her raptures implied, was the subject which had finally engaged Catherine Dessin in serious thought. I wondered what she would say if she knew the real source of my competence on this occasion.

Only days later my father's world was turned upside down. The Sorbonne had been functioning as a mere shadow of its former self since the beginning of the Occupation. The young men had disappeared and the young women needed to work so there were few students to benefit from the wisdom on offer and increasingly they were being taught informally. My father's subject was unlikely to appeal to the enemy and there was simply no job for him to do. He arrived home early one afternoon and announced that he was no longer required by what remained of that once great university. It was of little comfort then that he had lasted longer than most.

To my embarrassment he began to teach at the Convent, at first on an occasional basis but soon most days. Our regular English teacher had returned to her native country shortly after the outbreak of war and her place had been filled by a nun of uncertain health who was now very ill indeed. Outside help was drafted in and my father proved by far the most satisfactory substitute. The only other male lay teacher we had known was the science master who had not returned from the Exodus so the arrival of Professor Dessin was a matter of some comment and curiosity.

I found it disconcerting to address him as Monsieur instead of Papa and wondered if the girls in my sisters' classes giggled as much as those in mine whenever I had to stand up and answer him formally.

I often walked in or back with him and after an awkward start looked forward to our conversations. I learned a lot about his own youth, about my grandparents, about how my mother had not liked him at all when they first met. I told him the war was childish and remembered that Klaus von Ströbel had described it as an occupational hazard of being male. He laughed but talked earnestly about freedom and the dangers of Hitler.

During these walks my father indulged me by discussing fashion, films and skating, by exclaiming over the exploits of Bette, by lamenting the absence of ever more goods from the shops and only occasionally endeavouring to counter with more serious subjects. Confronted almost daily by classes of girls which contained as many gigglers and daydreamers as earnest pupils, he had begun to accept that it was Annette and Jeanne who were exceptionally bright not I who was exceptionally dull.

I began to believe that he might let me leave after all without attempting baccalauréat and I might have pressed the issue had I any particular job in mind or had I found the prospect of a daily work routine, unrelieved by long holidays, remotely congenial.

Despite the greater closeness to my father which came from these walks the atmosphere at home was becoming brittle. Annette was awakening to the realisation that no matter how clever she was there could be no glittering future in an Occupied country; Jeanne was becoming awkward and rebellious with adolescence; my mother worried about Jeanne, the absent Martin and the prospect of keeping us all nourished as rationing grew ever more stringent. My comfort was Edouard with his winning ways and happy but not always comprehensible prattle. I would swing him up and piggyback him through the two flights of stairs which led to my grandfather's room where we would collapse in a giggling heap while I regained my breath and the old man teased Edouard.

Sometimes we played hide-and-seek and sometimes Hunt the Horse. Edouard had a very worn toy horse, made by my grandmother while he was still in his pram, from which the stuffing oozed and the wool mane hung loose. He could not bear to be parted from it for long and we soon found that one way to keep Edouard occupied was to hide it and challenge him to find it. Once my grandfather sat absolutely still for ten minutes with the ridiculous creature balanced on his head while Edouard hunted high and low around him.

Even here the chill of Occupation made itself felt, in this case literally. I had always associated my grandparents' rooms with warmth, sometimes too much stuffy warmth, as their elderly, inactive frames required heat earlier and greater than did the rest of us. Now my grandfather wore two jerseys and a heavy jacket in a cold room. I hated the war on his behalf.

'Will it ever be over?' I asked him in frustration.

'One day it will have to be over but when or how none of us can know, so we must just keep going. In 1914 we all thought it would be over by Christmas and it lasted four years but it did end and so will this. The important thing is to make the most of what you have and not waste time waiting for a different world.'

It sounded a bit like one of Sister Benedicte's lectures so I sought refuge in playing vigorously with an enthusiastically squealing Edouard.

I was playing with him again but in imagination only as I dreamed my way through Sister Xavier's biology lesson. We were standing outside, hugging our coats close to us against the November chill, solemnly inspecting the construction of the roses which grew in abundance near the entrance to the Convent. My feet felt like lumps of ice and as I looked down at them I covertly inspected the footwear of my fellow pupils. It was scuffed, down at heel and often too big as older siblings handed down their shoes. Yet most of it had been polished, pride still flickering among the conquered. Even so, three of the girls were wearing homemade shoes with hideous wooden soles. I stared at my own uninspiring black laceups and wondered how long it would be before Annette or I or Jeanne were reduced to such measures.

When I looked up I saw him. He and a junior officer had just entered the gate and were walking up the steps towards the main door of the Convent. He appeared not to notice us, to be intent on whatever business brought him, his mouth tight with some anxiety. Immediately I wanted to wipe away that tautness, to protect him from worry. My reaction surprised me although I found the thought pleasant and warming in some way I could not quite understand.

Bette nudged me. 'It's him,' she whispered, 'Von whatever.'

'Ströbel,' I muttered to Bette. Klaus, I said to myself.

Sister Xavier told us to pay attention and challenged us to repeat what she had just said. Bette obliged, but I was again distracted, this time by Yvette Levin, who seemed to be shrinking into her coat, her eyes terrified.

'No, no,' I wanted to soothe her. 'He hasn't come for you. He saved you once before, remember. He is not the Gestapo.'

The words were uttered in my imagination only but for a few seconds I saw the world through Yvette's eyes, through the eyes of thousands of Jews, who lived in daily fear and uncertainty. The reality of their Occupation was different from mine. I glimpsed darkness and horror and it was no longer the November wind which chilled me.

Sister Xavier plucked a large, slightly overblown, whitish rose and asked us to examine its centre. We passed it around, but when it was my turn an insect ran out and I dropped the flower with a scream. Immediately everyone else jumped aside to avoid the harmless creature with loud cries of 'Ugh!'

Sister berated us for fools and infants but I sensed she was not really angry. I bent to retrieve the rose and, as I straightened up, I saw he had come out and was watching the scene with amusement and that the junior with him was the same one who had driven us to our homes that night.

Without thinking I waved. Klaus von Ströbel's face lit up with recognition and he waved back. Then they were gone and I turned to face a frozen tableau and the gaze of twenty pairs of scandalised eyes.

Later I faced the calm eyes of Sister Benedicte whose demeanour suggested disquiet rather than anger. I should not wave at men in the middle of a lesson and in particular I should not wave at *those* men at all. They were the enemy and my conduct was decidedly unbecoming.

I met her remonstrations with truth. I had acted instinctively, having recognised the officer in question. One did wave when seeing a familiar figure and I had forgotten both that I was in class and that the enemy should not be acknowledged. My tone stopped only just short of weariness, implying that the episode was too unimportant for all this fuss.

Yet I knew I should not have waved, that the others would not have done so, that it was a mark not just of recognition but of warmth. If Sister Benedicte thought my response to her rebuke insolent she did not say so but instead turned to my unsatisfactory work.

I left her small, cramped office feeling idle and wanton but unbothered. I yearned to escape the confines of the close supervision which school represented, to feel I had never to construe a Latin sentence or to evaluate an algebraic equation again. That afternoon I shook my hair free the instant I was outside the school gate, holding my satchel between my knees while I undid the plaits.

I walked home alone, but when I was nearly there Jeanne caught me up. 'I like your hair like that,' she commented.

'So do I,' I said mutinously.

'We're doing Virgil,' she announced proudly.

'So am I.'

My little sister stared at me, puzzled. I managed to smile. That afternoon I had struggled to translate Dido's anguished realisation that Aeneas was leaving her, called by fate and duty, driven by *pietas*. Cécile had sighed in sympathy with the tragic queen when I would have preferred her to be whispering the right answers to me. I could not empathise with Dido until I imagined Klaus von Ströbel as Aeneas.

I thought of Aeneas looking anxious as Klaus had looked that morning and of Dido wanting to smooth away the worry lines and I began to understand her better, but not enough to hate Aeneas as much as Cécile seemed to think appropriate.

On the Church Steps

'*Ite, Missa est.*'

With relief I watched the priest leave the altar, having spent the Mass glancing covertly at my watch every few minutes. It was a mystery to me why I did this, as I genuinely believed, but somehow my concentration would fail and by the *Sanctus* I was no longer trying, by the *Pater Noster* I was looking forward to the rest of the day and by the *Agnus Dei* I was unsuccessfully stifling yawns. I wondered if the priest ever allowed his mind to wander and thought it must be wonderful to be as holy as he.

Edouard raced down the aisle and Stephanie, a newfound friend, ran up it towards him. My parents were chatting to some neighbours while Annette and Jeanne had gone to light candles in the side aisles so I looked in vain for Bernadette who sometimes attended Mass at this time. I began to wander slowly towards the door, almost tempted to enter one of the confessionals in order to while away the time until the others would be ready to go home.

Some Germans had attended the service and as I left the church one was standing outside, drawing on a cigarette, the smoke a thin wisp in the late November sunshine. He turned and for the second time that week I recognised von Ströbel's junior officer. At once he bowed and clicked his heels and bade me good morning.

I returned the greeting uneasily. His French was poor compared to his superior's, but his smile was engaging. He addressed me as Mademoiselle Dessin and I did not wonder why he should remember my name; he asked casually if I always came to Mass at this time and I innocently said I did. Then, as if sensing that he was embarrassing me, he was gone with a formal nod of farewell.

I glanced around but the parishioners emerging into the morning sun did not appear to have noticed our encounter and I had all but forgotten it when members of my family began to join me on the church steps.

On Sundays we gathered in the dining room for our midday meal despite the awfulness of the food now available. My grandparents descended from their upstairs rooms, on my grandfather's part with increasing difficulty, and we congregated round the table as we had on every Sunday I could remember. On these occasions more than on any others I felt Martin's absence, wondering where he might be now, hoping his exploits with the Free French were not leading him into danger. Sometimes we were joined by our cousins, sometimes by our friends, but this did not happen so often as guests felt obliged to bring along food which was scarce enough at home.

Today, though, we did have a visitor, Mad Aunt Sophie, and she brought with her – doubtless with reluctance – some contributions from her hoarded stocks. I wondered if that was why Annette and my father had gone to fetch her when she would rather have stayed in her own apartment. At any rate she showed little enjoyment of either the lunch or our company and enquired querulously every quarter of an hour or so if it was time to be gone.

Whenever she did this my father would say, 'Soon, Sophie' and she would subside, muttering. I too yearned to be gone, to be free in the wintry sunshine, to inhale the crisp air, to trample fallen leaves. I resolved to suggest a cycle ride to Annette, but unluckily it fell to her and to me to see our aunt home, grimacing at each other when she wasn't looking.

Once I had settled the old woman in her preferred armchair, I made an excuse to visit the bathroom and flung open the cupboard door, half fearing it might be empty, my heart beating with hope and fear when I saw it was not. There stood the shampoos in their rows, most of them liquids rather than powders, bottle of Palmolive after bottle of Palmolive.

The previous day I had taken more than two hours to wash my hair in egg, rinse it in vinegar and painfully comb out the resultant tangles. All I could see through the tears which sprang to my eyes with each painful tug was a vision of that cupboard with its rows of shampoos, the promise of a return to normality, of making a once simple task simple again. If I could not wash my hair without so much pain then I would cut it and wear it as short as possible.

A rustle behind me made me start but it was only Annette. I sensed she wanted to tell me to leave the coveted bottles alone but that they presented as great a temptation to her as to me. Emile had long since been succeeded in her affections by first Pierre and then Henri but the young men were leaving Paris, seemingly just disappearing, and these days Annette's attention to her appearance was for pride alone.

It was still a fierce pride and she wanted the shampoo. She also knew that to take it was stealing and that asking for it outright would only meet with a refusal, but the privations of Occupation were biting deeper now than they had been when I had last looked so longingly in this cupboard and the claims of honesty, of conscience, of upbringing somehow felt less compelling.

'Try asking,' said Annette heavily.

'She won't understand,' I prevaricated, knowing that Annette would realise that if our aunt said no then it really would be stealing if we took even a teaspoonful.

'If she could understand,' I went on doubtfully, as my hand reached to the shelf, 'she would want us to have it. She wouldn't want us to suffer.'

We took one bottle each and rearranged the remaining bottles so that ours might be less easily missed. At home when I lied to my mother and said Aunt Sophie had given them to us she raised her eyebrows but did not press for any detail. With a small frisson of shock I realised that my mother was effectively conspiring with us in our dishonesty and that I did not really want her to, that the world would have been a more reassuring place if she had questioned us and insisted on the return of the shampoos. I felt vulnerable rather than triumphant, an uncertain adult rather than a secure child, a voyager without a guiding star. I had chosen to be bad and those who should have been curious or shocked were not.

Annette appeared untroubled by the whole episode while I agonised over whether it should feature at my next confession, afraid that if it did the priest might do what my mother should have done and suggest the return of the goods to their rightful, if senile, owner. I salved my conscience by giving Bette enough for one wash without telling her how I had come by it. She too asked no questions.

My hair was at its best when Klaus von Ströbel appeared at Mass the following Sunday. He greeted my father and mother, who responded coldly, and smiled at me.

'Mademoiselle Dessin.'

I found myself answering more warmly than I had intended purely because I was embarrassed by my parents' ungracious attitude and felt rewarded when he seemed pleased. As Christmas was now less than a month away I asked if he would be returning to Germany to see his children. He shook his head and I murmured something sympathetic, becoming uncomfortably aware of my parents' disapproving stiffness.

If he too was sensitive to the hostility around him he ignored it, talking determinedly with me for a few minutes before taking his leave. I watched him walk away from us, down the aisle, with a mixture of relief and regret. At the door he was joined by the young, fair-haired officer and together they went out into the driving rain without a backward glance.

Yet I knew that he had wanted to look back, to wave, to mouth goodbye, that only my parents' presence prevented his doing so. I realised too that I had watched his departure for too long, that I should have turned at once instead of following his walk from the church and that now my family was watching me.

'It's Sunday,' I observed defensively. 'And we are all equal in the eyes of God.'

No one argued and I knew that the defensiveness was in itself an admission of wrongdoing. Fraternising with the enemy was wrong, full stop, not just between Monday and Saturday. Yet I knew some other people who were less strict in their interpretation of enmity.

Still I believed what I had said. We were all equal. Yvette Levin was as important to God as the most senior, bemedalled German officer even if the Gestapo thought she was a subhuman and Klaus von Ströbel had not forfeited entry to Heaven merely because he was part of an invading army. Then I remembered mad Aunt

Sophie and how I had robbed her in a way I would never have considered had she been of normal mind. I touched my long, shining, soft hair and knew myself a hypocrite.

Bette's hair too was silky and lustrous when next I saw her. Sitting before her mirror we were twisting our hair into different styles and talking about Christmas. The first winter of the Occupation had been difficult but the current one was hell. At least I thought so then, in the December of 1941, not knowing the rigours and privations which yet lay in store for us.

I had more or less stopped growing but I was taller and had bigger feet than any other female member of my family so there was no handing down of clothes and shoes. Ironically Annette wore shoes which last year had fitted me. I knew that it was only a matter of weeks before I became the first of our family to have to resort to home-made shoes. I had let down hems and let out seams, but my clothes were worn and would not last another year.

Annette used some of my skirts and blouses for work. Despite glittering success in baccalauréat she was merely a secretary to the manager of a store which controlled and distributed rations, a position she hated but which was of some advantage nonetheless as it enabled her to obtain extra supplies. When I remembered all her bright hopes I could only wonder that girls like Bette and Cécile struggled on, their sights firmly set on the highest possible grades, when there was so little opportunity before them.

'The war must be over one day,' Cécile had pointed out when I asked her why she worked so hard.

'Yes,' another girl had put in. 'But by then we will be too old for university and work. It will be time to settle down and have families.'

I looked forward to having a family. I would have six children because otherwise there would not be enough to use all my favourite names. Louis would be my eldest, clever, the apple of his grandfather's eye. Then would come Marguerite but everyone would call her Margot and she would be a tomboy and compete with Louis whereas her younger twin sisters, Viviane and Madeleine, would be shy and domesticated, wonderful cooks, the kind of girls who doted on their father and knitted him jumpers. Next Henri and, after a very long time, Colette.

I would write down their names and attach different middle names and confirmation names. Occasionally I imagined a family photograph and arranged their names as captions with their ages in brackets. I dreamed of living in a large apartment and of their running up and down stairs to visit other children, of a concierge who was sometimes fierce and the unwilling victim of their tricks and at other times was beaming, tolerant, wistfully childless.

I had only the haziest notion of the husband who would help me produce such a family. He was just a gap in my imaginary photograph, nameless, formless, featureless, but recently I imagined fine lines around his eyes crinkling like Klaus von Ströbel's and realised that, as much as I wanted a reliable wage earner, he would be human too and vulnerable. I thought of the young, open-faced officer by the window of Le Printemps and of Robert as he played with Edouard and decided I preferred a few fine wrinkles.

I voiced this thought to Bette as she pulled my hair up so tightly that tears sprang to my eyes. In the mirror I could see Alphonse, relegated to the top of the wardrobe.

Bette paused and pursed her lips. 'An older man? Could be dangerous.' Her tone somehow suggested that such danger could be appealing.

'Why?' I asked reluctantly, thinking I might be demonstrating an amusing naïvety.

'He could be married.'

'Not everyone over thirty is married,' I protested.

'Then one must ask why not. He might have had a whole series of girlfriends and put them all off with his selfish ways or his meanness with money or perhaps being too forward.'

'Too forward?'

'Yes, you know.'

I did not know.

'He might want to do things. Things you shouldn't do before marriage.'

'Ah,' I said, faking the dawning of comprehension, and turned the conversation to Christmas, in particular to the absence of chocolates this year.

Bette was sticking pins in the huge heap of hair which she was holding on top of my head. She held three of them in her mouth, which I felt to be unhygienic, but it did not seem friendly to complain.

'I know how to get some.'

Because of the pins I couldn't understand what she had just said. Bette waited until she had jabbed all three into my hair and then repeated that she could obtain chocolate for Christmas.

'Where?'

'Montmartre. The girls there get them from the Germans and some of them are happy to pass them on.'

'Why do the Germans give them chocolates?'

Bette paused in the act of winding my hair into another coil. We looked at each other's reflections in the mirror. Then she said, 'Because they have given themselves to the Germans.'

Bette continued motionless, looking at my reflection, while I absorbed this unintelligible information.

'You mean they have decided to take Germany's side?'

'I mean they are prostitutes.'

This time I did not bother to pretend I understood. Bette knew that I did not.

'You know what we were talking about just now? About some men wanting to do things before marriage? Well, there are girls who will do it for money. That is why some people go to Montmartre, especially the Pigalle area.'

When we were much younger, Bette had often explained things to me before my mother or elder sister had thought it right to do so. To obtain such forbidden knowledge I crept under a large bush near the roses at the front of the Convent or into the cupboard where Sister Aloysius kept the stocks of exercise books and we sat back to back because it was too embarrassing to look at each other. Thus I learned, with varying degrees of accuracy, about what happened when women gave birth, about why Marie-Claire Delfont had left so hurriedly one term and been sent away by her parents, why I had heard Edouard described as a mistake.

Now we did not sit back to back but went on looking at each other in the mirror as Bette explained, using sufficient circumlocution and euphemism to leave me with only a little more knowledge than before. I reflected that if the women of Montmartre did what you had to do to have babies in exchange for money then there must be a lot of babies in Montmartre.

I was glad to return to the safer subject of chocolate and how we might get some. I asked Bette if it was not wrong to accept chocolate from the Germans, even if only at second-hand, but she replied that we were only taking back that which they had stolen from us. As I pondered this, a daring plan began to form in my mind.

For its successful execution it was necessary that Klaus von Ströbel appear at Mass again in the next couple of weeks, but he had only ever done so once, at least when I was there, and I was working on fallback strategies when I saw him the very next Sunday, this time outside on the steps.

I had come out towing Edouard by the hand, but otherwise alone. The rest of the family had come to an earlier service because we had a large family gathering in celebration of my grandparents' fiftieth wedding anniversary and my job was to keep Edouard out of the way while the grown-ups prepared.

I greeted him in what I hoped were neutral tones appropriate to a conversation with the enemy but even so I noticed disapproving glances from one or two other worshippers. He enquired after my family and I told him of the preparations at home, adding some bitter commentary on the likely nature of the meal.

For this I had good reason. One of my uncles had a smallholding in the country and, unable to get to the celebrations, his wife had parcelled up some food and sent it to us. Unfortunately the package took a week to arrive and all we extracted from it was some stinking remnant of what had once been fresh meat. Undeterred, my mother boiled it for hours with some vinegar and it was now to form a major part of the celebratory meal.

Von Ströbel looked sympathetic, but not embarrassed, and then mildly amused as I went on to anticipate a miserable Christmas without the usual huge feast and things like chocolate. I did try not to place emphasis on the word chocolate, less because I was retreating from my plan than because my complaint sounded childish. I should have spoken of the absence of silk stockings or perfume or some such sophisticated requirement, not chocolates.

He hoped my grandparents had many happy years to come and that my family would enjoy the celebrations, albeit within the limitations imposed by war. Then he teased Edouard who responded enthusiastically, being as yet unable to distinguish Germans from Frenchmen.

When we parted I was certain my plan would succeed. A few days before the end of term a car drew alongside me as I walked home from school and the fair-haired junior officer leaned out and handed me a parcel. I glanced around but there was no one who might have noticed and I stuffed the parcel in my satchel. At home I unwrapped the package in the bathroom because Annette and Jeanne were in the bedroom. Chocolates spilled out over the dark green linoleum but it was the small Christmas gift tag which held my attention.

To Catherine, with compliments, Klaus von Ströbel.

To Catherine. Not Mademoiselle Dessin. Catherine. It could have been the mark of an adult addressing a child, but I knew it was not. I knew that ahead of Annette and Bette I was admired by a man, not a spotty youth like Emile or Robert but a man. Then I remembered that the man in question was married and I looked again at the tag, it suddenly seeming urgent that it should, after all, bear no special meaning. It was all perfectly proper, it must be so. He sent not love but compliments and the full use of his surname was reassuringly formal. Here, surely, was no harm.

I lied to my parents on Christmas Eve, saying the chocolates had been obtained by Bette at Montmartre, noting that they exchanged glances and caring neither that I lied nor compromised Bette, who had in any event contemplated doing exactly what I claimed. I had hidden the tag amongst my handkerchiefs and often when I was alone I took it out and re-read it until it became grubby and dog-eared. I had before kept secrets from my parents but some instinct told me not to trust anyone with the existence of the tag.

I did not even tell Bette and therefore had to lie again when sharing the gift with her, saying we had been sent the chocolates by a relative. It cost me ten Hail Marys at my next confession, but the priest seemed more interested in why the Germans had given me chocolates in the first place than in the barefaced lies I had told.

Catherine, I thought to myself as I rose from the penance, Catherine.

Catherine, I whispered to the mirror as I used it to brush my hair, Catherine. I looked at the image it sent back with satisfied vanity. The privations of war suited me better than the rest of the family. I had lost my puppy fat and my face looked finely chiselled beneath my thick golden mane, whereas Annette's sallow face looked merely pinched and hungry. Her pride at last had worn thin and because washing it had become such an ordeal, she left her hair dirty for too long so that it lay flat to her head, lank and greasy. She wore her hair as short as fashion allowed to minimise the discomfort.

Looking back I wonder that we were so optimistic, that we spent hours in front of the mirror, looking at ill-fitting clothes, ankle socks and home-made wooden-soled shoes; that we looked forward to marriage and children despite the absence of young men; that we dreamed of our own little homes whatever the impossibility of heating them properly. I remember how the women spent days making hats out of paper to wear at the races at Longchamps where they fell apart if it rained.

I remember and I wonder and I forgive myself, but then it was much harder to face up to what was happening when I found myself arranging the names of imaginary children beneath an imaginary photograph and suddenly the blank occupied by the imaginary husband took shape and the shape was that of an oppressor of France.

seven

An Act of Injustice

I greeted 1942 with the same happy optimism I had brought to New Years in childhood. This would be a significant year, a memorable one in my personal history. Once I had imagined some future biographer writing, 'This was the year when the remarkable talents of Catherine Dessin were first noticed' or 'It was in this year that Catherine Dessin took a decision which was to alter her life and that of so many others'.

The talents were never specified in my dreams nor was the nature of the momentous decision but the thought of some great destiny unrolling before me somehow made up for all the disappointments, petty humiliations and sheer ordinariness of the past year.

Now I no longer coveted a place in history and had some time ago learned to place my talents in depressing proportion to those required for genius but I still saw each new year as a promise of an exciting fresh start and this time I had good reason, for in the summer I would get the dreaded baccalauréat out of the way – I had no grounds for believing I would pass – and then at last I could leave school.

I had decided what I would do, having come to recognise my skill with Edouard. I would mind children. Sometimes I pictured myself working in an orphanage, bringing happiness to small, sad toddlers, who would keep in touch with me all their lives. I had a regular fantasy in which I recognised a child as being one of those who became lost during the Exodus and reunited it with ever-grateful parents.

Occasionally I saw instead a young family which had lost its mother and was presided over by a grieving father who must give up the children to an orphanage because there was no one to look after them while he worked to feed them. I would save the day and far into the future he would realise that there was no better mother for his children . . .

I knew my dreams were childish, but still they came and comforted me and I had not the resolution to drive them out of my mind. I did however wonder what size of family I should have if I added six of my own to that of a grieving widower, but that was my only concession to the claims of reality.

As it happened I neither took baccalauréat nor looked after children in 1942. The reason for the first was simple: I was expelled.

The series of events which led to my shameful ejection from the Convent began when a girl in my class told me a very dirty joke and, failing to recognise it as such, I passed the story on to Cécile, who was suitably shocked and warned me not to tell anyone else. Bette was immersed in her work and spent most breaks with her head in her books and Cécile was not much better as a companion in those fraught months leading up to the examination. I therefore became more friendly with some of the other girls and Lisette, who told me the joke, was one of those with whom I spent break.

The friendship was tenuous and did not survive what happened next. When a girl three forms lower went home and told her parents the joke, saying she had heard it at school from an older girl, her mother visited Sister Benedicte in high dudgeon protesting that she had sent her daughter to a convent to be protected from such pollution, not exposed to it. The child was asked to identify the older girl and immediately pointed the finger at Lisette.

Lisette had been in trouble before and knew she faced expulsion so she took the coward's way out and said she had not understood the story but had heard it from me. Summoned to Sister Benedicte's study I fiercely denied it, staring at Lisette in disbelief. Normally my word would have carried the greater weight but Lisette was desperate and she insisted she was telling the truth. Mother Superior looked from one to the other of us before sending us back to our classroom where I sat and shook with indignation and terror.

Half an hour later Bette, Bernadette and Cécile were sent for, reminded that God heard every word they were saying and asked individually if I had ever told them, my close friends, a grossly improper joke. The first two gave instant denials but Cécile hesitated, momentarily torn between the demands of truth and loyalty, and Sister Benedicte pounced. Cécile did her best for me, saying that she was sure I did not understand what I had told her, but my guilt had been confirmed.

Lisette and I were told to write apologies to the younger girl's parents and also to Sister Benedicte herself for the disgrace we had brought on the school. Lisette complied with relief, but I steadily refused. I was innocent and would not therefore apologise to anyone.

My parents were called to the school but I stood firm through my tears and trembles. I had done no wrong. Indeed, wrong was being done to me. It was all so horribly unfair. Reluctantly Sister Benedicte told me that I must come to school next day with my letters of apology or not at all.

At home everything was unnaturally quiet. Annette and Jeanne crept away from the tension and grave faces in the kitchen. Edouard was above with my grandparents and the usual preparations for the evening meal were absent. There was no clattering of dishes, no smell of cooking, no steam on the windows, no low grumble from my grandmother as something was discovered not to be ready. The table was unlaid, the stove cold and silent.

My father said he believed me. He did not for one moment accept that I would have understood such humour and would have thought less of me if I had. Lisette's record was against her and he was surprised by Sister Benedicte's conclusion, but, although it was unjust, I must accept that life was full of unfairness and the question before me now was not how I could undo it but how I should react. If I apologised, I could still write a private note to the Mother Superior saying that I was only doing so to avoid being expelled and maintaining my innocence. Sooner or later Lisette would give herself away and my reputation would be restored.

'No.' The word was a thin squeak of sound. My mother moved to hold me but my father motioned her away.

'Then you must make up your mind to go to another school or to none at all,' he said. 'I suppose we must be stoical about it, my little woolly kitten, and accept that the outcome of bac was never entirely certain.'

I gave him a watery smile, reassured by the endearment left over from childhood, by his acceptance of my decision and by his calm appreciation of the future. I hated seeing my parents so sad, knowing that I would have preferred them to be angry. It did not surprise me when my father both gave up his post and removed Jeanne at the end of the term. She went to another school where there was no uniform and her academic prowess allowed her to settle down without fuss. My father began teaching part-time in a number of different schools and for the first time ever the Convent, which had dominated my childhood, played no part in our lives.

I wrote, at my grandfather's suggestion, a very dignified letter to Sister Benedicte thanking her for my many years at the Convent and wishing the Community all the best for the future. I said that I was innocent of the charge Lisette had laid, but that I understood the decision and that God would give me the strength to cope with the future. She replied in equally generous terms and my grandfather said he suspected she knew she had got it wrong.

Sometimes I wondered if I would have been so calm had I been destined for great success in the exams. Would I still have stood my ground, have written such a letter? I knew that for the first time in my life I hated, that I felt towards Lisette a deep, bitter and active ill will, not for what she had done to me but for the grief and anxiety she had inflicted on my parents. I remembered their taut, strained, disappointed faces in the kitchen and fervently hoped the future held some terrible punishment for Lisette.

I rejected Sister Benedicte's reasoning when she told me that I was being expelled for disobedience and defiance rather than for the joke itself. Had she herself not always taught us that it was wrong to obey an unjust order?

In the weeks that followed I often thought of school, of the whole class standing up each day to say the Angelus, of heads bent over the *Aeneid*, of whispered confidences in the playground, but gradually the images began to fade and I found I did not envy those still there for I was free of homework and earning my own money, able to dispose of my spare time as I wished without feeling guilty about undone revision.

The misery of my expulsion still lingered but that too grew faint and I looked to the future which at first was uncertain. I helped briefly serving in the shop of a family friend, hating the monotony, the dullness of the goods and the drabness of the clients, longing instead for the excitement and perfumed air of Le Printemps.

After two weeks of that I left to work in a café where I scalded a customer with boiling water on the first day, dropped a pile of plates on the second and refused to report for work on the third. My parents, with studied restraint, suggested I should train for office work, perhaps as a secretary, but I had had enough of learning and exams and insisted that I should eventually find work with children. A few days after the disastrous café experiment Annette announced that there were two vacancies at the Distribution Centre and my parents would take no refusal from me.

The work, which consisted of preparing rations for despatch to various retail outlets, was dull but easy and I got on well with the others. Somewhat to my own surprise I was happy, unpressured and largely content, escaping less often into fantasy and daydreams as the first bulbs pushed through the earth in the parks and I realised that I could enjoy spring in all its fullness without the daily, wearing round of exhortation and rebuke from angry or despairing teachers. The work was not well paid but at least my earnings were my own.

One evening Bette was waiting for me after work. She told me Yvette Levin and her siblings had not turned up at school that day and she wanted me to go with her to their apartment to see if they were all right.

Of course they were not all right, I thought, as I walked with her through the March chill. Did Bette seriously expect they all had the flu or something? I recalled Yvette's small sisters and brother, trying to imagine them woken in the middle of the night and dragged, crying with fright and bewilderment, to Drancy.

A grumbling concierge admitted us but said no one was in the Levins' apartment. Bette asked where they were and she shrugged. After we had rung the bell and knocked loudly for a while, a neighbour came out of the opposite door and told us in kindly tones that the Levin family had gone away.

Bette claimed she had come to retrieve a schoolbook and would ask the concierge to let her in, whereupon the neighbour said she had a key because she kept an eye on Mr Levin senior if Yvette's mother had to be out for any length of time. She did not come in with us and I wondered if she were afraid, trusting or simply believed the Levins would not return to hold her to account.

They had been taken in the night. Beds were tumbled and disordered, the contents of drawers spilled on to the floor and cupboard doors hung open. They must have packed a few basic necessities in haste for most of their belongings were still there while the bathroom was bare of toothbrushes. There was not a morsel of food in the kitchen and I wondered who had taken it all. The concierge? The neighbour? German soldiers?

Would they loot this apartment now or would some relatives arrive to pack up? The Catholic, non-Jewish relatives, of course. While Bette sank down on one of the unmade beds and held her head in her hands, I looked out of the window, down on to the darkening Parisian street. A pair of German soldiers walked past, the muddy green of their uniforms suddenly visible in a falling beam of light. Then, as we wondered and grieved in silence, there came a faint mew.

'Oh, my God,' whispered Bette, 'a cat.'

We finally traced it to its hiding place behind a suitcase under the bed. It shook as we pulled it gently out. Unlike its owners it was plump and I imagined the Levin children secretly feeding it scraps from their own plates.

For a while we just sat fondling it, seeking to reassure it, wondering what the small, fat, smoky creature, which wore a tartan collar, might have been called. Then I went to ask the neighbour if she could care for it. She shook her head, her eyes sad.

'What are we going to do?' I asked Bette.

'We had better take it.'

'But where? I can't take it home. It would kill Catherine the Second.'

'I doubt it. That hen would scratch its eyes out. If we leave it here the concierge will eat it.'

I too had heard of people eating cats and shuddered. I could do nothing for Yvette but suddenly the cat became symbolic and I would not abandon it to such a fate.

'What about you? Can you have it?'

Bette shook her head. 'I've never been allowed so much as a mouse. My father thinks animals in the home are unhygienic.'

Yet she had pulled out the suitcase from under the bed and was musing about whether we could carry the animal in it. Presently she went to the kitchen, rummaged for a while and returned with a hammer and sharp knife, but the leather defeated her efforts to punch airholes and in the end we settled for a pillowcase.

The cat had been a diversion, a welcome distraction from the horror around us, but, with the means of its transport solved, we were forced once more to confront what had happened – was happening – to Yvette and her family. I remembered her as I had last seen her, clutching her small, misbehaving brother with one hand while trying to shake out an umbrella with the other, laughing at her own efforts.

'We will have to ask your friend,' said Bette.

'My friend?'

'Von Ströbel. He helped Yvette before. You must see him at once and tell him what has happened.'

My friend. I could not pretend that I did not like the description, that I was not flattered and warmed by the notion that I might be thought to know Klaus von Ströbel better than others, but I was also surprised.

'He is not my friend.'

'Well, he likes you anyway. His face lit up that day he saw you at the Convent and you talk to him after Mass.'

I wondered how she knew, as she did not go to that church. A small cold knot formed in my stomach as I realised for the first time that my conduct might be the subject of gossip, to be dispelled by the much happier thought that I had an excellent reason for calling upon Klaus and that few could say I was wrong to make such an effort to help Yvette. I would go to his Headquarters and boldly demand to see him. This was what Bette must have meant when I confided to her my feelings for Robert and she asked if I felt powerful. I was powerful now. I could save Yvette. As we rose to go I pictured the Levin family once more in this home.

My mood of optimistic heroism was quickly punctured by farce. The cat struggled, scratched and yowled as we put it in the pillowcase, at one point escaping my grasp and obliging us to chase it round the apartment. I alternated between pity and frustration as we lugged the heaving cargo downstairs, wondering why we had bothered with the airholes when it must be scratching its prison to ribbons.

Then the concierge confronted us and demanded we release the animal at once. She and I fought over the pillowcase until she was distracted by a shout from above and we looked up to see a dozen or so of Yvette's neighbours peering over the banisters in amazement to find out the cause of the commotion. Bette took advantage of the pause to grab the sack and run outside.

The curses and threats of the concierge pursued us as we ran until the mobile weight of the loudly mewing cat forced us to stop, panting and laughing, bleeding from the ungrateful creature's scratches, our hair blowing wildly. I realised then that it was raining and neither of us had an umbrella. We had a long walk ahead of us and had not even decided where to take the cat.

'The Convent,' said Bette suddenly. 'We will ask the nuns to look after the cat until we find it a home.'

I did not in the least like the idea of facing Sister Benedicte again but Bette said she would go in alone and certainly I had no better idea to offer. We plodded on, taking it in turns to carry the furiously active bundle. As the rain grew heavier our hilarity turned first to misery and then to exhaustion, especially when Bette said the pillowcase would no longer take the strain if carried like a bag and we were forced instead to bear our unwilling burden in our arms.

It was with a premonition of rescue that I heard a car slowing down behind us, then drawing level. Even before it stopped I knew whom I would see.

I needed no second invitation before scrambling into the dryness and warmth of Klaus von Ströbel's car, but even in those straits Bette hesitated to accept help from the enemy, proud despite the rain and wind and ludicrous circumstances. Her resistance was only overcome when I reminded her of Yvette. Klaus sat beside the driver and asked us where we wanted to go, politely ignoring the wails from the pillowcase, his expression one of quizzical amusement.

An absurd thought entered my head and before I had time to dismiss it I heard myself asking, 'Do you like cats?'

He turned to look at the heaving pillowcase. 'My children have one,' he prevaricated.

Bette took over. 'Yvette Levin and all her family have been taken by the Gestapo and the cat was left to starve.'

He looked grave but kept his attention on the cat. 'And so you are taking it where?'

'We don't know,' I said before Bette could mention the Convent.

'Your own house perhaps?'

'We have a hen.'

I saw his lips twitch. 'What sort of cat is it?'

It was an odd question and I knew he was playing for time, time to think of a solution, perhaps time to decide whether he wished to involve himself at all.

'It is very fat, which is more than can be said for any other living creature in this city,' replied Bette, restoring her honour by reminding the enemy of her resentment.

'It is smoky coloured and has a tartan collar,' I added in more placatory tones. 'I don't know what they called it.'

Called. Past tense. I knew then that I did not really believe I could help Yvette.

'We could call it Mac.'

We. He was going to help. Beside me Bette stirred uneasily.

'Why?' I asked, baffled by the unfamiliar name.

'You say it has a tartan collar.'

I feigned enlightenment. Bette would have to explain later, I thought as the pillowcase jerked furiously.

'I don't care what its name is. I just wish it would stop fidgeting and that we could get it somewhere, anywhere dammit, *now*.' Bette's shame and frustration boiled over. I knew she meant that she wanted to be somewhere else, anywhere else, *now,* in dry clothes and away from both cat and enemy.

'Remind me of your address, Mademoiselle Bette,' said Klaus gently, 'and we will drop you there. Then I can take your friend home too. You may leave the cat to me. I shall call it Macfidget and it will be quite safe.'

'What about Yvette?' demanded Bette, unmollified. 'Her brother and sisters are very young.'

'I will make enquiries,' promised Klaus.

We absorbed that in silence. He could guarantee the safety of the cat but when it came to the humans he could only make enquiries. He might just as well have told us there was nothing he could do to help Yvette, that all his enquiries could achieve would be confirmation of her fate, that his writ did not run to Gestapo Headquarters or to Drancy.

Somehow, despite all that had happened, I still expected problems to be sorted out, that some grown-up somewhere would see to it. Since the unfairness of my expulsion that expectation had diminished but now it died altogether. Yvette would not be saved. Around me the city seemed to darken and I heard again in my memory the cry in the night which had haunted me in the early days of the Occupation.

I was angry with the world for its unfairness and I understood why Bette maintained enmity towards the Germans, even to those like Klaus von Ströbel who tried in modest ways to make things better for the Occupied. I thought he had about as much enthusiasm for the war as we had but still he represented the regime which was persecuting the likes of Yvette Levin and her family. I recalled suddenly the neighbour telling us of a grandfather too and tried to imagine how I would feel towards Klaus if it were my dearly loved Grand-père who was carried off to Drancy in the middle of the night.

Bette bade me goodnight and muttered something ungracious to Klaus when he delivered her home. He retaliated by accompanying her to her own door where, as I learned subsequently, he explained the circumstances to her parents. It was a warning, I thought, not to take his good nature for granted. I resented it mainly because it left me in charge of the pillowcase from which now emanated a horrid smell.

For the short journey that remained he asked questions about the Levins, calling me Catherine and twisting in his seat to face me. When we arrived at my house he again reassured me over Macfidget and promised to contact me about Yvette as soon as he had found out what had happened, before leaving me to face my parents alone.

A neighbour paused in the rain to stare at me.

'Are you all right?' he asked.

I nodded as I fumbled for my key and then, in an act of defiance, enjoyed the shock on his face as I raised my hand and waved to Klaus von Ströbel.

eight

To Shrug and Not to Know

'A *cat*?' My father's voice rose less in anger than in incredulity as I explained why I had been brought home by the Germans for the second time in less than a year. 'You took a cat from the Levins' apartment and carried it through Paris in a *pillowcase*?'

Annette and Jeanne were gaping at me and my mother was looking helplessly at my grandmother. My hair was still wet and I was sitting in the kitchen with a towel round my shoulders fighting feelings of irritation and mutiny as I answered a barrage of questions. Whose permission had we asked? Were we sure that it was the Levins' cat and not one they happened to be looking after? Had we left our names and addresses? What had the concierge said? Where on earth had we intended taking it? Indeed, if it really had to be taken, why not work out a proper plan and return for it tomorrow with the appropriate means of carrying it?

I refrained from telling him that I was afraid the concierge would eat the animal or that I had fought her for possession of the pillowcase in front of half the neighbours. Reluctantly I was beginning to see the incident from my parents' point of view, to recognise that Bette and I had acted precipitately rather than boldly, that we had subjected the animal to an unnecessary ordeal and exposed ourselves to ridicule.

'For heaven's sake, Catherine, you are seventeen not twelve. How can you have so little sense? And then you ask the Germans to sort out the very mess you created. Von Ströbel of course. I tell you I want no more favours from him and I do not want you to see him again.'

I was too weary with it all to argue but I saw Klaus the very next day. The young, fair-haired officer was waiting for me as I left work and, ignoring the hum of curiosity among my colleagues, I went with him to the same office I had sat in the previous summer when I had broken the curfew. On the way he told me his name was Kurt Kleist and that he had been posted to Paris about two weeks before that incident.

When I entered the inner office the first thing I saw was Macfidget, peering out from under an easy chair. Klaus followed my gaze and smiled.

'He is not yet used to his new surroundings or perhaps he is still recovering from the unusual journey he made yesterday.'

'We were fools,' I acknowledged. 'But we were so sorry for him.'

He let that pass and motioned to me to sit down. 'If anyone from the Levin family claims him, let me know. Meanwhile it is bad news, I am afraid, Catherine.'

Although I had expected nothing else I felt my heart jump and a coldness enter my stomach.

'Yvette Levin, her parents, grandfather and siblings are in Drancy. One parent was not arrested at first as there was no Jewish history – the mother, I think, but I am not certain. In the event, whoever it was put up such a resistance as to be arrested too. Catherine, I am sorry, I have no authority to release them from Drancy. None at all.'

'Someone must have.'

'Those who have such power will not be impressed by your reasons.'

'But the Levins have done no wrong.'

'They are Jewish according to the definition to which we must work.'

'They are Catholics but even if they were not, even if they were as practising Jews as Abraham and Moses what does it matter? How can it justify this?'

Klaus shrugged. 'It is not religious practice that counts but racial origin. I do not make these laws, Catherine. Therefore I do not have to justify them. If you are wise you will not question them too loudly.'

Loneliness, a great cold, dark cloak, floated down enveloping me in merciless folds. I was distraught for the Levin family, especially its smallest members, embarrassed by my own clumsy intervention which seemed crasser by the minute and disappointed by Klaus's helplessness but above all I felt myself deserted, utterly alone in my desire to help the Levins. The very fact that Klaus could not remember which parent had resisted arrest suggested that he must have made only the most cursory of enquiries.

My father had dwelt at length on what I should not have done but had offered no advice on what I could do, accepting Yvette's fate as readily as if it had been the cat which was snatched in the middle of the night. How many others, I wondered, were not turning up at their schools while teachers and classmates looked the other way, not wanting to see, to confront, to save?

'What will happen to them?'

Klaus looked uncomfortable and I stared at his hat where it lay discarded on his desk, focusing on the eagle and swastika, formerly the symbols of unwanted presence, of invasion and oppression, now suddenly of something I could not yet grasp but still feared dreadfully.

'There is talk of transfers from Drancy to ... other places.' Klaus's gaze did not meet mine.

'Other places? Where?'

'Poland perhaps. I don't know.'

I could not tell whether he did not know or simply was unable to say because the knowledge was secret. I pressed on, though fearing the answer.

'And what will happen there?'

'They will work.'

'But the little Levins cannot work. Yvette's grandfather cannot work. Why could they not be left in Paris while the others were taken to work?'

Klaus got up and came round to lean on my side of the desk. For a while he just looked down at me with pity, saying nothing, watching as I struggled to make sense of a moral order so brutally corrupted, watching as I finally accepted that no one would make things right for the Levins. What, I wondered, would I say to Yvette after the war? That I had tried and had immediately given up?

Despite my slowness in the business of growing up I had cried much less recently, but now I gave in first to tears and then to great, gulping sobs, searching unsuccessfully for a handkerchief until Klaus handed me his. It was time to go, to stop making a fool of myself in front of an enemy I should have despised but instead was in danger of loving. As I stood up he pulled me against his chest and stroked my hair while I sobbed, uttering the consolatory noises I had so often heard from my parents when I wept as a child and, seeking its comfort and warmth, I willingly embraced the danger and stepped into the abyss that was falling in love with Klaus von Ströbel.

The next few minutes were a blur of happiness and misery. I felt myself guided to the chair under which Macfidget had found refuge and from which I heard rather than saw the door open and shut. There followed a muted conversation and then Klaus returned, shortly afterwards followed by Kurt Kleist bearing a cup of coffee, good coffee, not ersatz.

When I had recovered enough composure to demolish the beverage, Klaus explained that he was on duty and could not see me home but suggested, with kind irony, that this might be a good thing in terms of family harmony. I managed a watery smile of agreement. As Kurt Kleist saw me out, I asked about Drancy and what happened there, at which he shrugged and said he did not know.

It seemed to me a fair summary of Paris's attitude to the Jews. Everyone shrugged and did not know.

At home I discovered Klaus's handkerchief and knew that its return could provide the excuse for my next visit, knowing also that I would need no excuse, that he had sensed my surrender to my feelings, that his comment on family harmony had an application beyond the context in which it was made, that he was effectively offering a promise of future discretion.

I privately washed and ironed the handkerchief, telling myself it was in preparation for its reunion with its owner, instead determined that it should join the scruffy gift tag in its secret place.

By the end of March 1942 when, had I but known it, the first trainload of Jews had left Drancy for Auschwitz, the thought of what had happened to Yvette and her family had become a dull ache rather than an active source of pain. I thought of her now occasionally rather than daily and I acknowledged that soon I should think of her only rarely.

I saw little of Bette, Bernadette and Cécile who were now in the last weeks of preparation for baccalauréat, but a great deal of Klaus, secretly, meeting well away from home and work. Quite often we went to Saint-Germain-des-Prés where I would watch the artists talking and drinking as I waited for him. Once I arrived pushing my bicycle with its back tyre punctured and a pair of rather bohemian men traced the damage with spittle and mended it for me.

Sometimes we met, as if by accident, at the theatre, sometimes in cafés. Occasionally he did not turn up at all and I would go home, deprived and disappointed, after half an hour, as he had told me I should. Work was by no means predictable, he had explained at the beginning, and sometimes he would have to break appointments at the last minute. Though I knew this to be inevitable I was miserable whenever it happened.

I hated the secrecy too while recognising it as imperative if I was to avoid hurting those I loved. It did not occur to me that there might be other means of giving myself away until Annette challenged me one night as we were getting ready for bed.

'You haven't heard a word I've said, have you?'

Startled out of thoughts of Klaus, I tried to recall what Annette had been talking about and failed.

'Sorry, I was daydreaming.'

'You always are these days.'

Yet now, I thought, I dreamed of what was real not of fairy stories. Klaus was real, the butterflies in my stomach when I saw him were real, the fluttering excitement which accompanied just hearing the sound of his name was real, the way his face lit up when he saw me was almost unbearably real. Yet so was the danger and Annette's words were a timely warning.

I remembered Robert and wondered how I could ever have thought myself in love with such a boy. How could Annette have pined for lanky, conceited Emile with that stupid Adam's apple in his throat? Only a man was worth loving, a man with plentiful dark hair greying at the sides and temple.

I did not always rejoice in the difference in our ages, sometimes feeling the fruit or chocolate with which he never failed to greet me in those early weeks the equivalent of a parent giving a child a treat, at others resenting his none too subtle attempts to supplement my education which had ended so abruptly. I was acutely aware that sometimes he sounded like my father, remembering a war which had been over long before I was born, displaying the attitudes of one for whom youth was scarcely experienced.

I asked him about his family and he told me he had three children: Johanna, who was twelve and must have been the girl in the photograph which had inspired Bette to trust him on the night we broke the curfew, and two younger ones, Willi-Lothar of the same age as Edouard, and Lotte, still a babe in arms. Johanna had an abundance of fair hair not dissimilar to mine and the boy was prone to what Klaus described as onomatopoeic giggles at the wrong moments.

He stumbled slightly over onomatopoeic, that being one of only two occasions on which his awesome command of the French language failed him. The second would be more dramatic but it was to come from a bleakness I could never have imagined in those heady, spring days of 1942, when in my wilder moments I could almost have wished the Occupation to last for ever if it meant Klaus's staying in Paris.

I closed my mind firmly against the still, small voice which whispered 'wife', 'Jews' and occasionally even 'traitor'. When it seemed to murmur 'Martin', I was resentful of, rather than chastened by, the fleeting sensation of shame. Klaus was handsome, kind, polite and, flatteringly, wanted my company. He was undemanding and made me laugh. Could it be any wonder I yearned to be with him every moment that I was not? What, I demanded of my conscience, could be so wrong then about our meetings? The reply was not even half formed before I brushed it aside.

I learned to lie about where I was going and what I was doing. Once I asked Annette to tell the Distribution Centre I was feeling too poorly to work and I told my parents I was going to see the doctor. Instead I spent the morning in Les Trois Quartiers inspecting ribbon, artificial flowers and other useless items. There was nothing which might make me more attractive to Klaus but I enjoyed the fantasy that I might find something.

It would be the same at the other big department stores, Les Galeries Lafayette or Le Printemps, but I began to search in my mind for ways of going there rather than back home or, worse still, to work. Absorbed with this problem, I did not at first notice the beginnings of a commotion, the sudden advent of fear among my fellow shoppers and browsers, the distant sound of someone shouting orders. By the time I emerged from my dreamland into the real world, the doors of the shop had been locked and the customers were being herded together. Hysterically a girl called out that a German had been stabbed in the store and they were looking for the culprit or for hostages.

Soldiers were pointing guns at us while others searched out those who had vainly sought to conceal themselves among the merchandise. I should have been terrified but instead was merely embarrassed that my petty deception might now be exposed. Beside me a woman wept that we would all be deported and her mother of ninety would be left alone in their apartment with no one to look after her.

The Germans were now demanding our papers. As I held out mine to a young officer he looked at me and I saw uncertainty enter his eyes. The woman with the elderly mother began to keen and he shouted at her brutally before calling over one of his colleagues who also stared at me quizzically then nodded to him.

Before the envious, contemptuous gaze of my fellow Parisians I was ushered out of the shop and left to go where I pleased. I understood well enough what had happened and began to hurry towards the Distribution Centre to work, to expiate, to drive away the memory of being spared from some ghastly fate, which still confronted those in the shop, because a sharp-witted German had recognised the girlfriend of his commanding officer.

I changed direction towards the Seine, wanting now instead of working to watch the early June sun sparkling on the river, to breathe the air of freedom, to imagine myself upon a boat sailing away from Paris and its horrors. I remembered the woman keening and wished that I knew where she lived so that I might do something for her mother, tormenting myself by imagining the old lady waiting for her daughter, waiting and waiting. I hoped they found and shot the culprit for surely that would spare the others, others as innocent as I but who had no friendship with the enemy to pray in aid.

I felt guilty, grateful, soiled, distinguished, but when the turmoil of my mind began to settle I was conscious of one thing only. If Germans recognised me as the friend of Klaus von Ströbel so must Parisians. I had been a fool to imagine I was capable of keeping the association clandestine and soon all my friends and relations would know as well.

Someone I knew was approaching me now, smiling. I wondered would she still smile if she had heard how I consorted with the enemy, would she even acknowledge me? A year ago it might have made no difference but now the impositions and privations were so huge and so many people had just disappeared that ambivalence towards the Germans had long since hardened into hatred.

Then, as I returned her smile still wondering for how long I could take such greetings for granted, I stood stock-still, my eyes fixed on the yellow star, my spirit screaming with shocked but silent protest. The order had gone out about a week ago that all Jews over the age of six must wear a yellow Star of David. Until now I had not seen any and had hardly paid much attention to this latest manifestation of persecution but now the cruel reality confronted me from the jacket of a girl younger than myself and I had not even realised she was Jewish.

Her smile weakened a little as she followed my gaze but she continued towards me.

'I'm sorry,' I said. 'I didn't know.'

'No? I'm afraid I always thought it was obvious.'

I looked at her and supposed it was, although now I came to think of it I had little idea what distinguished Jewish features. I recalled something about large noses and felt myself ignorant and insensitive. I glanced again at the star, remembered Yvette Levin and thought such a regime could be the product only of savages, not of Europe in the middle of the twentieth century.

'I am afraid I qualify several times over under the definition. Both parents, all grandparents. Not very assiduous, but it isn't that which counts. The time will probably come when you will be afraid to acknowledge me in the street.'

They are Jews according to the definition to which we are obliged to work . . . I do not make these laws, Catherine, and so I do not have to justify them. Klaus's words rang through my brain tolling moral desolation.

'It isn't fair.' How often had I roared those words in childish protest at some petty injustice, how pathetically inadequate they sounded now.

'Nothing's fair. Children lost in the Exodus, tiny babies sent to Drancy, not knowing what happened to some of the men who fought, old folk not having enough to eat *und so weiter, und so weiter* as those beasts would say.'

'I am in love with one of those beasts.'

Her mouth slackened and her eyes widened but she said nothing as she turned and walked away quietly with no trace of flounce, just a slight, defeated sagging of the shoulders, so slight I could not be sure I had not imagined it. I never saw her again.

I saw other yellow stars that day as I headed for the river but the sun had gone in, a chill breeze had arisen and I became preoccupied with feeling cold and then with the excuses I must think up to explain a day's absence from both home and work. The last outcome of my folly which I wanted was dismissal from the Distribution Centre where Annette was now given five kilos of rice, maize or rice flour each month. I hoped that I might also earn extra rations after I had been there a little longer, although I knew they would not allow too much for the same family.

I had not resolved my problem when I arrived home and found myself announcing, as I entered the house, that I was still unwell and was going to bed. As I was going upstairs my mother called after me to know what the doctor had said and I pretended not to hear. Surprisingly I slept at once, lying on top of the bedclothes, not waking until Annette came to bed. I came round reluctantly, aware of the taste of sleep in my mouth, knowing that once I allowed myself to wake fully I should feel hungry and that there was hardly any food in the house.

I muttered when Annette pointed out that I should undress and get into bed properly, wanting to return to the oblivion of sleep. Later I was briefly conscious of my mother laying an eiderdown over me before falling back into dreamless sleep.

In the morning I woke with a pounding headache and hunger cramps. My mother supplied aspirin and the congealed remains of my portion of the previous night's meal. After one mouthful I retched and realised that now I really was ill, too ill to be rebuked when I admitted I had not seen the doctor, making the excuse that I had suddenly felt better and had gone for a walk instead.

At my mother's insistence I stayed in bed, listening to the drone of the vacuum, Edouard's feet racing along the landings and the voices of my mother and grandparents. I slept for hours at a time, waking only to notice the change in the light which first streamed through the window with the strength of midday, then glowed red and then barely lit the room at all. I became vaguely aware of other voices as my father returned from teaching and Jeanne from learning but I did not hear Annette come to bed.

The following morning I felt weak but otherwise vastly better. I consumed one of Jeanne's government-issued vitamin biscuits and a large omelette for breakfast, enthusiastically thanking Catherine the Second, trying to ignore my craving for fried potato and real coffee. My grandmother observed disapprovingly that I had eaten nothing for twenty-four hours, making it sound as if my illness had somehow been specially designed to inconvenience the household with a requirement for irregular mealtimes. She did, however, side with my mother when we argued over whether I should return to work.

In the end we compromised and agreed that if I felt well all morning I should go to the Distribution Centre for the second half of the day. I looked in on my grandfather who was sleeping by the window upstairs, wheezing gently, a rug over his knees despite the heat of the June day; I played hide and seek with Edouard who never failed to betray his whereabouts with giggles; I tidied Jeanne's small, cluttered bedroom.

I thought of Bette, an only child of parents who both worked, so often alone in that quiet, immaculate apartment and pitied her. I wondered what Yvette Levin was doing and how people lived herded together in those camps day after day with no family privacy or how, like Sister Benedicte and her colleagues, single women joined together to pool individual isolation. One day I would have a home and a family of my own.

I pictured Klaus coming home to his evening meal in a room with a blazing hearth before which small children played and for the first time in months began again to christen an imaginary brood but this time with German names, my imagination getting little further than Fritz or Eva and, of course, Klaus. One of the boys would surely be called Klaus and he would be my secret favourite.

I knew myself a fool, that Klaus already had a family, that the cosiness of my present home would dissolve into icy wasteland if I were to invite him into it, that the future I wanted for myself was achievable without Klaus but not with him, that our friendship alone was enough to destroy the bonds which held my happiness together.

I knew myself a fool, but I willingly dreamed on until my fantasies were dispelled by a small but discernible commotion downstairs and I hurried, curiously rather than anxiously, to find the cause. The back door was open and immediately I knew that something had happened to Catherine the Second, that she had been mauled by some other animal or stolen in broad daylight. Fleetingly I wondered if she had produced chickens, having only the haziest idea as to what might bring this about, but rejected that as impossible because the stir of human reaction was tinged with sadness not joy.

By the time I joined my mother and grandmother in the small back garden I was prepared for what I saw. Catherine the Second had died, quite naturally and peacefully. My first response was a sentimental one, remembering her gentle clucking, as she scratched hopefully in the back garden for bits to eat, her rustle in the kitchen at night. My second was one of horror and I looked at my mother with anxious eyes which pleaded for anything but that.

She put her arm round me. 'Catherine, we must.'

'But she was ours. We loved her.'

'Farmers love their animals too but they raise them to be killed and eaten.'

I screamed and my grandmother called me an imbecile but there was no venom in her voice and when she bent to lift the hen she handled the corpse gently and not, I felt, just for my benefit. In the end, after Jeanne cried too, we bartered the hen for bread and vegetables and I tried hard not to think of what happened to it next.

The creature's death left a gap in our diet as we no longer had the advantage of fresh eggs and from time to time Annette or I would cycle into the country to beg from some cousins, who lived out towards Brie, hoping that eventually we might even obtain a chicken to replace Catherine the Second. Twice Annette was stopped by Germans, who 'confiscated' the goods, but my own experience was worse, being attacked on one occasion by three French lads who, fighting me successfully for vegetables and potatoes, left me to the dubious hygiene of trying to save some of the smashed eggs which had fallen from my grasp in the struggle. Weeping and bleeding from my scratches, I was then stopped by Germans who went off in search of the miscreants, leaving me perversely frightened on the wrongdoers' behalf.

After that my parents put a stop to any expeditions unless we could find a male friend or relative to accompany us and as this was not often possible we resigned ourselves to doing without fresh produce other than that grown in our own back garden. Jeanne missed it most and, as she showed no reticence in bruiting her dissatisfaction to anyone who would listen, I cannot believe that I was not more alert when one Sunday, as we prepared to walk to Mass, she told us she intended to cycle and would catch us up.

Jeanne had not said where she intended to cycle, which was afterwards her excuse for the deception, but when Mass was over and she could not be found amongst the departing congregation I knew she must have gone to my cousins'. My father ran home ahead of us, but we did not expect him to find her there.

Annette and I were sent cycling after her, hoping to meet her as she headed back to Paris but, determined to avoid the experiences with which we had met, Jeanne had devised a different route and we arrived at our cousins' house hot, exhausted and worried to be told that our little sister had left for the city hours ago.

It was early evening before we arrived home still lunchless and worn out with pedalling at anxious speed. The perspiration was pouring off me and soaking my clothes. Sweat plastered Annette's short hair to her head and she was shaking with fear for Jeanne, a child of thirteen, who had travelled alone into the country to obtain goods which all Paris and many Germans wanted.

Relief coursed through me as I saw Jeanne in the kitchen. She was crying and shaking but she had no cuts, bruises or torn clothes. My mother took her up to bed while my grandmother told us what had happened.

Jeanne had arrived safely at our cousins' who were surprised that she had made such a journey alone. By her own admission Jeanne had lied and said her older sisters could not come. Concerned, they decided that their elder daughter should accompany Jeanne to the outskirts of the city but when the older girl's bike developed a puncture less than a kilometre into the journey Jeanne sped off on her own, heedless of calls to stop. She then embarked on the circuitous route she had devised and for a while all went well.

Two kilometres from Paris she passed a German with a young Frenchwoman. He stopped her and questioned her and the woman said surely she was young to be cycling alone with such goods but neither made any attempt to take them and Jeanne pedalled on, growing confident of success and a good supper, but she was also tiring and began to make increasingly frequent stops to regain energy. As she was now on the fringes of the city she encountered more people but they ignored her, seeing nothing remarkable in a young girl on her bicycle out for a Sunday ride.

During one of her rests a woman in a cycle taxi stopped to ask if she needed any help and Jeanne realised that she must be looking harassed. Certainly she was uncomfortably hot and when she saw a church she decided to go inside in search of a cooler temperature. Unfortunately, just before she did so, she slid a sandwich, given to her by our cousins, from her pocket and consumed it on the church steps, putting down the other parcels while she ate.

Jeanne had been in the church less than a minute before two Germans came in, looked around the seemingly empty space and walked straight up to her, snatched the parcels, turned out her pockets and then began patting her in search of hidden food. They had just located a bunch of vegetables concealed in her petticoat when a priest, alerted by her screams, burst out of the confessional with an outraged face.

The tormentors ran off with their plunder and the priest summoned an assistant who brought Jeanne and her bicycle home.

'So much for German correctness,' observed my father. 'They didn't even bother asking for the food. Just damn well seized it and in a church of all places.'

'Searching her underwear too. That is what upset her most – wondering what the priest might have seen,' added my grandmother.

Annette asked my father a question with her eyes. He shook his head. 'Not as far as we can make out. They just wanted the food which Jeanne had so obligingly displayed on the steps, maybe for girlfriends or bribes.'

'Did the priest report it?'

'No. He thought we should make that decision, given Jeanne's age.'

'There can't be any doubt surely, otherwise they'll do it again,' I pointed out. 'This must be a matter for the German army rather than the police. We should go to the Kommandantur.'

I expected grim agreement. Instead there was a short, explosive silence before my father looked first at Annette and then at me.

'The trouble is my daughters no longer appear to tell the truth. Jeanne led us to believe she was cycling after us to Mass when she knew very well she intended to do something her mother and I would never have allowed. It is no defence that she did not tell a direct lie because the essence of a lie is the intent to deceive and if she had not been punished enough by what has happened she would now be getting the hiding of a lifetime.

'You, Catherine, are too old for punishment and a fine example you set. Deceit has now become a way of life. You tell lies about where you are going, whom you are meeting, what you have been doing. If you want to complain about German soldiers I doubt very much if you need to go to the Kommandantur. You can just tell von Ströbel the next time you whisper sweet nothings in his ear.'

nine

The Truth in a Photograph

My father had just told me I was too old for punishment but my first reaction was to fear his wrath. I had always known that he must find out eventually but, in so far as I had given the matter any thought at all, I had supposed that somehow I would have some warning of impending discovery, some time to decide how to react. I had thought often enough of the aftermath of exposure, of being nagged by a disappointed family with disillusion in its eyes, of being cold-shouldered by friends, of seeing disapproval written on the faces of all I encountered, but I had never given much heed to the actual moment of being unmasked.

Fear was followed by confusion because I could not determine whether to defy the censure around me, to dismiss it or to plead for understanding. Then confusion was in turn swallowed up by relief as I realised that there was no longer any need to fear this moment because it had already arrived and was no longer menacing me from the uncertainty of the future. I need weave no more complicated deceptions, sustain no more lies.

I became aware that Annette had evinced no surprise, was not gasping with shock or staring at me with incredulity, and I remembered the soldier who had recognised me in the department store. My infamy appeared to have a wide currency and I had been deceiving only myself in my attempts at secrecy.

'I'm sorry. Truly. I couldn't bear to hurt you or worry Mother.'

'Does being sorry mean giving him up?' My father's voice held menace as well as challenge.

'I can't.'

'You mean you won't. You realise this man is responsible for whatever has happened to Yvette Levin? That he commands men who would kill Martin? That every time you hear a shot, a scream, a bullying order you can thank him?'

'He is not directly responsible for any of those things.'

'How do you know?'

'I know he is a good man.'

'We all know he is a married one. He is not being so good to his wife, is he? Or to you? What does he imagine he is doing to you?'

If my father had asked merely the first question I might have been discomfited, but the second stung my pride and released me from any trap of principle.

'He is not causing me any problem. I can take care of myself.'

My father shook his head in disbelief. I watched him struggle with himself, knowing that he wanted to forbid me to see von Ströbel again but that he also realised I would disobey him either openly or in secret and that short of setting a guard over me there was no way he could stop us meeting. It was unlike him to admit defeat over anything but now he was facing a situation familiar to so many as their offspring grew up and developed minds of their own and he was not going to court the indignity of issuing an edict he could not enforce.

I learned many months later that he actually appealed to Klaus himself who told him there was nothing to worry about: we were just good friends. What he thought of that I do not know but at that moment of discovery I wanted, clumsily, to give him the same reassurance and could not because I refused adamantly to face up to such a possibility. I was sure I was in love and would not belittle Klaus by describing him as just a friend.

In the end my father resorted to forbidding me to let Klaus come to the house, insisting that the rest of the family were patriots who should not be touched by the remotest suggestion of association with Germans. He sounded both tired and urgent and because it was an easy promise both to make and keep I agreed, somehow believing that this subtly made the rest of my conduct more bearable for those around me, despite my mother's red-rimmed eyes and my grandmother's tight, disapproving mouth.

There was urgency also in Annette's voice when we were getting ready for bed with Jeanne's intermittent snuffles still audible through the wall between our room and hers.

'Poor kid. You must tell your friend. Do you think they might be shot?'

I pondered that. 'I don't know. Do you want them to be?'

It was Annette's turn to become thoughtful. 'I want them to think they will be, to be seriously frightened, to shiver all night.'

'And then?'

Annette suddenly exclaimed over a missing button. I helped her look for it but was not deflected and when we had given up the search I repeated the question.

'I suppose I'd be happy if they had to clean Jeanne's shoes for a week.'

I smiled. It was what my mother had made us do for each other in childhood when we had acted meanly.

'Oh, of course it is much more serious than that,' Annette conceded. 'I meant I am sick of this war and people dying.'

We had put out the light and settled down to sleep when Annette whispered, 'Give him up.'

'I can't.'

'You can if you really try. You remember how I used to adore Emile? I thought I would be in love with him for ever but now I can't think what I saw in him. I couldn't recreate those feelings I once had if my very life depended on it. It will be the same for you. One day you will wonder what on earth was so special about a middle-aged German officer. So why wait? Get rid of him now.'

My mother offered the same advice in clumsy disguise as she and my grandmother suddenly took to reminiscing at length about their youth and early suitors and how it was for the best that none of these starry-eyed romances had led to marriage. It was hardly subtle and I was amused rather than irritated but it was a hugely different approach from that normally adopted by my parents whose love for us had always led them to nag rather than guide and stand back. I remembered the rows over my poor showing at school and my irresponsibility towards Aunt Sophie, the prohibitions which had curtailed my liberty in activities already permitted to some other girls of my age, the over-protectiveness which had hung over my early childhood and was now manifesting itself in their love for Edouard.

I wondered whether they feared that if they tried to insist on a break with Klaus I would draw stubbornly closer to him or perhaps that he would himself intervene, using his position to wreak vengeance. Perhaps they hoped that I – or he – would see sense if left alone, unpressured.

Once, when I had come downstairs unheard, my father was saying to my mother in a raised voice, 'If we try to stop her, he will stop us. Which is more important?'

'My daughter,' she replied and I detected a flash of uncharacteristic spirit beneath the words.

Fearing to be caught eavesdropping I crept back to my bedroom. I did not understand what I had heard but I was relieved that my family appeared content not to bludgeon me and, although I knew I deceived myself, I interpreted their attitude as indicating a reluctant acceptance of what I was doing. I was not able to think this for long but for a time it gave me false comfort and false hope and led me, fatefully, to abandon concealment.

Klaus's eyes darkened when I told him about Jeanne and he insisted on a formal complaint. My sister wept all through the interview as she was forced to describe her humiliation in graphic detail and I began to regret that we had not decided to let the matter rest. My father had confiscated her bicycle and she had to walk everywhere. We would now rely on occasional parcels from our country cousins, he had announced, and possibly the odd train trip to see them. Jeanne was left with the guilt of having deprived us all.

I began meeting Klaus openly, feeling the pride of ownership as we walked or were driven together, smothering the small hammer of reason which knocked at my mind to tell me that I could not own what had already been given elsewhere. Occasionally I left work early and knew no one would dare protest. Once or twice I procured some small favour for a workmate. Heady with love and power I did not at first notice the withdrawal around me.

If I arrived home after the normal mealtime I would find my supper uncooked.

'I wasn't sure if you would be eating here or with him,' my mother told me on the first of these occasions.

Him. Never Klaus, rarely these days even von Ströbel. Him.

'I don't want to hear his name in this house,' shouted my father after I foolishly told Edouard in his hearing that a nice man called Colonel Klaus had given me some chocolate for my little brother. 'And we don't want any favours from him.'

He did, however, let Edouard eat the offering despite my grandmother's view that he should have sent it back.

'I don't want to discuss it,' Annette repelled me one night when I tried to confide in her.

Then I began to come home late to find no supper at all.

'We thought you were eating with him,' was my mother's amended refrain.

One morning I could not find my keys and when I returned just before curfew the front door was secured. I rang and pounded on the door for a full five minutes before Annette let me in.

'Oh. We thought you weren't coming back.' Her insolent tone alone would have provoked me but the associated insult was too much and, before I realised what I was about to do, I drew back my hand and gave her face an enraged slap.

At once I was appalled and remorseful but Annette, turning loftily from both the assault and the apology, walked upstairs, her back emanating affronted dignity. When I remembered the insult I felt less sorry and when, the following morning, I discovered my keys in the very place I had looked for them the previous day I did not feel sorry at all.

When Klaus told me that he would not be able to see me for ten days he might as well have said ten months. It was nothing unusual but my family's hostility left me feeling isolated and vulnerable. His presence was now reassuring as well as exciting and I needed him as much for comfort as for companionship. Yet I was wise enough not to protest, aware that if I became clinging he might feel less flattered than burdened, that he looked to me to lighten not increase his load. For the same reasons I had not confided to him the persecution I now endured almost daily at home.

My expression must have betrayed my thoughts for he first

laughed and then began a gentle enquiry but I shook my head, earnestly denying that anything was wrong and he desisted with a relief so evident that hurt and anger burned through my miserable spirit. My problems were my own, his attitude seemed to say, not his.

Not wanting to spend evenings with my disapproving family, I sought out Bette who had left school with huge success in baccalauréat but who, like so many, found it now of limited value. She had been snapped up by the nuns to teach the younger children after one of the regular teachers contracted tuberculosis. She pulled her face into the moue I remembered so well as she told me that too many children were a nuisance, they were all stupid and I would do the job much better. I was not sure whether I believed her but certainly she did not look much like the frumpy or demure teachers I recalled from what now seemed like far-off schooldays, for Bette had turned *Zazous*.

She wore a jacket with padded shoulders, a short pleated skirt and striped stockings. Despite the rain she affected the dark glasses of the fashion and carried her umbrella resolutely furled. It looked ridiculous and I yearned to be *Zazous*. The adherents of this craze, which was now sweeping Paris, followed jazz and cultivated an insouciant stare. I asked what her parents thought.

'They think it's funny because it's one in the eye for the Boche. Shows we've still got spirit and can have fun despite their efforts. In any other circumstances they would probably cast their eyes up to Heaven in disbelief.'

When I told her about Klaus and my family she groaned and wished we had never broken the curfew.

'We must have been mad. You would never have met him if we hadn't done it.'

Bette did not, however, appear shocked or to feel the need to decamp from my company and over the next week I saw her often, looking forward to our meetings, but when I suggested we should try and get together with Cécile and Bernadette she muttered some excuse and turned the subject. A small, sad chill whispered that they no longer wanted to know me.

Then, as the ten days were close to expiry, I forgot them as my thoughts turned to Klaus and I was picturing the happiness on his face, which never failed to make me fall in love with him anew, when I realised that I was seeing him in the flesh a hundred metres or so away and, then, that it was not Klaus at all because he was standing beside the man I had noticed.

They had not seen me and I stared incredulously as I drew nearer. They might have been twins and I knew at once that the man I had first mistaken for Klaus must be his brother Willi, of whom he had often spoken, and that his presence in Paris, not some piece of urgent work for the German army, was the reason for our temporary separation.

It was not particularly odd that Klaus's family should visit the conquered city, which was a great prize for the Germans and frequently visited by off-duty soldiers sightseeing. Hitler himself and half the German high command had come soon after the Occupation started. Yet he had not told me and I understood that he was no more eager for his family to know about me than I had been for mine to know of him.

I began to walk to where they were standing, engrossed in the view of the Eiffel Tower which Klaus was pointing out, and had almost reached them when Klaus saw me. With satisfaction I saw the alarm flare in his eyes but I passed by without speaking, as if I saw only strangers in my path, and did not look back.

I fought back tears as I turned for home. I was becoming estranged from my own family and I had no place in his. Although I had not expected it to be otherwise and knew well enough that in his case the need for secrecy was even greater than in mine, it still seemed to magnify my isolation, to leave me a stranger between two foreign lands, to undermine the security of belonging which, until now, I had taken as much for granted as the air I breathed.

Starkly, too, the incident told me there was no future with Klaus. His family would hate me and especially his children. They would hate me not because I was French – there could be little point in hating a foe crushed and subservient – but because I would have broken his marriage. They would see me not as a beautiful, mysterious temptress, but as an immoral young woman, a floozy.

The thought caused me to stand still, my face on fire, my insides full of ice, as I came to terms with a realisation that, until now, had flitted unheeded and shapeless in the furthest recesses of my mind, like a moth, unheard, unseen, but known to be there. Friends and strangers were assuming something which was not true.

I knew that I was not a floozy, but I was not quite sure why. Certainly I courted a married man, which was horribly wrong, but I knew there was some other dimension, the dimension which gave gossips such pleasure, which caused curious stares or unkind comments, which gave rise to a woman having 'a reputation'. Bette, of course, had a reputation but I was sure that what I now struggled to understand was different, more reprehensible, more indelible, final.

I remembered Bette telling me about the women of Montmartre and how they and the Germans did the thing which produced babies and I recalled Marie-Claire Delfont, who had suddenly disappeared from school because, everyone whispered, happily scandalised, she was having a baby.

Did people think I was having a baby? How would I know if I were? Bette had told me once as we sat back to back in the stock cupboard that women could feel a child moving about inside them and we had giggled, wondering if it tickled. Surreptitiously I placed my hand over my stomach and held my breath in fear. Nothing moved.

Common sense reasserted itself. I knew that there was a line to which I could not put a name but which I had not crossed. Why else had I reacted so angrily when Annette had taunted me with something I only half understood? Would not my parents send me away if they thought I was in danger of having a baby?

Suddenly I remembered Dido's words uttered falteringly by Cécile as she translated from the Latin: 'If only I had a little Aeneas . . .' Dido had wanted a baby even though Aeneas was deserting her, driven by some higher duty to his gods. I grappled unsuccessfully with that for a while before being swallowed up once more by the mortification of realising how I might seem to others.

That thought, together with a lingering resentment that Klaus had made so little enquiry about the state of my relations with my family and the memory of the alarm in his eyes when he thought I might be about to meet his brother, made me want to punish him. I decided I would turn *Zazous*, proclaiming my indifference to his disapproval, but there was no time to make the necessary garments and, when the ten days were at last over, I threw myself into his embrace.

'Was that Willi?' I asked.

'Yes. After you had walked past he asked me if I had noticed that girl's hair. He was very admiring.'

'And you said?'

'I said I recognised you as a young lady who had once broken the curfew and your wonderful hair had made me overlook it.'

'Was that the reason?'

He smiled. 'Partly. I might not have been so tolerant had you been bald and ugly.'

'Did you introduce him to Macfidget?'

'Yes. I told him I confiscated a pillowcase and found a cat in it.'

We were in the Café Flore at Saint-Germain-des-Prés and several diners turned their heads as I laughed, not believing him. I tucked my arm in his as we rose to go, uncaring what people thought of me, proud to be with Klaus von Ströbel, ready to take on anybody who said I should not be.

We walked for a little to a secluded spot I had come to think of as ours, from where we could look back to Paris or out towards the countryside, and sat down on the grass. I asked him about the rest of his family and he said all were well according to Willi who had brought a collection of letters and presents from his mother and sister, Angelika.

I commented how much he looked like his brother and he said all his siblings had inherited their looks from his father's side of the family except for Angelika who was fair. Thinking how I also stood out from the rest of my family, I asked what Angelika did and Klaus said she ran the house for her mother, Willi and his other brother, Gerhardt. Willi's wife had been ill and they and the children often stayed there for long periods.

I asked if that meant Angelika was a good cook and Klaus gave a great guffaw. His sister neither cooked nor sewed, he assured me, she merely organised others to do these things and had vowed never to marry because she could not face such drudgery and saw no reason to be any man's property. She was an ardent believer in female emancipation and was both wilful and strident in its cause.

'No *Kinde, Kirche, Kuche* for her,' observed Klaus. 'But for the fact that we live miles from anywhere and I think she has some preference for staying alive, she would be in the most awful trouble by now with the authorities. Decidedly unorthodox.'

Sometimes I wondered that he trusted me so freely and I trembled, thinking he deliberately took risks, wilfully courting the ire of the regime he served.

As if in confirmation of the thought he gazed out towards the countryside and said, 'Willi enjoyed his trip to Paris but I wonder when we shall all be free to travel again, to see the English Lakes, perhaps, or when the English will be free to drift along the Rhine? War is such a damn waste.'

I knew he did not mean a waste of life but of liberty, of time, of opportunity. I had not travelled much beyond France but I too had once been to England with Annette and my father when he was visiting Cambridge University. We had been left with some of his English friends in that city, who spoke no French and served dreadful food. I had hated it and, though I was nearly nine, cried for Mother.

'When the war is over you can take me to Scotland,' I said, recollecting that he had specialised in Scottish history, 'and we can dance on a mountaintop.'

Immediately I wished the words unsaid, instinct always having told me that it was unwise to let him know that I expected a continuing relationship after the war, when he doubtless intended returning to the life and family he had left behind.

He did not, however, appear to attach any significance to my unguarded reference to the future but instead jumped up and pulled me to my feet.

'We do not need to wait so long,' he said, 'and we do not need a mountain. I will teach you Scottish dancing now.'

'I can already do it,' I laughed, remembering Madame Paschale and wet days at school. 'But we have no music.'

'It is in my head,' he cried and immediately began to hum a reel. We danced wildly, with Klaus leaping and whooping, and I felt like a child whose parents were making fools of themselves for its entertainment until I began to share his enjoyment and to abandon all dignity myself. We danced until we were exhausted and collapsed on the grass on top of each other, gasping for breath and consumed by immoderate laughter.

He looked down into my eyes, still laughing, before rolling off and lying on his back staring up at the sky. For a moment I had sensed a hesitation, as if he would stay on top of me in that undignified heap, a frisson I could not name, a movement in his eyes so elusive I might have imagined it but the moment had passed and as we lay back on the grass the hazy impression fled from me altogether, as insubstantial as Creusa's ghost.

We sat up suddenly and hastily moved apart as running footsteps came along the road. Kurt Kleist's voice called urgently and Klaus replied, 'Over here' as he got to his feet. Reluctantly I followed suit, aware that there was grass on my blouse and wild disorder in my hair, knowing he was about to be summoned from me. Kurt came into view and spoke in rapid, urgent German, receiving an answer which sent him moving off in equal haste.

Klaus turned to me. 'I'm afraid your countrymen have spoiled our fun for today. Three of them are dead as a result of some incident involving a stabbing on the Métro. My men are involved. K.K. has gone for the car.'

As the car raced back into the centre of Paris, Klaus scarcely spoke to me but instead fired questions at Kurt and occasionally urged the driver to even greater speed. He left me outside the Kommandantur and I hastened away, not wanting to be associated with the forces who had killed three Frenchmen. As I hurried home the occasional yellow star jumped out at me from the dull clothing of the Jew who wore it and I hated not the Germans but myself.

I began to form a resolution which, a few hours earlier, I would have thought impossible and by morning it had hardened and lasted through the day. I would go after work and leave a note at the Kommandantur if I could not see Klaus, telling him it was over, that I was French and our friendship was wrong.

An early curfew, imposed as a reprisal for the previous day's trouble, made the plan impossible and I spent that and five succeeding evenings in the cold bosom of my family, by which time my resolution had evaporated so when, on the day the curfew returned to its normal time, I received a note asking me to go to the Kommandantur after work I did so with hope not hardness in my heart.

It was rare then for him to ask me to go to his place of work, so rare that on the few occasions it happened I feared trouble, but he explained that he would be delayed a while longer and left me with Macfidget in the inner office. The delay proved substantial and I began to prowl about. A spare jacket from his uniform hung on a peg and I began to toy idly with one of its sleeves, to run my finger along the insignia on the shoulders, when I noticed a button hanging loose on the front.

My grandmother had taught me always to carry a needle and thread and however impatiently I had received the advice in the past I was now glad I had listened. I took down the jacket and, spreading it over my knees, began to sew, dreamily picturing a future in which I would sit at home by the fire sewing on Klaus's buttons while he played with our children. The task took but a few minutes and was interrupted only by Macfidget playfully catching a dangling sleeve.

As I bent to inspect my handiwork I caught the scent of the jacket, of its cloth, of him. I held it over my face and breathed deeply, longing for him to come back, to hug me, to be with me. Then, embarrassed, I returned it to the peg and as I did so I saw the letter, lying half out of the inside pocket, doubtless disturbed by my activity. It was in German but I pulled it out to stare at the handwriting, which was very neat with curly capitals. Only a woman could have written in such a script and I knew it must be from his wife. The writing was too neat for the headstrong sister, too firm for the ageing mother.

I glimpsed only the salutation before footsteps and guilt led me to return the missive hastily to the pocket. *Mein Liebchen, Liebchen Klausi.* Even my German was up to that, I thought. His wife called him her darling, darling Klausi and he kept her letter next to his heart.

I felt deserted, knowing the reaction to be both unfair and irrational, and when the footsteps passed by in the outer office I sought to augment my isolation by looking more closely at the photographs on his desk: a gap-toothed boy smiled cheerily back at me, a pleasant, kindly-faced grandmother held a chubby baby, a rather blurred group of three men and a young woman held tennis racquets. In the final photograph mother and daughter smiled self-consciously into the lens.

The wife was attractive in a homely way but it was not she, whom a few seconds earlier I had almost hated, who held my attention. As I stared down at the girl with the tumbling blonde hair, I gasped as the humiliating, reassuring, disconcerting truth entered me.

Klaus von Ströbel, mein Liebchen, Liebchen Klausi, was missing his daughter not his wife.

ten

At the Farmhouse

I do not know what inspired me to say, when Klaus asked me what I would like for my eighteenth birthday, that I wanted to have him to myself for a couple of days, away from the call of duty, away from accusing looks.

I had expected him to say it was impossible but instead he was quiet for a moment and then said hesitantly, 'I know of a place but . . .'

'But what?'

This time I was impatient with the hesitation, longing for him to say that yes, it could all be arranged, that nothing would stop us going away.

'Liebchen, you know I will never leave Ellie?'

I stared at him stupidly, wondering what his wife had to do with the conversation. He was looking at me intently when I saw him relax and something like wistful amusement replace the temporary uncertainty in his eyes.

'What will you tell your parents?'

'I see no need to tell them anything.'

It was a hollow, childish statement of defiance and he said no more, but indeed I faced a choice between telling them the truth and enduring another bitter argument or telling a lie and enduring a bad conscience. In the event I did neither and left by stealth, writing in a note placed on Annette's pillow that I was going away for two days and failing to specify where or with whom. I knew I was postponing a terrible confrontation, a thought which did not fail to recur occasionally and attack my peace of mind.

I was at first disappointed by the realisation that I would not be absolutely alone with Klaus but he said someone must cook our meals and clean up after us and that his batman had a few days' leave owing to him and would welcome the jaunt into the countryside. Of course he would make himself scarce when he was not needed. It required only the briefest consideration of my culinary skill, inadequate and in France's current exigencies woefully so, to reconcile me to the arrangement.

I was less easily reconciled to the presence of Kurt Kleist, but Klaus insisted that in order to get away at all he had to bring some work and that for security reasons he could not be wholly unprotected at some remote farmhouse. Kurt, too, he promised me, would be largely invisible. I sulked a little, asking if an entire regiment was coming with us, but liked Kurt enough to overcome my resentment.

I made but a passing enquiry about the owners of that large, tranquil farmhouse, as I excitedly explored the rooms, and received but a vague reply from Klaus. From the windows I could see evidence that some husbandry of the land persisted and I assumed the property to be normally occupied.

I put my small, battered case on the large bed in the main bedroom and trailed my hand over its scarred leather, remembering the first time I had ever packed it. I was six and going to stay with my other grandmother who lived by the sea. Happily I had filled it with my favourite toys and books, before watching in tearful disbelief as my mother discarded my efforts in favour of clothes, soap and toothpaste.

It had since been my companion on numerous family visits, a school trip to Lourdes and that tedious occasion when I had accompanied my father to England. Once my mother told me not to bring my adored rag doll, Caroline, in case I lost her and I disobeyed, smuggling Caroline in the bottom of my case, unpacking the bag myself lest my mother discover her, tucking the doll up in the case each night as though it were a bed.

'This is your greatest adventure yet,' I said aloud, patting the luggage fondly, and was immediately disconcerted when the batman came in and placed Klaus's much smarter version on the other side of the bed.

I did not like Heini, who always looked at me with deferential contempt, certain that he resented my friendship with Klaus and as a result despised us both. I blushed, thinking myself foolish to be caught talking to a suitcase. Perhaps misinterpreting my confusion he asked in French, so heavily accented as to be almost unintelligible, if he should put Klaus's case elsewhere. I shook my head and he began to unpack, laying out pyjamas on the side of the bed.

When Heini had gone I too unpacked and moving the pyjamas to one of the pillows laid my nightdress beside them. Then I ran downstairs to join Klaus. I exclaimed with delight at the sight of the flames in the grate of the large, old-fashioned fireplace in the lounge for there was neither wood nor coal for such a luxury at home. We drank wine and I became a little light-headed which helped to repress the guilt when we proceeded to a supper which would have fed my entire family. I tried not to think of what even then they were eating and took an unsatisfactory comfort from knowing that at least they had my share.

After supper we talked, of his brothers and sister, his parents, grandparents, Macfidget, childhood, career, hobbies and of mine but not of Ellie or his children. Nor did I tell him, as I had intended, of picking up a clutch of delivery notes at the Distribution Centre and finding the words 'Nazi Whore' scrawled in capital letters on the back of an envelope, nor of the three colleagues who would no longer even say good morning, but I did tell him of Bette and her sturdy loyalty.

During one pause when I was expecting a response and none came I glanced up to see him gazing absently into the fire though he still played with my hair, feeling its weight and thickness, letting it fall away from him in ripples. I asked him what he was thinking about and he said the war and how but for the hostilities we might never have met.

'Thank God for the war then.' I spoke without thinking but was shocked less by what I had said than by his failure to agree with me. His reaction seemed to confirm my fear, always nagging but rarely confronted, that I meant less to him than he to me. I thought that he must still see me as a daughter and daughters grew up and made their own nests but I wanted him for life, to possess all the years that lay ahead of him and make them my own.

Upstairs as I sat at the dressing table waiting for Klaus to come back from the bathroom I felt the first twinge of doubt as a picture of Edouard danced unbidden into my mind. Supposing someone stole our father or mother from him, from Jeanne? Was that not what I was trying to do to some equally helpless, innocent child? To three children, one of whom giggled onomatopoeically?

I remembered the contempt in Heini's eyes, the coldness in my workmates', the misery and anger in my family's. I knew what I was doing was wrong; I knew I had the power to stop; I knew that I would not stop. Klaus had once said to me, 'You owe it to yourself to think of all the consequences, not just to your parents, your friends but to yourself, above all, my sweet Catherine, to yourself. So if one day you send a message saying it is all over . . .'

I had put my hand over his mouth, refusing to hear more, wilfully blind to the future. When on another occasion he had hinted that it was unlikely he would be posted to Paris for ever I had reacted in the same way: I would neither see nor hear anything which threatened my dream. Tonight we would be close, snug, warm and Ellie would be miles away in another country.

I expected him to return cosy in his pyjamas and when he did not I was shocked and embarrassed, politely looking the other way while he retrieved the garments. My father, grandfather and Martin all wore pyjamas, stripy, friendly things which spoke of home, family and closeness as did the nightdress I now wore, which was ankle-length and flannelette against the October cold.

I risked a glance in the mirror and saw Klaus approaching me rather than the bed and pyjamas. I froze and he hesitated momentarily before bending to kiss my hair.

'Are you sure you really want this, Liebchen?'

I had very little idea of what 'this' might be but I did know that I was afraid of something, feeling some very panicky butterflies fluttering loose inside me. Then I plucked from a store of knowledge I scarcely knew I possessed a time-honoured prevarication.

'Yes, I mean no. I don't know. I'm afraid I have a headache.'

He gave his great guffaw, the one I had last heard when I had asked whether his sister was a homely soul, then turned from me to collapse on the bed, still gasping with a laughter which strangely also contained pain. Eventually he got up and located the pyjamas, which might have reassured me had I been certain I understood what had just happened.

'I'm sorry. Darling, you are not disappointed, are you?'

The helplessness of his renewed mirth told me that, unwittingly, I had turned my beautiful dream into a farce of significant proportion. He looked at me fondly but I recognised it as the look my parents used to bestow on me. From somewhere came the thought that a man would look at Bette in a quite different way.

When I knew him asleep I let my tears flow, afraid my unhappy shudders might disturb him, until I woke in the weak light of morning. I propped myself on my elbow to look down at him, expecting to see a grown-up version of Edouard, sweetly asleep, no worries on his countenance. Instead I saw a man of my father's age, with the bristles of the temporarily unshaven, snoring contentedly through open mouth. The farce, I thought, was now complete.

When Klaus told me after breakfast that he would shut himself up for a couple of hours with Kurt in order to get the work out of the way and leave us free for the rest of the time I was almost relieved, wanting to be alone to rerun the events of the previous night in my baffled, unhappy mind. As I wandered through farmland and lanes I thought of the simplicity of the life I had once known when only my poor performance at school tarnished otherwise undiluted happiness.

I was almost back at the farmhouse when I met a woman coming from it, a Frenchwoman, poorly clothed but better fed than her city counterparts. Silently she barred my way, staring at me. She did no more than that – she did not visibly sneer or place her hands on her hips or take up any other threatening attitude – but in those few seconds as I tried to steady my gaze against her silent, contemptuous one I was immobilised with icy fear.

She looked as if she were studying a slightly repellent but largely incomprehensible alien phenomenon and I saw myself through her eyes, through the eyes of any loyal, oppressed Frenchwoman. She had just come from the farm where I guessed she had been delivering milk or butter to the Germans who occupied it. She had seen Heini and maybe also Klaus and Kurt and now she saw me and had made the appropriate connection.

I pushed past her, muttering, 'Good morning, Madame,' and she made no attempt to stop me but I knew she watched my retreating form until I ran the last few metres to Klaus and safety.

In the afternoon I walked again, this time with Klaus in whom I sensed a greater wariness, not, as I had expected, towards me but towards the surrounding countryside. More than two years into the Occupation, resistance had begun to assume a more tangible shape and a senior German officer unprotected and miles from anywhere could provide an irresistible temptation to any homicidally inclined patriot. I asked him if he were afraid.

'No, just cautious and so should you be, my Catherine. I am glad I did not know you were out wandering alone this morning.'

'I am not known out here.' It was true enough, but my encounter with the woman gave the lie to any comfort I might take from my anonymity.

'No, but the farmhouse is.'

So this couple of days was not unique to us, not special. Other German officers used it for the same purpose – no, not quite the same, I thought as I recollected the previous night and the shame burned through me. I saw myself afresh in the eyes of Heini, of the woman, of my poor mother, and it was an unpleasantly ignoble image.

I asked him who owned the farm and where they were now and this time he answered me.

'They were arrested a year ago and shot.'

I absorbed that in silence for a while. 'Were they Jewish?' I asked eventually.

'No, not as far as I know. The family had farmed the land for generations. Now some people from a nearby smallholding keep some of it going. It is vitally necessary that food production is maintained.'

'Have you been here before?'

He shook his head and I felt obscurely relieved.

'And before you ask why they were shot, I don't know.'

He never seemed to know the important things like the fate of Yvette Levin or why his colleagues had seen fit to kill the people whose home they had requisitioned. I no longer wanted to stay in the farmhouse and I despised myself for not saying so because I was afraid that he would take me at my word and cut short the break.

A bird rustled in a nearby bush and I jumped in fright, thinking of resistants and stabbings. Klaus did not so much as twitch.

'Have you ever been afraid?' I asked wonderingly.

His laugh was a short, sardonic bark. 'God, yes. I was old enough to join up towards the end of the last war and they sent me to the trenches. If any man tells you he wasn't terrified to near insanity in the trenches then you can tell him he's a liar.'

I had heard my father, who had fought at Verdun, say much the same thing. He had always told me how grateful he was to the shrapnel and three bullets that had caused him to be invalided out of the French army a few months later.

'Were you at Verdun?'

'No. That was in 1916 when I merely wanted to join up. The reality came somewhat later and it was not killing Englishmen or Frenchmen, but cowering in a trench with the dead exploding around me. I tell you when I first heard the order to go over the top I cried in sheer terror.'

I did not want to hear any more. Men did not cower and cry, that surely was the lot of women, and yet he showed no embarrassment by what he had told me. I recalled that when in uniform he wore the Iron Cross.

'Oh, yes. Iron Cross, *pour le mérite* – the Blue Max no less. You name it and I won it as soon as I decided I wanted to die, but I never did damn well die. I fought right up to the armistice and was demobbed with a few scratches and grazes, pompous plaudits and memories which took years to leave me alone at night.'

We were walking back towards the farmhouse which glowed golden, mellowed by the evening sunlight, warmed by thick creeper. A light shone from a downstairs window. I could not imagine anyone wanting to die, especially not someone of my own age. It seemed fearsomely selfish towards his mother who must surely have spent the war worrying that her sons would not return. God, I thought with satisfaction, had overruled such sinful nonsense.

By an association of ideas I asked where we should be going to Mass the next day, which was a Sunday, and received a look of surprise.

'Mass? I am sorry, I had not given it a thought.'

'But it's mortal sin not to go.'

'It is?'

I looked at him and a sharp doubt entered my mind. 'You are a Catholic?'

'No. Lutheran.'

My mind rebelled against the words. Nearly everyone of my acquaintance was a Catholic. Annette and I occasionally whispered about the exceptions, arguing over whether they were bound for hell. Catholicism was so obviously right it seemed impossible to reject it. For eighteen years I had heard at school, Church and home how the Pope was the guardian of absolute truth. It had not occurred to me that I might marry a Protestant, that my children could be taught anything other than what I had been taught.

'But I used to see you at Mass.' Only now did I recollect that these days the one place we did not meet was Church.

'Generally outside the church, if you remember, and I came to see you not the priest.'

I gaped at him and he began to laugh at me.

'Oh dear, oh dear. A married man, an enemy of your country and now a heretic to boot. It seems, Catherine, that the last gives you the greatest trouble.'

It did. Patriotism had been required of me for less than two and a half years, having been unnecessary in any active sense for most of my life. The temptations of a married man had confronted me for much less long than that, but the demands of the Church had been drummed into my consciousness from the moment I could think at all.

Lightly, Klaus explained that from the moment he had seen me on the night I broke the curfew he wanted to meet me again. He knew where I lived but could hardly come to my front door, given my age and the likely attitude of my parents, and I was so obviously uncertain when we met at the Quai d'Orsay that he himself doubted whether he should try to press the acquaintance further. Then, when he saw me at the Convent, he realised I was a Catholic and saw the perfect solution to the problem of inventing a chance meeting. Between them, he and Kurt set out systematically to track down where and when I went to church.

I wondered that I had not worked it out before, remembering how I had found Kurt on the steps outside church and his asking me if I always went to Mass at that time. Somehow it did not sound like a man in search of a daughter and my confusion grew even as I felt flattered: my instinct when reading the Christmas gift tag had been right after all.

Nevertheless I wished he were a Catholic. Of course it was perfectly possible to marry someone of a different religion. At some time or other Yvette Levin's parents had done just that. Before I realised what I was going to do I found myself asking Klaus urgently what had really happened to Yvette.

'I know no more than I told you. Drancy, then somewhere else.'

'And what's happening to them there?'

'Again I cannot tell you more than I already have. It is a work camp for Jews and . . . others.'

'Just work?' I ignored the allusion to others.

'Yes. Look, I hear these rumours too. When we first arrived there were rumours that Germans ate children, now there are rumours that we kill Jews in the camps, thousands at a time. Dear God, there is even one version that says we make soap and buttons from dead Jews. It is all equally preposterous and only credulous fools could even begin to think that sort of thing might be true. Soap and buttons indeed!'

I laughed, reassured.

I *laughed*. As we pondered an evening of eating and drinking, warmed by firelight, thousands of my fellow human beings were suffering and dying in the most appalling manner and I laughed. By comparison falling in love with a married oppressor of France was nothing. I spent most of the war hurting people: my parents, my siblings, my friends, teachers, mad Aunt Sophie. The Jews I did not directly hurt at all but, though there is much that I look back on with shame and might wish undone, nothing stands out more than that moment, that fleeting moment, of laughter when Klaus dismissed truth as falsehood.

The evening passed peacefully with no repetition of the previous night's fiasco and next day my spirits had risen to playfulness. We had to return to Paris that afternoon and I wanted to make the most of the morning so when Klaus settled in an old armchair and began to read a German newspaper, now well out of date, I protested bitterly and tried to pull it away from him. Exasperated, he jumped up and I ran off with him in pursuit. He tripped and swore while I ran up the stairs and along the landing where he caught up and grabbed me. I broke free and tore off in the other direction.

To me it was like the games I played as a child with Martin or some temporarily condescending grown-up. That there might be a different quality in it for Klaus never entered my head until he did catch me and holding me, laughing, looked at me with fleeting expectation as he had after the ludicrous display of Scottish dancing, but this time as he let me go I saw a flicker of impatience in his eyes, so transitory that I might have imagined it, but I knew I had not done so.

I straightened up and put out a hand to steady myself, inadvertently sending a small glass ornament crashing to the floor. I had noticed it earlier in the visit, a small hedgehog with an umbrella, a child's ornament which Klaus had looked at with a grunt of amusement and I with an exclamation of delight.

'Oh! What will the owners say?' I cried in dismay. 'I must see if I can find another.'

We looked at each other in silence as my words echoed in my head and suddenly I was looking not at the ruins of an ornament but at the ruins of Catherine Dessin, of a character which I had assumed would never change no matter what the circumstances. There were no owners. They had been shot by men dressed like Klaus and I had moved in without their permission or blessing, had used their bed, their plates, their bathrooms, indeed their very absence through death itself to disport myself with one of their murderers, for if Klaus had not been directly involved he was still part of that massive killing machine, the German Army.

No wonder the woman at the farm entrance had looked at me with silent hatred. She had probably known the owners.

'Klaus, we shouldn't be here. We must go.'

He did not oppose me and we went to the bedroom to pack. While he changed into his uniform I sat at the dressing table staring at myself in the mirror, trying to detect signs of my gross misconduct in my face. My grandmother had always said you could see character in a face.

Eventually he came and sat on the end of the bed behind me and spoke to my reflection, at last saying the words I had been dreading.

'Catherine, we must give this up. I have treated you very badly.'

'I don't see how.'

'You know it's wrong. That's how.'

The words made no sense.

'It's wrong,' he repeated, 'and it can't work.'

'Why not?'

'Because of this.' He rose from the bed and took my hand, placing it on the eagle and swastika on his uniform.

'What of it? It's only a symbol, as real or unreal as we care to make it.'

He smiled ruefully. 'And this.'

He bent down until his face was level with mine and together we gazed at our mirror images; my clear skin, which glowed despite the rigours of Occupation, lay next to his crow's feet and laughter lines; the greying wings of his dark head were almost lost in the tumble of my fair hair.

'It doesn't matter. Lots of women marry older men.'

He drew back sadly. 'And that is the most pressing reason of all. You deserve lasting happiness, Liebchen, real happiness. In short you deserve marriage and that is exactly what I cannot offer you. I already have a wife and very young children. We must give each other up now before I make it even more difficult for you to find a young Frenchman.'

'I do not want a young Frenchman. And you do not want to give me up. Is it because . . . of what happened two nights ago?'

He denied it at once but I was unconvinced and on the way back to Paris Kurt Kleist kept his eyes on the road and pretended he did not know I had been crying.

eleven

Interlude

I had not been to confession for many months because I did not want the priest to tell me it was my duty to give Klaus up or to suggest that absolution might depend on my at least making some effort to do so, but now I had missed Mass on a Sunday and I must make a confession or abstain from Communion, which would cause comment. A considerable amount of circumlocution was necessary but I managed to convey to Father Tessier just how close I had come to a significant extension of the sin I was already committing and waited for the suppressed shock I expected to hear in his voice.

There was indeed a silence. Then:

'Surely the Grace of God was in this man,' said the priest in tones of wonder. It was the last reaction I would have predicted and the unexpectedly light penance did nothing to lessen my surprise.

Bette also mentioned the Almighty and in equally awestruck tones. 'Dear God, you were lucky.'

I was beginning to believe it but I also knew that there was too much I did not understand and I had been blunter with Bette than with the priest because I wanted her to explain to me what I did not know.

'Not here,' she said, 'Not in a café, for heaven's sake. We had better go home. Frankly, I wish we could go to the stock cupboard and sit back to back.'

In her room, with Alphonse staring down from the wardrobe, Bette told me what I supposed my mother would have told me if I had been about to marry or perhaps not even then. Maybe I might have been left to find out for myself.

I asked an unguarded, prying, perhaps unpardonable question, believing I already knew the answer. Bette hesitated only fractionally before saying, 'Yes, I have.'

She spoke neutrally without shame, pride or defiance.

'And the others? Cécile? Bernadette?'

'Good heavens, no. Quite unthinkable. If they were sure that I had they would make a pariah of me.'

Bette had not been able to withhold a slight emphasis on the last word and I winced. For a while I absorbed what she had told me in silence then we spoke simultaneously, using the same words.

'You are lucky!'

'Yes,' said Bette sadly. 'You are. You will find it quite easy to live within the conventions, to marry in white. So will the others. I wish I could be like that too, life would be so much more straightforward.'

'But you are so certain, so unafraid of it all. And no one could call my life straightforward at the moment.'

At that she began to lecture me. I had taken a risk of enormous proportions and might not be so lucky next time. Von Ströbel was married and quite apart from any moral considerations I would never see him again if things went wrong. Instead I would end up in some awful place run by nuns and no respectable man would ever marry me while my lover would run back to his wife, his world untouched. It was, she assured me, the theme of much great literature.

Had my parents spoken to me in such a fashion I would have resented it, but I could take it from Bette, not least because I knew she was right. When at last her speech ended I shook my head and, unlike my parents, she knew when to give up or perhaps, loving me less, felt no imperative to continue.

'Then God help you,' she whispered with grim friendliness, 'because nobody else will.'

At home no one made any reference to my absence over the past two days. Having dreaded a confrontation I now perversely wanted one, the silence seeming to augment my alienation, to signal that I was no longer worth saving. My grandfather alone among the grown-ups still treated me with active affection and patience but the sadness in his eyes was a continuing rebuke and I sought him out less than I might have done.

At work I found another scrawled note, much more abusive than the last. I stuck it on the wall with a comment of my own underneath saying that I would send the next such document to the Kommandantur. Both pieces of paper disappeared and I knew that by my threat I had confirmed for any remaining doubters the justice of the rumours that surrounded me but had also purchased safety. My love for Klaus had placed me in jeopardy but his for me was my protection.

Annette told me I had disgraced her and that if I did not leave the Distribution Centre then she would. I ignored her and we both worked on there, lured by extra rations and oppressed by the mental inertia of Occupation which so often defeated the will to make major changes to lives preoccupied with the pettiness of daily shifts to obtain an extra morsel of food, an extra minute of heat, shoes in which one could actually walk.

When Klaus told me at the end of October that he was to take two months' leave in Germany and would be away until mid-January I tried to be grown up about it, to be pleased for him, and failed abjectly, leaning against him and weeping while he stroked my hair and said that at least he would be coming back, that this tour of duty would still continue.

I snuffled that I could not bear it and afterwards berated myself for a fool. Had I not always resolved I would not drive him away by being possessive? I knew too that he had taken no substantial leave since being posted to Paris and must be in need of a proper break, that he must badly miss his children; but as often as I thus reasoned I thought of his wife, of how he would be daily reminded of what he stood to lose, of the weakening of his feelings for me which must occur if he was to be away so long. Self-pity swamped me and, unforgivably, I hoped his holiday would turn out badly.

We planned to meet the night before he left but a punitive curfew frustrated us and I spent the cold November evening alone in my room in bleak contemplation of a separation which fear told me could be permanent and hope pleaded was not.

When he had told me he was going to Germany I had said, 'Der Vaterland?' in tones as playful as I could manage and he had replied, 'Heimat' and my heart sank. Homeland. Klaus was going home which left me representing a foreign interlude, a land of strangers.

Home. I thought of warmth, welcome, children running to greet him, a smiling Ellie embracing him, all cruelly oblivious of me, and whatever fear or longing possessed me was quickly swallowed up by misery as I imagined him surrounded by small, familiar objects, throwing aside his uniform, relaxing into a long forgotten routine, adoring and adored.

It was poor consolation that, for a while, my family seemed disposed once more to consider me one of its members rather than an outsider to be shunned, because I discerned their intentions as surely as if they had told them to me. It was their plan to throw every possible diversion in my path, to distract me from thoughts of Klaus, to provide the prospect of other men in the forlorn hope that I would cease to miss him.

Robert was invited to the house more often and Annette brought young men home. Even my friendship with Bette received unusual encouragement for while I was with her I would be less likely to mope. I received it all with amusement rather than resentment, rejoicing at least in the thawing of the atmosphere at home where recently only Edouard and my grandfather seemed to regard me with undiminished affection.

There came a period in which I really did begin to lay aside my preoccupation with Klaus's absence as I entered one of those phases in my life which were abnormally eventful, absorbing me despite myself. In the week before Christmas Mad Aunt Sophie died and various relatives arrived in Paris to sort out her belongings, implement her will and attend her funeral.

My mother and aunts took me to her apartment to begin what I could only think of as dividing the spoils despite the heavy sighs and exclamations of 'poor old Sophie'. With only the slightest twinge of conscience I hurried to the bathroom under the pretence of needing to use its facilities and, as soon as I had locked the door, flung open the shampoo cupboard.

It had been emptied, so completely emptied that not even a

packet of old-fashioned powder shampoo or a dusty bar of cracked soap remained. I gasped and stood there, staring stupidly, expecting that at any moment all the goods I had so coveted would rematerialise before my eyes. I had not planned to take all the stock I had last seen in this cupboard, but I had intended to help myself to a generous proportion, concealing the items in my pockets (I had deliberately chosen to wear a cardigan with deep ones), in my underwear, my handbag. When I ran out of such places I would have hidden the shampoos on top of the cistern, under the bath, anywhere, for later retrieval, but I would have left much more than a token amount for others. Whoever had pre-empted me had been troubled by no such qualms.

Now I expostulated with moral outrage at the unknown person who had frustrated my plans and deprived both myself and others, abusing her as a common thief, forgetting my own intention to take more than my fair share, for there was a meanness here which transcended even the moral fudging to which Occupation had reduced all but the most fastidious, a scale of cheating which shocked. My outburst brought the rest of the party to the bathroom and we all stared at the empty cupboard and at each other, suspicion flaring.

The concierge? Who else had a key? My mother and one of my aunts glared at each other. When had any of us last looked in the cupboard? What about the doctor, the undertaker even? I no longer cared, I merely ached with disappointment as my visions of comfort and scent evaporated. I cursed the thief once more and turned away, hoping we might yet find something in the apartment to alleviate the misery of Occupation.

Whoever had raided the bathroom had done the same with the larder and wardrobes. No one could have carried out so thorough a looting without being noticed by the concierge and when I explained the matter with mounting indignation to an unmoved gendarme I could not repress the hope that he would accompany me there and then to the scene of the crime and immediately search the concierge's rooms. Instead he wrote down my story in a laborious hand and told me it happened every day.

I repressed the temptation to head straight for the Kommandan-tur to see if I could interest the Germans where I had failed with the French forces of law and order. Klaus would not be there and nobody else was likely to care, except perhaps Kurt Kleist, but it seemed unfair to expect him to risk intervening in matters which were probably well beyond his jurisdiction.

All we had left from Mad Aunt Sophie's hoards were old newspapers, battered books and useless bric-a-brac. We did, however, also have the bedding in which she had died – the thief was either too nervous or too fastidious to take it – and this, along with curtains and the cover of the bedside table, was cut up to make various garments over the next few weeks. Jeanne had a wonderful velvet dress from one of the curtains.

Among the mourners who returned to our house after the funeral was a cousin of my mother who had eight children and a large Labrador dog called Simon. As a pretext for getting away from the din of the youngsters I took Simon out into the back garden, where he immediately flopped down on to the grass and looked up at me in mute protest at the noise, the reduction in the scraps on which his family now fed him and the weight of his years. His black fur was flecked with grey and, as I fondled his elderly head, I remembered the grey in Klaus's hair and looked at Simon with helpless love.

For the first time in a very long while I began to laugh at myself. To feel emotion for an ageing dog because his grey hairs reminded me of Klaus was not merely ludicrous but pathetic and I was glad that I alone knew that such a thought had entered my head. I was a long way from making the sort of detached analysis which might have led me to conclude I was in the grip of a schoolgirl crush rather than the passion of a lifetime but that small act of self-ridicule could have been the beginning.

Then Simon's owner emerged from the house and, in the manner of one addressing the youngest of his vast brood, told me that I was a disgrace to France and to all my family. I responded with restraint but also a hardened resolution, my doubts dissolving and with them my self-mockery.

Three days after the funeral my grandmother was taken ill and had to spend a week in hospital. Once we knew she was in no danger of dying or being permanently invalided I found myself positively rejoicing in her absence as it meant I spent a great deal of time upstairs with my grandfather and Edouard who, despite the current thaw in family relations, were still the only ones in the house with whom I felt truly at ease.

Once when Grand-père mentioned the Great War I remembered what I had meant to ask him after my conversation with Klaus at the farmhouse.

'Were you ever in the trenches, Grand-père?'

'No. I was well beyond anything other than a desk job by then. Why?'

'Did men cower and cry?'

He raised his eyebrows but answered straightforwardly.

'All the time, I should imagine. Your father fought at Verdun as you know. They say you could hear the noise of the German bombardment a hundred and fifty kilometres away. Whole woods were uprooted and blasted into the air, while the trenches were full of rats and decaying corpses and among them men fought and slept and fought and slept. The Germans started using flame-throwers and men were burned alive. Indeed, your father told me that he was in a trench when the timbers which shored it up caught fire. Every so often the men were ordered over the top of the trenches straight into the battlefield hell. I expect they all damn well cowered, but they went. That is what matters, Catherine – not that a man should blub as he went over the top, but that he should go over the top even while he blubbed.'

My grandfather gave me a few moments to absorb that before saying, 'Catherine, I don't know why you are asking this but I can guess. All I can tell you is that men – even handsome, brave men in uniform – do not act like the heroes of films and books. They are flesh and blood but the measure of a man is what he does when he is afraid, not that he feels that fear in the first place.'

He pressed the issue no further but I looked at Edouard and inwardly cringed when I thought of his future. I prayed that he might never have to fight in a trench, surrounded by rats and exploding corpses.

The Christmas of 1942 was undiluted misery. We ate cattle food and a pathetic quantity of meat while I imagined Klaus and Ellie spoiling their children with food and presents in abundance. Again I had to repress the instinct to ask Kurt Kleist for help.

As the festive season came to an end and our thoughts turned to work I began to count down the days until Klaus's return. I sensed my parents again withdrawing as if conceding that their strategy had failed and resigning themselves to a renewal of shame and betrayal.

There was still a week to go when I saw him. He was sitting in the front of a car beside a driver I did not recognise. I raised my hand to wave and then dropped it when I saw his taut, set face and his eyes which stared grimly at a scene he did not see.

My selfish spirits soared: it had not been a good leave. I fairly danced on the way home as I wondered what I should wear for our reunion. At work I hummed to myself, making light of tasks that normally bored me.

I made excuses when there was no word for a week. He had after all returned early and presumably for some purpose which he was now preoccupied by fulfilling. After a fortnight my spirits were low and I began to reason that his grim expression might have stemmed not from bad memories of his leave but from contemplation of what he must now do in Paris. I wondered that I had not before thought of the obvious explanation: he was determined to break off our relationship and was tormented by how he was to do it, by how I might react.

When, in the third week of his return, a note arrived asking me to meet him outside Paris at a place we knew well, I was cold with premonition, wondering if I would be able to control my reactions or if I should break down, wondering if there might be any way I could change his mind.

It was cold at our trysting place and I shivered but when he at last came he seemed oblivious both of my discomfort and his own, sitting on the ground in the open air as he gazed unseeingly at the rolling French countryside. Numbly I waited for him to mention his wife. Eventually he said, 'You remember my brother?'

Willi. At once I was overcome with remorse. He was going to tell me that Willi had been killed. Poor Willi, I thought as I remembered how I had seen him sightseeing, carefree, just a little while ago. Their poor mother, I exclaimed inwardly as I moved to comfort Klaus.

His stillness stopped me. Then he said, 'You remember I told you about my brother, Gerhardt, who was . . . not very bright?'

They were the last words anyone ever said to me in childhood or youth. As I looked at Klaus I realised he had aged, that the lines around his eyes and mouth were deeper etched and I knew the same was about to happen to me, that I was starting a journey with him into a land which knew no innocence, no kindliness, no good and that if once I went there I could never return.

twelve

But Deliver Us From Evil

As soon as our relationship had reached the stage where I found it impossible to talk about Klaus's wife and children without guilt or embarrassment, I had deliberately taken to asking him questions about his parents and siblings. So when he asked me if I remembered his brother Gerhardt I at once recalled the family which lived in a large house, deep in the countryside of northern Germany.

Klaus had been born on the very first day of the century which always seemed to me to have some dramatic significance that was irritatingly elusive. His eldest brother Lothar was four and Willi two. Three years after Klaus's arrival his mother, Lotte, had given birth to a fourth son, Gerhardt, who from the beginning was what Klaus had described to me as 'not quite right', thriving in physical growth but unable to walk till he was nearly four and never capable of uttering more than a few disjointed words. He was a loving and gentle child, fond of animals, upset by the tears of any of his brothers, content to potter about in a world he could not understand.

The three elder children adored Gerhardt but his condition had convinced their parents that they should have no more children. This accounted for the gap of fifteen years between Gerhardt and Angelika, whom Peter and Lotte von Ströbel always described as a surprise.

It was a happy family in which Klaus grew up, the children playing on the large estate his parents owned, Gerhardt spending hours with cows, pigs and hens. 'He became helpful to my parents before the rest of us,' Klaus had once observed, telling me how, from the age of eight, his youngest brother loved to help with the farm and could calm an agitated animal as if by magic.

The Great War came close to annihilating an entire generation but, when the von Ströbels gathered around their dining table to welcome the New Year in 1919, Peter and Lotte had indeed much to be thankful for in the survival of all their sons. They knew of no other family as fortunate.

Lothar had joined the air force and eventually flew with von Richthofen's circus, writing home with tales of the Aces, Boelcke and Voss, outliving them all, becoming an Ace himself before being shot down by a Sopwith Camel near Maranique and spending the last six months of the war in hospital. He returned home in 1918 with only a slight limp to remind him of his suffering.

Unlike Lothar, Willi was not old enough to enlist at the beginning of the war but eventually joined the navy before finding himself in the sea at Jutland, cold, terrified but alive and, having been pulled out of the water by the British, doomed to the safety and frustration of a prisoner-of-war camp for the duration.

Unsurprisingly Peter and Lotte resisted any attempt by Klaus to join up before he was obliged to do so and even more strenuously opposed his wish to enter the army from which young men were dying in trenches by the million, but he pleaded a dislike of heights and water and, as the German Army was by then so desperate for recruits that men younger than he were joining up daily, his will prevailed.

Gerhardt spent the war peaceably among his animals, missing his brothers, often wandering from room to room looking for them. As they returned so he clung close to them, neglecting even the cattle he cared for to make sure his brothers were still at home. Willi was the last to arrive, having had to be repatriated upon release and, his lungs having been affected by many hours in the freezing seas of Jutland, Gerhardt would listen to his wheezing with an air of surprise so comical that even the worried Lotte laughed.

They had survived but Germany's economy collapsed and large tranches of the estate had to be sold off. It was imperative that the men found occupations and a means to sustain themselves in a future which now looked very different from the one they had so long anticipated.

Lothar decided upon aviation, then still in its infancy, while Willi became a schoolmaster and Klaus began to study history at Heidelberg. Peter von Ströbel put money into Lothar's flying venture, taking an active interest in the business, and life appeared to be settling down for all of them. Then, when Angelika was barely five and Klaus was wondering if it was too soon to spend a couple of years in Britain to pursue his new-found love of Scottish history, Peter and Lothar were killed in an aerobatic display.

It was a devastating blow for the close-knit family which had come unscathed through so much, but none felt it more keenly than Gerhardt who appeared to understand the meaning of the coffins being lowered into the ground. For many months he was visibly distressed if Klaus or Willi were not about and frequently set out to check on Angelika even when she was safely asleep in her bed.

As if in compensation for the misery of the early twenties the rest of the decade proved a good one. Both Willi and Klaus married, bringing Lotte the joy of grandchildren. Klaus and Ellie travelled in Italy and Britain and by the beginning of the thirties Klaus was teaching at Heidelberg and set for a life in academia. He and Ellie moved to Oxford in 1932 and watched the rise of Hitler from another country. Meanwhile he developed an undying love for the rugged bleakness of the north-west Highlands, hunted in Leicestershire with his new English friends and detailed in letters to Lotte all the progress of his daughter Johanna.

'You need not expect the English to do much fighting,' he commented in one letter to Willi. 'They had enough last time even if they did win. Yesterday evening I went to a debate at the Oxford Union where the students decided they would not "fight for King and Country". So perhaps we shall have a peaceful century. I hope so for our children's sake.'

None of the von Ströbel family had much patience with National Socialism. Lotte pronounced Hitler common and Angelika, now a self-willed young woman in her teens, said nothing on earth would induce her to dress up in the dowdy uniform of the

Association of German Maidens, the female equivalent of the Hitler Youth.

Willi hated red flags and socialism, fearing that the challenge to a social order still reeling from the deposing of the Kaiser would now be complete but Klaus thought not, citing the bitter opposition of the communists. He was vastly more concerned with the militarisation that seemed endemic in the Movement and accurately forecast that it could only end in war. He was certainly uneasy enough to return to Germany at the beginning of 1935 but, instead of once more immersing himself in academic life, he found his linguistic skills increasingly in demand and began to work at first occasionally and then regularly for a number of Government departments, finding nothing to reassure him despite the undeniable growth in prosperity and fall in unemployment.

Nevertheless it became apparent that whatever doubts any of them had should be heard only within the family and even Angelika learned discretion as the oppressive nature of the new regime was daily more apparent and active persecution of the Jews became an unacceptable but accepted part of life in Germany. Angelika returned from a visit to Berlin with stories of Jewish women scrubbing pavements and Willi raged in vain when one of his fellow schoolmasters lost his job, having been denounced for some obscure Jewish connection.

Klaus became aware that not all his friends shared his reservations and watched in disbelief as men he had once respected became fanatical devotees of Hitler, but he thought them misled rather than evil. When war broke out Klaus and Willi resigned themselves to being called up to desk jobs and positions of moderate seniority. Whatever they thought of Hitler, they were loyal to Germany, resenting bitterly the humiliation of the Treaty of Versailles, so without enthusiasm, but also without any attempt at resistance, they became active participants in the war effort.

This much I knew, as I thought I also knew that Gerhardt, who was by this time nearly forty, still tended the animals and played with Lotte's grandchildren who outstripped him in ability even before they could speak.

Now Klaus told me that he did not. In order to protect Gerhardt from a regime which did not allow the right of the mentally handicapped to live, the family had long played down his disability when filling in official documents and, as they lived in a remote location and Gerhardt was employed in real farm work, they had been successful in keeping him safe. Unfortunately they had been too successful.

A few months earlier Gerhardt had been called up. Thinking the summons to active service a ludicrous error, Lotte had not bothered her other sons but had sent the papers back with a letter of explanation and the name of Gerhardt's doctor who had taken some risks in the past when classifying Gerhardt's condition. To her amazement, soldiers arrived at the house two weeks later and took Gerhardt off by force so that when Willi and Klaus, at last alerted, had begun to act their idiot brother was already employed as a guard at Dachau, where, they could only assume, his ability to carry out tasks mechanically and diligently without having the least understanding of their meaning was regarded as a highly-prized asset.

For a while the family persisted in the belief that it was all a mistake and that Gerhardt would not last five minutes in such a role, fearing that instead he might become a victim of the regime, but as the weeks passed and officialdom proved unmoveable both Klaus and Willi made arrangements for leave in order that they might pursue the matter more vigorously. That was why Klaus had left Paris. The family began to gather at Lotte's house, but three days before Klaus arrived his brother was returned home as unceremoniously as he had been taken and with as little explanation.

During those three days Gerhardt simply hid in the barn, refusing to be coaxed out, wailing in a fashion which no one had heard before, not eating, rarely sleeping, often shaking in every limb with eyes staring at something the rest of the family could not see. The doctor could only tell them what was already obvious: Gerhardt must have received a serious fright and would take a while to recover.

Klaus greeted his wife and children and went straight to the barn where he found Gerhardt gibbering incoherently and this time it was not only the incoherence of his limited communication but of terror. Klaus tried everything, singing nursery rhymes, putting his arm around Gerhardt, fetching the cat to comfort him, talking of food indoors but all to no avail. Willi joined him and they stood looking down at their younger brother as he hid in the hay, in turn looking back at them with large, frightened eyes; eyes which seemed to plead with them to take away monsters, to pull him to safety and drive off some hellish fiend.

Eventually they took Gerhardt by force into the house where he hid under a bed. Severely worried, tired out by his journey from Paris, unable to make sense of what was happening, Klaus cut short his first evening with his family and, to the bitter protests of Johanna and Willi-Lothar, went early to bed.

He was woken, gently, a few hours later by Willi who whispered that the rest of the household was asleep but that Gerhardt was downstairs and demanding 'Aus', which was all he could ever make of Klaus's name. Reluctantly Klaus crept out of the room, careful not to wake Ellie. On the landing he asked what time it was and Willi said four in the morning.

'We found Gerhardt in the kitchen,' Klaus spoke without looking at me, still gazing, unseeing, at the French countryside, 'and then he told us everything.'

'*Gerhardt* told you everything?'

'Yes. Not in words, of course, but for the first time in his life he communicated. He must have talked to us for half an hour in gestures, imitating actions, miming, showing us more graphically than any verbal description could have done what went on in that camp.'

Then, shockingly, Klaus began to imitate what he had seen, idiot actions accompanied by idiot noises which left no doubt as to what atrocities were being described. I turned my head away but the recital went on and I forced myself to look once more.

When the grim pantomime did stop, the silence was dark and menacing. I remembered how I had laughed when Klaus had dismissed the rumours about Jews being tortured and ill-treated and knew the revelation was my punishment. Others would find these things out when the war was over and they were placed in no moral quandary but we knew then and must ask what we should do.

I thought no more horror could be possible but Klaus had resumed the tale in his normal voice, albeit dulled to monotone.

'We sat there, saying nothing. Willi had his head in his hands but I just went on looking at Gerhardt, wondering what on earth to say. All his life we had murmured platitudes to him when he was upset, had addressed his needs in childish language, offering childish solutions. Now suddenly it was he who had brought us knowledge and needed an adult response. I failed him, Catherine, I failed my little brother in the hour of his greatest need. He looked at me and knew that I was as shocked as he, that this was one we weren't going to sort out, that I had no answer. If only I'd had the presence of mind to tell him it was over and he didn't have to go back, to say I would tell the nice policeman and he would put a stop to it, to say all those poor people were up in Heaven and wouldn't want him to be sad. Anything. If only I'd said anything.

'Instead I just sat there numb and when Gerhardt ran out of the house to his barn I didn't stop him. I wanted to talk to Willi first, to ask how we should handle it. He wasn't much use because he was in essentially the same state as I was, but while we were talking Angelika came down in her dressing gown and slippers to ask was that Gerhardt grunting just now and what was going on?

'Willi shook his head at me but I gave her a censored version of what had happened and she immediately said she would go to Gerhardt. I left the kitchen door open to light her path and the next thing we heard was the most almighty scream which seemed to split the very night.

'We ran like hell to the barn and there he was. He had hanged himself from the – how do you say it? – bits of wood.'

'Rafters, beams,' I spoke mechanically as his French failed him for the second and last time in the whole period I knew him.

'Rafters.'

The silence darkened.

'You see,' continued Klaus, 'he couldn't have formed any intention to do that, have worked out that he could kill himself by finding a rope and putting it round his neck. It takes logic to throw a rope over a rafter, form a noose, stand on an upturned bucket and then kick it away and Gerhardt was incapable of logic or working out a sequence like that. That too must have been an imitation. He had seen people hang themselves and find peace. And that was all he wanted: peace, somewhere where the horrors of that bloody camp couldn't follow.'

I held him, trying to comfort a comfortless soul, subconsciously aware that our roles had for the moment reversed, that it was he who depended on me. When at last he moved away I whispered a question, 'What will you do?' I feared his answer, dreading his saying that he would confront those responsible, shrinking in spirit from whatever his despair might lead him to do.

'Do? What do you suggest I do? Shoot Hitler? Gather a force together and storm the camp? Or perhaps put in a report and hope that nobody would have known these things if I hadn't kindly told them and that they will be suitably horrified and galvanised into action rather than just moved to make Ellie a widow?'

Perversely I then wanted him to act, not meekly accept Gerhardt's terrible fate or the lot of those even now imprisoned in Dachau and its like, people such as Yvette Levin. Assured he stood in no danger of acting rashly, I now deplored his caution.

Despite my thoughts his sarcasm was almost a relief after the toneless recital of horror, broken only by that dreadful pantomime, but he fell silent again, holding his hat in his hands, staring at the swastika, at the symbol of the regime he served, at the emblem of evil.

'*Sed libera nos a malo.*' Without realising it, I uttered aloud a line of the Lord's Prayer which I said mechanically every week at Mass, and which suddenly had meaning; real, urgent, meaning. Evil was no longer a vague, if faintly disturbing, concept but an actual force which had disfigured our lives, had managed to permeate the mind even of an idiot. *Sed libera nos a malo.* But deliver us from evil.

'Amen,' said Klaus. 'He knew before the rest of us, sensed evil where we saw only folly. I've never had much time for all that stuff about a sixth sense in those who are short of the normal quota but now I'm not so sure. A few years ago, well before the war, I was staying with my mother when the Nazis were putting on a torchlight procession in a nearby town. We had a small relative with us and she wanted to have a look at the spectacle so Willi, Gerhardt, Angelika and I all set out with this kid in tow.

'It really was quite a sight. There must have been thousands marching in that small town, singing patriotic songs, carrying flaming torches. Some of them were pretty young too but we had got used to that. Then the child, Gisela, became scared of the crowd that was pressing round us and Willi swung her up on his shoulders. When I turned round from helping with that I couldn't see Gerhardt and for a while we were all in a bit of a panic because we knew he would be utterly incapable of finding his own way home.

'In the end Angelika stayed with Willi and Gisela while I began to push back through the crowds, looking for Gerhardt until I found someone who knew him and who said she had tried to stop him, but Gerhardt just carried on. This lady said he looked frightened. When I got right to the back of that mass of people I saw another acquaintance who had also sought to stop him, this time actually holding on to him but he pulled away and ran off.

'I hunted high and low, calling for what seemed like hours and then he came to me but when I tried to take him back into the crush to find Willi and the others he just wouldn't have it. Of course I thought the crowds had alarmed him but when we were all going home we heard them singing again and Gerhardt simply bolted, if you could call that lumbering run a bolt. Say it's just my imagination if you like but now I think he felt the evil in that parade, that he knew he was close to something bad and cruel. God help him, he *knew*.'

Klaus rolled over on his side to stare once more at the horizon and, as I fumbled for something to say, for some illusory comfort, he began to sing.

The voice, pure, tenor, operatic, exquisitely pitched, arrested me until I focused on the words. Klaus sang not in German but in French so that I understood every filthy syllable of that bawdy, obscene, soldier's song which echoed around the countryside through five or six explicit verses and seemed to hang in the air when it ceased.

I sat and looked at his back, blushing but unoffended, knowing that he was scarcely aware of my presence, that the song was not aimed at me but that what I was listening to in that pure voice and impure verse was the sound of a man cursing his fate. Cursing, cursing, cursing his fate.

thirteen

Risks

The hanged idiot swung in my dreams, his features, those of Klaus, distorted into pain and fear as he mouthed urgently at me and flailed his arms in uncoordinated imitation of some horror he had seen. Angelika's scream was my own as I seemed to become entangled with the swaying form which had begun to shake me.

I woke, violently shaken by Annette, who asked me in scared tones what was the matter and did I know I was screaming in my sleep? From the next-door room Jeanne called out and further away Edouard started crying. By the time my mother arrived to see what was happening, I was sitting up and trying to pass the incident off as just a bad nightmare but when exactly the same dream caused me to rouse the household for the second time that night, I abandoned sleep altogether and lay awake shivering, endeavouring to recall every horrible detail of Klaus's story.

In my imagination I saw its sequel, picturing Lotte being woken by her three surviving children to grief and loss, the hasty conference which decided how to explain the death to the authorities and what Klaus and Willi should tell their children, the dreadful task of telling their wives the truth. Klaus had described none of this to me, but I knew it must have happened much as I now saw it in my mind. I thought of Willi-Lothar's onomatopoeic giggle and wondered if there had been any laughter among the children of the household over Christmas.

Of course there would have been: children are resilient and adults try not to burden them with grown-up worries. I found myself pitying Ellie and knew I would not hate her again, knew also that I could no longer take Klaus from her, that they had all been through enough already.

I slept once more, fitfully but dreamlessly, and woke unrefreshed for the day's work. I was surprised, therefore, to find that I applied myself with more concentration than usual and with increased attention to detail.

At lunchtime I slid a small mirror from my handbag and examined my features which looked reassuringly familiar. It was apparently only inside that I had aged ten years, being impatient with the giggles of two young girls who had just joined the Distribution Centre, feeling grateful rather than excluded when I was left out of the usual workplace banter. I wondered what my colleagues would say if I told them what went on in the camps.

Most of us knew someone who had been taken away or had inexplicably disappeared and we looked the other way, pretending it had not happened, that we did not know. At least, I thought, I had tried to help Yvette Levin but it was an unlucky recollection for it unleashed fresh horror as I imagined the Levins as victims of the atrocities Gerhardt had described and found myself praying they were dead.

It was more than I could cope with alone but I hesitated to tell even my grandfather, fearing that Klaus might be in mortal danger if the story got out. I knew that, although I would have trusted her with my life, Bette could not help me. I yearned to cast my woes upon my mother in the hope of a magical solution, as I would have done only a year ago, to confide to Annette that she might condescend to wipe away my fears but I recognised that I was alone, that ultimately we are all alone.

In the end I unburdened myself to Father Tessier, under the seal of confession, assured he was bound by his vows to tell no one. He was gentle and sympathetic and seemingly so little surprised that I wondered if he had heard it all before, if German soldiers had blurted out similar tales seeking absolution from their involvement with the regime they served. I remembered the officer I had seen by the window of Le Printemps and wondered how such a man would handle the knowledge which had come to Klaus.

Klaus himself looked at me sadly when we next met. 'It's gone,' he said. 'Forgive me, if you can.'

I could make no sense of the words. 'What's gone?'

'Whatever it was that was you – the innocence, the youth, the fun, that faintly puzzled look I adored.'

He watched me absorbing his words and I realised he was right. Despite my quandary I was less puzzled, very certain of my relationship with him, knowing there was a new dimension and that I no longer feared it. He read my thoughts and smiled but there was a sadness about him which made me want to howl. I could hardly believe that I was the same Catherine Dessin who had positively rejoiced to see him looking taut and unhappy as he returned to Paris.

We were sitting in the Café Flore. It was not a place where Germans were welcome and usually Klaus enjoyed being there for that very reason, mischievously discomfiting his enemies, pretending to be oblivious to the sudden silence which greeted his entry. Sometimes I thought he had a more serious purpose and was perhaps noting which dissidents were there and on those occasions I felt uncomfortable, used even.

It now occurred to me that maybe he brought me there to test me, to let me experience the coldness of my fellow French, to let me judge whether I was strong enough to withstand it. Yet today I felt he was consciously absorbing the icy atmosphere and I wondered if he was punishing himself, if he was wanting to feel morally isolated.

Outside, however, he gave his usual humorous grimace, the one I knew so well, which could be prompted by ersatz food or drink, by uncongenial company, by overt hostility, by any unseemly display. It reassured me, suggesting at least the possibility of a return to normalcy. I had long ago christened that turn of his countenance his Flore face.

'Have you told anyone?' he asked me once and when I said only Father Tessier he looked relieved and urged me to keep it that way. As he had always been indiscreet and seemingly unworried by it, I felt a frisson of alarm that he should now attach importance to secrecy.

Sometimes I wondered if Willi and Angelika looked furtively

over their shoulders as they walked in the streets, if Lotte jumped at every creak in that old house, if Ellie held her children more tightly to her. Fear stalked us all, I thought. We had more to be afraid of from our own countrymen than from each other.

Had Kurt Kleist noticed the change in Klaus? Did he pretend he had noticed nothing or had he made a seemingly solicitous enquiry, in reality determined to be satisfied with any airy reassurance Klaus might offer? I was certain Klaus would never confide in his junior, that he would protect him with ignorance.

'K.K. is not a fool,' was all Klaus said when I asked and I was left to guess whether that meant Kurt would never put an indiscreet question or that, having asked, he would know how to interpret the doubtless uninformative reply. I tried to picture Heini's reaction if he were ever to stumble on the truth but it was a challenge to which my imagination was not equal.

Yet for all his discretion Klaus took risks. One day as we strolled slowly towards the Kommandantur a lad of fifteen or so erupted in our path and in the same instant that I noticed his yellow star I saw the men, two in plain clothes, one in the uniform of the SS, racing behind him. Klaus grabbed the youngster by the collar and hissed, 'Stand still and don't speak.'

A rapid conversation followed in German before the Gestapo man stood aside with surly reluctance and Klaus propelled his trembling captive towards his Headquarters. Within he made for his own office and snapped some order at Kurt who departed swiftly while Klaus began to question the boy.

Eventually Kurt returned and, in response to Klaus's raised eyebrows, nodded. Klaus told the lad to go home right away and preferably not by the main streets. I often wondered if he arrived safely or if the Gestapo thugs were lying in wait unseen by Kurt when he checked if the coast was clear.

'Wasn't that a bit risky?' I asked as I stroked Macfidget and tried to get him to settle in my lap instead of circling and kneading my thighs with his claws. 'Ow!'

'He remembers the pillowcase. No, not really. Those brutes are very junior and as they have ugly reputations even by the unexacting standards of the Gestapo I don't think anyone will complain that I clipped their wings a bit.'

'Don't they have kids of their own?'

'Probably, but they don't think Jewish children qualify as human beings.'

'But that's nonsense,' I said indignantly. 'Jews can feel fear and pain and grieve for loved ones just the same as Germans.'

'Indeed, there is quite a lyrical passage to that effect in a play by Shakespeare, when a Jew makes that very point.'

'Didn't Shakespeare live hundreds of years ago?'

Klaus smiled. 'Yes. Behold the progress of the human race.'

Kurt put his head round the door and Klaus disappeared into the outer office. I looked round the room, noting the jacket on its peg and wondering if it still held Ellie's letter in an inner pocket. I was deeply uneasy at what had just happened, despite Klaus's reassurance, realising that he was beginning to kick against the regime he was supposed to serve and that it was a regime which knew few limits when kicking back.

When he returned I surprised myself by saying, 'I believe it was in Shakespeare's time that traitors were boiled in oil? If the human race has made so little progress that means you should be more careful.'

'I rather think boiling in oil preceded Shakespeare. Man had progressed to hanging, drawing and quartering by then. At least English man had. Over here they preferred to tear people apart between four horses. Ravaillac . . .'

'Oh, stop it,' I protested. 'But please, Klaus, stop taking risks as well. Please.'

'If one quarter of what Gerhardt told us was true then modern man is no better than those of the times we have been discussing. It has to be worth a risk or two to drag us a few inches further forward. Dear God, here we are in the twentieth century, in the middle of Europe, with fine music, literature, art and apparently we're just a pack of savages. We might as well run ululating from mud huts and hurl spears at each other.'

I was uncertain how to counter his anger, knowing that grief and incredulity had plunged him into the deepest winter of the soul. I found myself wondering if what had happened in Germany could have happened in France and when I recollected how so many ran and told tales to the Kommandantur, denouncing troublesome neighbours as Jewish, settling old scores, regardless of the victims' fate, I started to agree with Klaus. Savages all.

I voiced the thought aloud but then again went on to beg him to be more careful, while some inner, more detached being noted that I spoke with greater authority these days. Indeed, after a while the bitterness drained from his voice and the evening ended on a lighter note, but as Kurt Kleist saw me home I prayed that Klaus would not allow himself to be goaded into overt opposition to that terrible regime. While I could not bring myself to regret his helping the Jewish lad, even if it were only a drop of kindness in a stinking, polluted ocean, I could not bring myself to want him to do it again.

Yet, two days later, when I saw him as part of that regime, I condemned him. I had finished work early and was walking slowly home, wondering whether to call on Bette who would by now have finished teaching for the day, when I noticed a kerfuffle near one of the big hotels used by German generals. There were five or six cars, much bustle and heel clicking and heiling of Hitler. Clearly someone of considerable importance was arriving and I joined a small knot of Parisians who had gathered to watch the spectacle.

I had been gazing at the scene for a few seconds when I saw Klaus and watched, repulsed and sickened, as his arm flew up in the Nazi salute and he bowed to whoever was the cause of the ado. I knew my reaction to be illogical, for what had I expected him to do? Salute like a Frenchman? Yet the gesture was horribly at odds with everything he had said: it looked fanatical, *unKlauslike*.

Then, as the grandee made his way into the hotel and Klaus walked towards his car, I saw him make his Flore face, the grimace saying louder than words, 'What a damned fuss.'

I laughed aloud. He had not seen me and, unusually, it was not important that I had passed unnoticed when so close. In those few seconds I felt closer to him than if I were in his very arms, for he had punctured the pomposity of the occasion with a small, comic, private reflection and somehow that suddenly seemed worth more than any amount of moral expostulation.

I was still smiling to myself when I arrived home and my

mother gave me a half-angry, half-worried look. Since Klaus had told me about Gerhardt I felt little guilt about what I was doing, believing he needed me and that, given his own circumstances, I was no longer being disloyal to France. It was not a position which could have withstood much examination but it gave me both comfort and courage in dealing with my family who reacted with suppressed and impotent wrath, doubtless thinking me to have become brazen as well as immoral.

I helped for a while in the kitchen and then went to find Edouard for whom I had brought home a piece of chocolate that I had obtained by barter from a workmate. I found him playing Hunt the Horse with Jeanne who refused to return my greeting and flounced off into her bedroom. She and Annette were in a phase of refusing to have any dealings with me at all.

Sighing, I turned to Edouard. 'Guess what I've got for you?'

Edouard looked down at his jersey. 'Don't care.'

Ice moved inside me but I persevered. 'Shall we give Horse some nice chocolate when we find him?'

'No. You got it from the Germs.'

'Germans. No, I didn't. We were swapping things at work.'

Edouard continued to look down, his small mouth set sulkily.

'Don't you love poor Catherine? I shall cry.'

It was an approach which had never failed to have Edouard throwing his arms about my neck but now he just shook his head and when I tried to hug him he pulled away and ran along the landing to Jeanne's room, calling her loudly. Jeanne opened her door and they both looked back at me.

'I hate you,' said Edouard fiercely. 'You like Germans.'

I gasped, looking stupidly as he disappeared into Jeanne's room and she firmly closed the door. I was momentarily tempted to fling open that door and challenge both her and Edouard but instead went to my own room where a further shock entered me as I took in the significance of Annette's stripped bed and the absence of her belongings.

My sister would no longer share a room with me and she or Jeanne or perhaps both had made Edouard join in the hostilities. I sat down on her old, stained, slightly lumpy mattress vowing not to cry. I almost succeeded and spent the next hour rearranging my own belongings in the greater space now afforded, before dragging Annette's mattress to Jeanne's room where I guessed my elder sister to have set up camp and then collapsing the bed and standing it against the wall.

By the time I had finished I was covered in dust as I had been obliged to lie on the floor under the bed in order to locate its key and I made a mental note to clean more thoroughly next time my mother or grandmother handed me a mop and sarcastically suggested its use. My exertions had however restored my equilibrium and I took a gloating satisfaction from the knowledge that my reactions were the last that anyone would have predicted. In the same spirit I joined my family for supper without referring to what had happened, greeting Jeanne and Edouard in airily chatty tones.

Jeanne glared mutinously but Edouard looked unhappy as if even at his age he felt embarrassed. I saw that despite himself my aplomb had amused my father who was looking covertly at Annette to see how she was taking it. She too pretended not to be put out and the meal proceeded peaceably while its participants seethed with fury and resentment. I guessed they might like to tell me to eat elsewhere but could not do so while my rations contributed to the cooking.

Through a week of early curfews I divided my evenings between my room, now blissfully my own, and my grandfather's whenever I was sure my grandmother was downstairs. To Grand-père alone did I admit that I found Edouard's withdrawal almost unbearably painful, to him only did I confide the hurt which my isolation brought.

Gently he tried to persuade me to think of the future, asking me what I thought would happen after the war. I said Klaus would eventually return to Ellie, that he had never deceived me in that matter and, win or lose, I did not suppose the Germans would always be in Paris in the force they were now.

'Catherine, you are telling me that one day he will go and you will never see him again. Why wait for that day? What sort of man is it who offers you such a future?'

I shook my head, but for once he pressed me.

'You deserve a good man, marriage, children. You are putting yourself beyond that, creating a character which is not really you, building obstacles for any decent man who might in the future love you.'

'If he loves me he won't be able to help himself whatever people may say about me. You can't just reason away that sort of feeling. Anyway, I don't intend to stay in Paris when it's all over. I shall start again somewhere else.'

'That is not so easy for a woman but let's suppose you do go away where no one knows you and that you do find someone you want until death do us part, what then? It is one thing to fall in love but quite another to marry, when parents want to meet each other and make enquiries about families. Then whoever it is will know all about you.'

'I cannot prevent any of that by giving Klaus up now. If you are right, then the damage has been done and I might as well enjoy it while I can.'

I saw that I had shocked and saddened him and, in an effort to mitigate my shamelessness, I told him that Klaus needed me, that things had happened in his life which I was not at liberty to divulge, that I knew what I was doing was wrong but that to abandon Klaus now would be a greater sin. I did not expect to convince him with such an explanation and knew that if I had simply stated I was hopelessly in love and could not help my appalling conduct my grandfather might have respected me more.

I cared so much for what the old man thought of me that I had to fight a seriously urgent temptation to tell him about Gerhardt but my fear for Klaus's safety prevailed and I was silent.

I saw Grand-père looking at me curiously.

'Is there something else?'

'No. It is as I have just said. Something terrible has happened to him but I cannot tell you what it is without placing him in mortal danger.'

'Then it is gross of him to burden you with it. He should have found an older confidant. If only you realised how much you have changed, Catherine. We used to be afraid for you, afraid that you had no idea what this man wanted, afraid of what he might do to you but what he has done is worse than anything we could have imagined. He has aged you ten years.'

'Grand-père, I want those burdens because they are his. If you were all so worried then Mother or Annette could have tried warning me instead of shunning me, explaining rather than condemning. There is little for me here, but when I am with him I feel as if I have the world and if there is any crumb of comfort I can give him then I will. Anyway he did not especially want what you doubtless all feared.'

I realised that the use of the past tense was an eloquent admission, that by saying, 'did not' rather than 'does not' I had shouted my guilt from the rooftops.

The old man sighed. 'It was bad enough when you merely thought you were in love with him, but now you really are. You may be a beautiful woman, Catherine, but you have placed an ugly blight on your life.'

He said no more but he would normally have rationed his advice more stringently and I felt another door at home stood merely ajar which in the past had been wide open.

As if reading my thoughts he said, 'Next time Edouard comes up here, follow him and we will see how long it takes to make him forget he is supposed to hate you.'

Edouard, egged on by Jeanne, did not often forget and when he did was reminded by my obliging little sister whom I began to hate. Soon he too appeared in my dreams running into the barn and shouting, 'Germans! Bang! Bang!' as he pointed at the swaying body, but now I woke alone, wondering if I had screamed only in the nightmare or if my family was too used to the disturbance to bother with its cause.

In the cold winter mornings of the first part of 1943 I lay shivering in bed, looking at the ice formations on the window panes, waiting for the remaining wisps of dream to fade, wanting only the warmth of Klaus's embrace, praying for some formula to restore his peace of mind, battering Heaven's gate with contradictory petitions that he might take no risks and that he might bring down National Socialism. When I was fully awake I became more realistic and wanted merely to be warm again.

fourteen

A Friend to all the Enemy

I started to look for somewhere else to live and wondered that the idea had not occurred to me before. My parents received the news without comment but Klaus strenuously opposed the plan, ironically motivated by the view that however badly my family treated me they would at least protect me from outside harm. He said that the war could be turning, that privations could get much worse and that a clan would do better than any individual.

I asked Bette if she would share digs with me but she replied bluntly that she could not put up with visits from Germans and I realised that I would not be able to be fastidious about any sharing arrangement: respectable or patriotic girls would not consider my company suitable. Hypocritically, but with great conviction, I refused to set up home with collaborators and my predicament became manifestly hopeless. I maintained the myth that I was still searching long after I had abandoned the idea and occasionally daydreamed about having enough money to rent an apartment without the necessity of sharing.

Then Bette told me she knew three girls who shared lodgings in another part of Paris and who would welcome a fourth if I was likely to continue working for the Distribution Centre and bringing home extra rations. I guessed the daily journey would make unacceptable inroads into my pay but went on the Métro to view the place anyway. The girls turned out to be dancers who, as long as they were earning a living, did not much care whether they performed for French or German audiences. One was from an orphanage, another had become separated from her parents in the Exodus and the third had left home because her father drank.

They were resourceful and hard-working, but we had nothing in common and I knew I would be uncomfortable there. We conversed politely but stiltedly over tea made from leaves which must have been used a dozen times and I understood their desire for extra rations, hoping someone would be found to fulfil it.

It was late when I arrived back in the centre of the city and the Métro was packed with people who had just left cinemas, theatres and restaurants and were hurrying home before curfew. As I pushed through the crowds I noticed a small knot of German officers and recognised Kurt Kleist. I did not wave for fear of arousing the hostility of those pressing round me but I began to make towards him with some vague notion of giving him a message for Klaus. I was only a little way behind him when, just as we reached the exit, I saw the knifeman.

Kurt had become detached from his group because he had stopped to retrieve something dropped by a middle-aged French-woman who took it from him with a bad grace. As he smiled and turned away I saw a thin, bald man with ill-fitting clothes sidle up to him and pull something from the pocket of his worn trousers, an item I do not think I had even identified as a knife blade when I screamed.

Everyone looked in my direction including Kurt and his would-be assassin. The latter interpreted the situation correctly and began to run for his life, almost immediately followed by Kurt and the other officers who had come racing back. They were obstructed, as if accidentally, by Frenchmen who immediately apologised, but then a shot rang out and everyone pelted for the exit.

I held back, wondering where the man had gone, and just as I realised that I was alone on the platform, I saw him sneaking towards the exit. I called out to Kurt wherever he might be and then froze as the man came towards me. He did not stop but, heading straight for the way out, threw me a single look of anguished disbelief before he disappeared from view.

Seconds later the Germans came running up, but, after a search of the area around the Métro, returned empty handed. By then I had left the platform and was standing in the main entrance, shaking less in reaction to what had actually taken place than at the dreadful thought of what might have happened. Kurt thanked me effusively and, as I re-ran the tableau in my mind, my trembling became uncontrollable: he had come within centimetres of death.

Had I merely screamed I might have got away with it, have been regarded as just a frightened young girl who spontaneously cried out when she thought she was about to witness a murder. I had, however, waited to see the end with the confidence of one who stood in no danger of being harmed by the pursuers and had called out to alert the enemy when a loyal servant of France was trying to effect his escape.

In those few minutes I had exchanged my image as a silly young girl besotted by a single German officer for that of a friend to all the enemy and I had done so in, of all places, a crowded Métro station. Thus ran the strictures of Bette who visited my home for the specific purpose of explaining what her friends were now saying about me. Reports of the incident had spread quickly and I had been identified in them as a collaborator, a traitor even, who willingly sided with the oppressors.

I was obliged to accept that much of what was being said was true. When I had been taken back to the Kommandantur to make a statement the warmth, light and bustle had seemed more like home than my cold room among my disapproving household. Klaus had been summoned from his hotel to which he had already retired for the night and he, Kurt and I had discussed the incident from which, from their point of view, I had emerged as a heroine.

Klaus had expressed himself even more warmly than the man I had saved and in my statement I had held nothing back, describing the Frenchman in detail. It was true that I been a friend to the Germans on this occasion and I had no regrets. I did not see murder in the same light as fighting and I did not admire the man with the knife, though I did feel a little compunction when I remembered the look of fear and incredulity he had cast at me. Stabbing soldiers would not make the Germans leave Paris; such incidents always led to arrests, hostage taking, deportations and executions as well as reprisals and early curfews which could last for weeks.

I remembered the Bishop telling us that we should love Germans as individuals while hating the creed they promulgated.

School, the white dresses, the procession in honour of Our Lady, my nervous revision all seemed distant memories from another century, from a foreign land where they spoke a different language, but I recalled those words as if I were hearing them anew.

Klaus and Kurt, together with one or two others with whom I now came in contact, were my friends. Perhaps, had I ever met him again, the young officer I had seen by the window of Le Printemps would have become a friend. By contrast I knew Heini was an enemy and it was the same among the French: Bette was my friend, Lisette was not. I was incapable of deciding relationships according to uniform or national symbols.

I knew I was rationalising an action which, performed by someone else, might have scandalised me but I was certain also that I had been right and I argued stubbornly with Bette who believed it to have been nothing short of treachery.

'Saving Kurt Kleist was one thing but helping them try to catch the man was another. Surely you can see that?'

'No, I cannot. He might have tried again with someone else and created a widow and orphans to no good purpose. It isn't as if he was fighting a battle.'

'He was. We all are – or most of us. For goodness' sake, Catherine, can't you see that people think of you as just another collaborator? Aren't you worth more than that?'

'*Kurt* is worth a great deal more than a knife in the ribs. He could have been in the morgue by now.'

'A lot of men are dying in this war.'

'In battle, yes, but not through cowardly murder. I despise that man, whoever he was.'

'Will you denounce him if you see him again?'

'Yes,' I said stoutly but I was uncertain, remembering that expression of fear.

Bette got up, her face set. 'You know, you are making things very difficult for me. I've stuck by you because we're friends, because you never deserted me when most little darlings' parents were telling them to stay away from Bette of the bad reputation, because I thought you were just being led on by Klaus von Ströbel, that you were an innocent abroad who still had secret hankerings to play with Alphonse. Now I'm not so sure. You've changed.'

'No. I've just grown up and recognised the utter futility of war. A madman sets out to conquer the world and we are all expected to act like savages. Well, some manage more easily than others.'

At that Bette left and I wondered when and how I could make up the quarrel. It was not as if I believed all I had said. The war was not futile if it could save the Levins and everyone else who suffered so appallingly, but I held to my view that murder was pointless rather than patriotic when committed at random and to no effect other than a fresh wave of oppression.

A friend to all the enemy. It might not be true but it would be a dangerous label to carry.

Kurt sent me a letter and flowers and to my surprise my mother did not sneer when she handed them to me. 'I would have screamed too,' she said. 'But now show wisdom and if ever you see the culprit again, pass by quietly on the other side. And one more thing – if you really must be friendly with von Ströbel and Kleist then we know we cannot stop you, but do not be led by this incident into enlarging your circle of German friends.'

It was good advice as several Germans were to stop in the streets to thank me, but I had to bite back a retort to the effect that if I had more friends among the French I wouldn't need to look to the Germans. It would have been an unjust comment as I had created the vicious circle myself.

My mother's advice also carried with it a reassurance I had long needed, for she would not have bothered me with her views had she no concern for my welfare. Klaus had once told me that my family would always love me more than they would hate what I was doing but I had seen little evidence of that until now.

Klaus repeated his own thanks when we next met, saying he dreaded to think how close they had come to losing K.K. His superior, a much-decorated general, summoned me to his office in the Kommandantur to tell me the same thing. I began to feel uncomfortable. A friend to all the enemy.

I commented to Klaus that Kurt appeared to be very popular. 'He is the nephew of some top brass. The General probably thinks we might have all ended up on the Russian Front if your compatriot had been successful.'

I laughed but then said soberly, 'I had begun to forget you are all the enemy.'

'Then remember it again and keep remembering because France will not forget.'

It was one of several oblique references he had started to make about the possibility of Germany losing the war. The prospect both reassured and frightened me as I tried to face my own future.

'War is so silly,' I protested. 'What is the difference between Kurt Kleist and a Frenchman his age?'

'None, but you could have asked that question during most wars in history. It is a rather sad fact of life that one moment two young men may be friends and the next they are obliged to dress up in different uniforms, wave flags and kill each other. A German mother does not weep less than a French one when her sons do not return. A French widow is no less bereaved than a German one. None of this is new, Catherine. Indeed, in civil wars friends and neighbours kill each other.'

'But what on earth is the point of it all?'

'I wish I had the smallest coin from the poorest realm for every time I've asked myself that. If you think this war is bad you should have been there last time round. I can't believe that any man, whether he was in the trenches or falling through the air in a burning plane or suffocating in a sinking submarine, really felt that the Kaiser's differences with the rest of the world were worth it. Yet sometimes war is simply necessary.'

'Why?'

'Well, a country may be invaded and if so it has a right to resist.' I heard the trace of contempt in his voice and knew he was thinking of how little France had resisted, of how eagerly her government had come to terms. I too believed we should have fought, not surrendered to the threat, but I also recognised that people were alive now who would not have been had France been able and willing to risk a bloodbath.

'Like Yvette Levin?' Klaus challenged me when I voiced the thought aloud. 'If ever there were just cause for war, Gerhardt told me what it was.'

'But you still want your side to win?'

'Oh, yes, I very much want us to win and to win pretty convincingly because we can't afford to be trounced again, not after what they did to us last time, but I want us to win with a different vision, Catherine, not the hideous, twisted one we are fighting for now.'

'You can't have it both ways.'

'I know, but you asked what I wanted and that was the honest reply. You also want things both ways – you want me to fight all that is wrong and at the same time to take no personal risks. In our oh so lucid thoughts you and I are as muddled as Gerhardt was when confronted with counting beyond three.'

'I still say war is daft. Perhaps if women ruled the world it would be run more sensibly.'

He gave a loud guffaw, the first I had heard since his return from Germany. 'Well, you're welcome to try, my dear. You couldn't make a bigger hash of it than the men have managed for a few thousand years.'

The fullness of his laughter pleased me for it seemed as if that dense black cloud under which he had walked since coming back to Paris might at last be dispersing a little, but now that Klaus was laughing again I longed for Edouard to do the same, but still he stubbornly ran from me, sometimes dramatically hiding behind Jeanne.

Jeanne herself was causing more than enough trouble with her almost nightly rows with one or other of my parents. To both Annette and me, my mother and father had seemed as gods who must be respected and obeyed, who could magic away problems, sort out any injustice. Only very slowly did we come to perceive them as human beings in their own right, complete with the normal quota of faults and foibles. Jeanne had arrived at this stage much younger, was rude and intolerant, and spoke to them with as little respect as she might have accorded children she disliked at school.

The calmest evenings were when my father had students to the house, teaching English in the dining room to a motley assortment of failed baccalauréat candidates, secretaries who had performed brilliantly at school and were now receiving what would have been a university education in an informal manner and small boys and girls whose parents were ambitious enough to secure them extra tuition.

Jeanne was inhibited by the presence of strangers from causing her usual arguments and I could not help reflecting that it would be a more peaceful household if the students came every evening. Soon they were arriving four or five nights a week, inhibited only by curfews, and I wondered if my father had any fears for his current teaching job or if for some reason we were short of money. Discreet enquiries to my grandfather revealed that neither was the case but still the students came and I would hear a comic buzz as a group struggled with the sound represented in English by 'w' or 'th' or pause to listen to my father's clear, didactic voice elucidating some feature of the work of Jane Austen or Charles Dickens.

One evening Annette came out of the dining room as I was pausing in the hall to take off a wet mackintosh. I looked at her in surprise.

'Brushing up your English? I thought it was still good.'

'I'm helping Papa,' she answered, sweeping past me in an endeavour to avoid further communication.

On another occasion, when I wanted to find something in the dining room, I paused outside the door listening to make sure no one was within and heard urgent whispering not in English but in French. I turned away, unable to identify the cause of the sudden unease which stabbed at my stomach.

Soon I forgot the students as I entered a period in which Klaus was more available than usual and we drew closer by the day, our lovemaking sometimes leisurely and sometimes urgent. I felt as tongue-tied as a blushing schoolgirl when I tried to tell him how much I loved him, the right words seemingly always elusive. I wanted to be poetic and lyrical, extravagant and original but what I said invariably sounded banal. I felt men had all the advantages in such conversation, able to extol female beauty to make comparisons with dawn on the mountains, exotic flowers and all the other sources of poetic inspiration. Women did not appear to write such verse or if they did I could not find it.

'Oh, just talk to him as you would to Alphonse or Edouard,'

was Bette's unhelpful advice. 'Men like baby talk sometimes and paying them compliments only makes them conceited.'

The rift between us had been mended and rather than go home to Jeanne's noise I often took refuge with Bette if I had time to kill and Klaus was working. She was still *Zazous* in her time off and entertained me with stories of teaching at the Convent.

One evening, as we were talking scandal about someone we had known at school, the bell rang and in walked Cécile and Bernadette. We looked at each other awkwardly and I half expected them to find an excuse to leave. Instead they sat down and a stilted conversation ensued until I departed earlier than I had intended. Bette grimaced as she saw me out but, reassuring her, I began to walk home in an untroubled frame of mind, knowing they were now gossiping about me and not caring. As long as I had Klaus I would be happy and others might be as spiteful as they pleased.

As I turned into our road I saw students spilling out onto the pavement and fully expected to hear Jeanne in full flood by the time I arrived indoors but the only sound was that of immoderate laughter from the kitchen, where I learned that Jeanne had been impertinent to my grandmother and the old lady had chased her with a stick.

The rest of the family was consumed with helpless mirth and for the first time in many months I was allowed to join in, exasperation with Jeanne's conduct temporarily outweighing disgust at mine.

When I found Bette waiting for me outside the Distribution Centre the next day as I left work I assumed she had come to apologise for Cécile and Bernadette, but then she told me that Sister Benedicte had died and for a moment we held one another and fought back tears. It transpired that the Mother Superior had been ill with cancer for some time but, typically, had struggled on, telling no one.

Although she had expelled me unjustly, I could think only of her kindness, guidance and gentle advice. Of course she was a dragon and I had been afraid of her but time had given me a different perspective. I told Bette I would go with her to the funeral but when the day arrived I went alone because she had gone down with influenza and was too weak to get out of bed.

When I saw the huge number of pupils, parents, nuns and old girls who had turned out for the funeral I wondered if Paris had been brought to a standstill. The sun shone down on a prodigious assortment of black garments as hundreds paid their respects and a lump rose in my throat when, remembering the frantic stratagems to which we had been driven in our quest for white dresses and mantillas, I realised that almost as much effort must have been put into finding appropriate clothing for today.

The old girls gathered naturally into their year groups as they sought out people they knew. I saw Lisette who, catching my eye, blushed and turned away. I had no more hatred towards her, Gerhardt's legacy being a wonderful new sense of proportion. What she had done to me seemed no more important than the things Jeanne did when she was throwing a tantrum.

In church I stood squashed at the back before following my contemporaries to the graveside. We stood some way off but I could still hear the priest and I looked only at him until the interment was over. It was then that I glanced about me to discover that I was quite alone, that the other girls with whom I had shared desks, lessons and secrets had moved pointedly away. I looked to right, left and behind but there was no one within twenty metres, despite the crush elsewhere. Everywhere I looked there were clusters of black figures but, as a shaft of sunlight fell on me, bathing my dark garb in bright light, offering a warmth which did not touch my heart, I stood alone, a solitary, shunned figure, untouchable, disdained.

fifteen

A Forecast of Judgement

My increased sense of isolation made me more appreciative of Klaus's.

'Is there really no friend you can trust? Surely some of the other officers? People you share the Mess with or at the hotel? Isn't there anyone you trained with or have known for ages?'

'There are many with whom I would trust my life, none with whom I would share my secrets.'

He was lying on a sofa of an apartment we sometimes used, while I sat on the edge, idly swinging one of his hands. It occurred to me that he must be very confident in me given the extent of my own knowledge. I supposed that, if he already trusted me enough to be sure I would let him go back to his wife without any active protest, the rest of his confidence was just a natural extension. I knew that it could not be mere complacency, a belief in his power over me, an assumption that I was besotted enough to agree to anything, because since his return there had sometimes been a hesitancy, an uncertainty, in him that had been absent from our earlier encounters. I was no longer just a pretty girl whom he liked and half-desired: we were as one and the one was alone and could look to no other.

I replaced his hand and leaned against him, burying my head in his chest.

'At least we have each other, mein Liebchen, Liebchen Klausi.'

He froze at the words and too late I heard what I was saying. Ever since I had read the opening lines of that letter from his wife I had been tormented by them. The script danced before my eyes, taunting me with Ellie's possession of Klaus to which my logic bowed and my passion did not. I had no plan to wreck his marriage, I wanted him and his family to be happy and even in my most selfish moments I did not wish him a widower, but I still hated his being her darling, darling Klausi. I wanted him for my own and so I allowed myself to call him mein Liebchen, Liebchen Klausi in my thoughts, convinced that they would never betray me because we spoke only in French and all my endearments, some of them ludicrous, came from my native tongue.

He could not have known that I had seen the letter but must instead have thought the words a terrible coincidence, a warning from Providence sending him a none too subtle reminder of his sin. Had I stopped at Liebchen, he would have been unbothered as he occasionally used the same term to me and it would have been a normal endearment, but the repetition and the effective use of Liebchen as an adjective were, as I was later to realise, eccentric, presumably stemming from some private joke between him and Ellie. Certainly I had never before called him Klausi. In truth I had never thought the name to suit him, much preferring Klaus, which I now always pronounced with a German intonation and accent, frequently drawing mockery from my sisters. By contrast I pronounced Kurt and Heini as though I were speaking French.

'Spare me the Klausi,' he said, trying to speak lightly.

I was tempted to ask why but I had the wisdom not to do so, although somewhere in a miserable corner of my heart a voice whispered that he kept the name only for her and resented my use of it.

If those around me had been less preoccupied with Klaus's status as enemy they might have challenged me more often with the existence of Ellie and their children. I knew that if Klaus and I had been reduced to the sordid arrangements that normally characterised an affair with a married man I would have broken off the relationship long ago and indeed thought it unlikely that he would ever have embarked upon it. As it was I had never seen Ellie or the children; Klaus did not have to lie about where he was; we could be together quite openly, going where we pleased, without fearing that we might suddenly meet his wife. Ellie was too far away to prey upon my conscience and I used my acceptance that Klaus would one day go back to her as justification for conduct I knew to be seriously wrong. Only rarely did thoughts of Ellie come to me as I gave myself to our wild, ecstatic, all-consuming lovemaking.

Klaus was looking at me and I turned to a more immediately pressing problem.

'I am so hungry I could eat the entire zoo.'

'I am not sure there is anything left in the zoo, but I know where we can get a four-egg omelette, some semi-decent potatoes, fresh fruit and tea which has been poured over its leaves only twice.'

'Can you throw in a glass of wine?'

'That is easy.'

It was not easy for the French. Even the Germans were now feeling the pinch but the Occupied were living on Rutabaga, a form of turnip used for cattle food, which we boiled for hours or fried for quicker but less satisfactory results. It was revolting and most of my family had seemingly perpetual stomach upsets. Mine were less frequent only because I so often ate with Klaus, who ensured even throughout the deepest privations that I enjoyed a superior diet to that of my countrymen. Once I might have felt guilt but my isolation had quashed such finer feeling.

Rutabaga occasionally gave way to Topinambour, a different type of root also normally reserved for cattle. It was a kind of artichoke and I wondered how any self-respecting farmer could feed anything so awful even to a cow. My father, with his usual prudence and foresight, grew tomatoes in pots in the back garden and as we had once done with the hen so we did now with the tomatoes and brought the tall plants in at night to forestall thieves. There was insufficient sun to produce really large, fat fruit but the product was more than adequate.

The coupons with which we were issued were often meaning-less, Jeanne only rarely receiving her quarter of a litre of skimmed milk to which she was theoretically entitled daily. Until Edouard had been persuaded to shun me I smuggled food into the house for him, including milk, which Klaus or sometimes Kurt supplied. I was fairly certain my parents knew but preferred to turn a blind eye if it meant a normal rate of growth for their small son. Recently I simply gave the goods to Grand-père, without disguising their provenance, and he in turn ensured Edouard thrived.

An attack of Colorado beetle destroyed the potato crops, with the Germans predictably seizing all that could be salvaged. It was rumoured that Parisians had begun to resort to rats but I did not believe it.

We made soap from candles and burned anything in sight to produce heat. My father had brought back boxes of old files from the Sorbonne and we used them all as coal disappeared completely. That had been going on for a year and there was not a single file left. We at least had thick eiderdowns and could burn newspapers which in some families were used as an extra layer of warmth on top of bedclothes.

As spring was promising to give way to summer in 1943 I gave thanks for the heat to come and marvelled that we had all escaped with nothing worse than flu. I knew of some households where the old and young had contracted, and sometimes died of, pneumonia.

I began to learn German, discovering a late enthusiasm for study, and solemnly asked Klaus in a laborious and ill-pronounced way if Willi's lungs were all right and if it was cold in Germany. He replied in his own language with exaggerated clarity and slowness.

'Willi's lungs are much better, thank you. It has been very cold but now we look forward to summer.'

'I am glad. Good night.'

'What?' asked Klaus, startled. He made his Flore face. 'Unless you really meant to bid me good night in the middle of this promising Sunday afternoon I suggest we stick to French.'

'I was endeavouring to say it is good not to have bad lungs and was just trying to assemble some words but I said *Nacht* instead of *nicht*.'

'Humph.' He made it sound like a word and I was just about to ask what it meant when I saw his expression and we both gave way to mirth.

Within a fortnight bad lungs were no longer a joke as I went down with a massive attack of bronchitis and felt pains that could only be pleurisy. It did not turn to pneumonia but I lay in bed coughing and wheezing, my temperature soaring, my nightclothes sometimes soaked with sweat and at others pulled closely round me as I shivered with cold.

My mother came, shaking an old thermometer, murmuring worriedly as she examined its reading. Annette and Jeanne brought in trays of unappetising food which I refused to eat. The doctor arrived and spoke gravely about warmth and nourishment and after his visit some medicine appeared which was to cure me.

I knew the time of day only by the strength of the sun when I woke briefly between long hours of delirium-laden sleep. Emerging from one such fitful slumber in the pre-dawn hours of a Monday morning, I knew something was different and eventually identified a cosy warmth and from somewhere in the room a flicker of flame. An old familiar smell penetrated even my blocked nostrils and I struggled to identify it.

As my brain cleared from sleep and fever I knew that my room was being warmed by an ancient oil heater, which my mother used to light when we ailed as children, but I had not seen it in use at all during the Occupation and had forgotten its comforting existence. My mother must have hoarded oil for an emergency such as this. No sooner had this realisation entered my mind than I yearned miserably for those old comforts of childhood illness: hot drinks, warm rooms, attentive parents. It appeared they were still around after all, my parents' love of me not, as I had thought, forfeited by my own love of a married German colonel.

I longed for the security of those far-off days when home had been a refuge instead of a battleground, but when I next woke I knew, without having consciously reasoned myself to such a conclusion, that it was almost certainly Klaus who had obtained the oil and when, a few hours later, my mother brought me a cup of nourishing broth I needed no further confirmation. This soup had certainly not been constructed from cattle feed.

My mother watched worriedly as I tried to sit up and leaned back weakly against the bedhead, but at least I was not tossing about in delirious sleep so I supposed she must have thought it safe to withdraw some sympathy. The soup appeared three or four times more during the course of the day but she never once stayed while I drank it.

The following day I had the strength to hurry a little as I staggered to the bathroom along the chilly landing and the day after that I was able to sit up and read between the soup visits. In the afternoon Edouard pushed open my bedroom door and peered cautiously round it. He looked half pleased and half frightened to find me sitting up in bed but I greeted him encouragingly and he sidled in, still regarding me with caution.

I guessed that my grandfather was asleep and the women engaged in housework, leaving Edouard with no attention and no playmate. I patted the blankets and, after only a little hesitation, he climbed up on the bed and showed me the drawing he was clutching. I peered at it for a moment before discerning a ship and watched his face light up as I correctly identified the scribbled object.

He asked to play Hunt the Horse but I said I was too ill, although if he would like me to read to him I could manage that. In fact I found that I could not manage it for long as it brought back a soreness in my throat. He seemed happy to accept this and occupied himself running a toy car up and down the bed.

When he tired of that he sat still and hummed, then suddenly asked, 'Catherine, why do you like Germans?'

At once I was wary, knowing that if I gave the wrong answer I would undo the companionship so suddenly reborn, doubtless out of his boredom, and which might yet be too fragile to last.

'Because they are mummies and daddies and have lots of little boys like you.'

'They're bad,' he insisted, unconvinced.

'I like only the good ones.'

'They should go away. We're going to make them go away.'

'Yes. They shouldn't be here.'

Disconcerted by my agreement he let the subject drop and shortly afterwards my mother called him and he rushed off as if in expectation of a treat. I winced as he let the door slam behind him but I was elated. I had regained Edouard.

Once she saw that I was better, Jeanne reverted to her old ways, slamming down the soup by my bed, leaving the room without speaking, sniffing haughtily. I thought about taunting her with a mention of my grandmother's stick but had not the energy. Annette was reserved but displayed no overt unpleasantness.

I had recovered sufficient interest in my surroundings to become aware that I was the most unpleasant part of them. My hair was greasy and lank, having not once been washed throughout my entire illness, I had not bathed properly since I had taken to my bed and I was sure that were my nose not so blocked up I would be able to smell the results. At least my nightdress was clean as the fever-induced perspiration had meant frequent changes but my room was stuffy from the oil heater, as summer proved tardy, despite a daily airing. It was therefore with horror that I heard an altercation below and then a booted tread coming up the stairs.

My mother followed Klaus to my very bedside, probably regarding such a visit as indecent as well as insolent. At any other time I would have laughed. Seemingly oblivious to my profoundly unattractive state, he bent to kiss me, asked me how I was and put two oranges on the bedside table. I had not seen oranges for at least a year.

I told him I was much better and then, to irritate my mother, asked after Kurt, Willi, his mother and Angelika. I sensed that he knew what I was doing and did not admire it. My parent, however, remained resolutely present and after a quarter of an hour or so Klaus turned to go. At that moment my father appeared in the doorway with an outraged face, asking Klaus how he dared to be there and demanding that he leave. I half expected him to make his Flore face and go, but instead he spoke calmly to my father neither in French nor German but in English.

The effect was immediate. My father blanched and my mother drew in her breath sharply, plucking anxiously at his sleeve to deter him from further confrontation. Klaus said no more than a quiet farewell to me and then he was gone, leaving me trying to understand what I had just seen.

What I had heard did not matter because I could not understand a single word and I wished, bizarrely, that I had paid more attention to English lessons at school. I remembered how Klaus had paid Bette back for her rudeness on the night we had rescued Macfidget by going with her to her block and giving her parents an unvarnished account of her misdeeds. I had reflected then that he was not a man to put up with anything he considered had gone too far and for all his humour and kindliness he knew how to assert his authority when he had to. Presumably it was in something of that spirit that he had just so spectacularly quelled my father's fury, but there had been another quality to his actions. Klaus was not a bully but he had just made my parents very afraid. Why? And even more importantly how? What on earth had he said?

I did not expect enlightenment from my parents so I did not seek it and Klaus repelled my enquiries gently but firmly, leaving me puzzled and uneasy. The last thing I wanted was a conspiracy of silence between him and members of my family. Then I almost forgot the incident as Klaus began to pressure me to go away into the country to complete my recovery.

'You need the air, my darling. You are still weak and you look terrible.'

'Thanks, O Gallant One.'

'Also you need time to yourself, to think.'

'No.'

'Do you remember anything about St Augustine?'

I goggled at him, unable to follow the change of subject.

'He asked God to make him good but not just yet. That is effectively what we are doing. We know we are behaving badly and that what we have cannot last, that one day I shall be posted somewhere else or the war will end or whatever, but somehow neither of us can act to bring that moment forward, to say it has to be faced one day so we might as well take charge of events and face up to reality now. It will be harder, not easier, the longer we leave it.'

I remembered my grandfather advancing much the same argument and a chill entered my soul.

'Where would that leave you?' I asked quietly.

'It would leave me where I would have been if we had never started this.'

'And that is what you want?'

'No. It is the last thing I want, but it is what we should now do.'

His persistence puzzled me. 'Why is this suddenly all so urgent?'

'Do you realise how ill you have been? Who cared for you? Your parents.'

'Who brought soup and oil for the heater? By the way, who made that wonderful broth?'

'Heini.'

'*Heini?* But he hates me.'

'No. Like most decent people, he does not approve of our conduct, but he can hardly say so and when I told him to make the soup he just got on with it. The point I am trying to make is that you have just given your family a pretty sizeable fright – it could so easily have turned to pneumonia – and, however reluctantly, they have been forced to reassess their priorities, to realise how very precious you are to them. You can build on that or you can squander it.'

'No. I am not going to the country. I want every minute there is to be with you.'

He tried only a little longer and then gave up, probably with relief, doubtless telling himself his duty was done, but before he did so he said something which was later to haunt me.

'You are a Catholic and I am not, but there is one thing of which I am very sure: judgement always comes and if not in this world then in the next.'

Afterwards I realised that he had been asking me to go away as much for his sake as for mine, knowing the only way to resist the temptation I offered was to put it beyond reach. I then wondered if he had thought my illness a judgement, if in some way he would have blamed himself had I been left permanently weakened or perhaps even died. Whatever he had thought, it was obvious the incident had produced an imperative to urge me at least to consider restoring some morality to my life.

My parents reacted with resignation to my renewed relationship with Klaus and my sisters sank back into sullenly pretending I was not there but Edouard stayed friendly and that alone had made my illness worth it. I learned that my grandfather had insisted on giving up some of his rations to me during my suffering and that twice he had struggled down the stairs to my bedside, alarming my grandmother who was sure he would catch the infection. Annette had cajoled a colleague at the Distribution Centre into letting her bring home a small amount of additional rations and Bette queued for more than five hours to obtain extra milk.

I was humbled and reassured by so much love, which, among my family, proved to have been dormant rather than dead, and, despite the resumption of domestic hostilities, I began to have confidence in the future.

For a while longer the broth was occasionally produced and I shared it with Edouard, then, in July, I lost my job at the Distribution Centre and with it the extra rations I had always brought home. The manager said he was sorry, my work had been much valued over the last few months but the after-effects of my illness were causing me to tire too easily.

'It's all nonsense,' I protested to Klaus. 'I am fully back to normal.'

'No, you are not, as I tried to tell you some weeks ago. However if you want me to ensure you go on working at the Centre, it can be done.'

I did not want in the least that he should start pressurising the Centre's management but I was not too proud to accept his help in finding a new job, specifying only that I would not work for the invader. A week later I found myself in the typing pool of Le Printemps, despite having neither secretarial training nor ability. If my reputation went before me no one hinted so and for the first time in a very long while I was surrounded by colleagues who included me in their conversations and activities. I realised that as the Germans now formed the major part of the store's clientele, no one who worked there could afford to fall out with them. I attribute much of my eventual return to health to that change of job, especially as I mastered typing with more ease than I had expected.

Amused, Klaus presented me with an ancient typewriter on which I practised with a steadiness of application that would have made Sister Benedicte proud of me. I composed paragraphs in German and soon he moved from correcting my grammar to suggesting improvements in style. I enjoyed it all and regretted that I had not treated my schoolwork with equal enthusiasm.

'You are looking so much better,' commented my grandfather. 'I wish you had found this work before.'

No one had mentioned the loss of the extra rations and a cold truce prevailed, my father even forgetting himself so far as absent-mindedly to correct my German one day when he overheard me composing a sentence out loud as I concentrated fiercely on a new rule. I considered learning English to please him, to provide a safe topic of conversation, but knew the relationship was too strained to be repaired in so facile a way.

It was around this time that Bette fell seriously in love so that for a while I saw less of her and then a very great deal as the romance ended explosively and she came to me almost daily to rage or cry. I never did meet the object of all this emotional energy and, saddened, realised that Klaus and I would never make up a foursome with any of my friends and their partners. Indeed, we never went into company together, the irregularity of our relationship precluding my attendance at military social functions and the enmity of my friends making it impossible for him to be welcome among them, not, I thought sadly, that I had many friends these days other than Bette and the girls in the typing pool.

I could have met more of Klaus's companions informally but did not want to become any further embroiled with the oppressors even had they not all been his age, causing me to feel out of place among them. I remembered the warnings of my mother and Bette not to be a friend to all the enemy.

Even now, when she herself was vulnerable and unhappy, Bette resolutely refused to see Klaus as anything other than just another German soldier who had no business to be where he was and who should be shooed back to his native land without ceremony. In an endeavour to win her round, I put her on her honour to tell nobody and then related the whole episode of Gerhardt, choosing to convey in words rather than mime what Klaus's brother had seen in Dachau.

Bette's eyes widened with horror and for half an hour or so she appeared to forget her own miseries but I failed in my principal aim. She was sorry for Klaus and even more for his mother and the younger sister who had discovered the body but she could not forgive him his presence in France. She would be friends with Germans only when they had returned home defeated and not a second before.

I might have argued with her but soon she was too swallowed up by her own chagrin and grief. With insight I realised that she would often suffer thus, her reputation attracting men who might look for greater respectability when they wanted marriage. Soothing, consoling, rallying, I wondered if this was how I should be when Klaus finally left and, if so, to whom I would turn for the comfort Bette now sought.

sixteen

Resistance

For the first time I could not rejoice in autumn, there being no new beginnings to celebrate and only the misery of another freezing winter to which to look forward. I was seeing little of Klaus because he was intensely busy with some special work which not only absorbed his days but made him irritable as well. In the restricted time that we had together his mind always seemed elsewhere and occasionally he said things I did not understand and which, although I dismissed them as random and meaningless, left me with a vague unease.

Once I heard him mutter, 'Do not hate me, Catherine.' He was not even looking at me or consciously addressing me and, when I tried to bring him back to the present, he started as if he had forgotten I was there.

I had made a full recovery from my illness earlier in the year and had regained both looks and energy but if I had even the smallest sign of a cold both Klaus and my family fussed over me as though I were an invalid, the first tenderly, the second gruffly.

Klaus had not returned to the theme of judgement, except to comment occasionally on what might happen to his country if it lost the war. On those occasions I had little reassurance to offer as I very much wanted it to lose, for Hitler to face retribution, for those who suffered in concentration camps to be spared any more. Each week after Mass I lit a candle for the repose of Gerhardt's soul, believing it would only truly rest in peace when the terrible atrocities were over.

Although I rarely missed Mass, I had stopped taking Communion, certain I was making a mockery of the Sacrament by persisting in my sin without the remotest intention of trying to do otherwise. It was an honest decision but it augmented my isolation, leaving me in the pew with Edouard and censorious looks for company while my family gathered at the altar rail. Klaus was sympathetic but, not sharing my beliefs which he was inclined to dismiss as superstition, lacked any real understanding of the anguish caused by what amounted to a self-imposed excommunication.

Father Tessier tried to tear some of the brambles from my path by inviting me to see him at the presbytery, where he laid aside the ritual pretence that he did not know who said what in the confessional and suggested a compromise. 'You do not need to promise never to see your friend again. Just promise to try for one week. All God wants is some effort, not for you to make yourself an outcast.'

I wondered how he could be so sure of the Deity's views on the matter but thought it tactless to enquire or to challenge his kindness. I hated disappointing him but I shook my head and answered matter-of-factly rather than defiantly.

'I couldn't promise for one day, much less a week. I'm sorry, Father.'

'Well, let me see you at Communion on Sunday.'

'Adultery is mortal sin.'

'So, my child, is cutting yourself off from God.'

I guessed he would have taken a stricter line had I been older or had I not told him about Gerhardt or, for that matter, the ludicrous scene at the farmhouse. I remembered how he had surprised me by saying, 'Surely the grace of God was in this man' in tones of wonder which I now fully understood. I smiled weakly at the recollection.

It occurred to me that Father Tessier must have seen in his time the whole gamut of wickedness and that what he was offering me now was his own judgement that I was not so far along the scale of sin as to make me an outcast. He spoke with gentle authority and although in my heart I remained unconvinced, I was willing to grasp at any straw if it promised the return of even the smallest normality. When I put to him Klaus's view of judgement I was surprised to find he did not demur.

'We reap what we sow.' Nor did he add to the proverb any qualifying statement about God's infinite mercy. It was a surprisingly stern attitude from one who had just persuaded me to take a less serious view of sin.

'I hope so,' I surprised myself by saying. 'Annette, Bette and Cécile worked their brains well nigh to a standstill at school and where is the University? The Germans have been here for three years and who suffers but the people they have conquered? Jews are being tortured and who pays but a poor fool who hangs himself because he can't understand the beastliness of it all? Where is the reaping, Father?'

He looked at me sadly. 'Moses wandered for forty years before seeing the Promised Land.'

I tried to picture myself in forty years' time and failed. I would be a grandmother perhaps. Stubbornly my imagination showed me Klaus's grandchildren and then, shockingly, an old man in his eighties. Klaus. I turned from the vision, telling myself that I was barely nineteen and old age was a long way off. Somehow, on the increasingly rare occasions when I permitted myself to fantasise about a future with a man who had always made it clear that he would return to his family, Klaus seemed frozen in middle-age where I gradually caught him up. I had not thought about a day when he would be a frail old man and I would still be under sixty.

I went out into the October sunshine, a little lighter in spirit, but as soon as I pushed open the front door at home I knew something was terribly wrong. Too many things were absent: the sound of work from the kitchen, the clatter of feet upstairs, Edouard's babble, Maurice Chevalier crooning on the wireless. Instead, in their place was a tangible sense of shock. In the kitchen all but my grandfather had assembled round the table, grim-faced. My mother was quietly weeping and at once I thought of Grand-père and rushed upstairs, but he was there, well, if grief-stricken.

I knew then that Martin had died.

'Killed by your bloody friends,' spat Annette and no one gainsaid her. They were the last words I can remember my elder sister saying to me for from then on she disowned me so completely that she would not acknowledge even my presence in a room.

I crept upstairs and sat in my room, alone, crying, remembering. I could see him as he was more than three years ago, a tall, kindly young man, who, while he piggybacked Edouard and teased Jeanne, had begun to pay compliments on our appearance to Annette and me. I stared down at my feet encased in his old slippers, unable to believe the waste of life that war brought daily.

Klaus tried to comfort me but there was an awkwardness about the conversation which contrasted starkly with the effect that the death of his brother had brought to our relationship. I half-expected him again to urge me to go away and give myself a chance to take a different view of our future but he did not and beneath his love and gentleness I thought I could detect a suppressed desperation, almost a clinging, which might have been more manifest had he not felt obliged to be strong for us both. I was too preoccupied with my own misery to try and tease out his or I might have pressed him on the subject.

As the days shortened, the cold grew and early curfews became the norm I took to going to bed early, finding it now as difficult to face my family as its members found it to have me in their midst. Inevitably I woke in the night more often, sometimes from dreams in which the swinging idiot pointed a gun from the rafters and shot Martin.

After one such dream I tried to switch on the light for comfort only to find we were in the middle of yet another power cut. Tiptoeing out on to the landing, I realised that everyone had retired for the night and that it must be the early hours of the morning. Needing to shake away the dream, I began to make my way downstairs, intending to use the stove for warmth as years ago Robert had done. A small shaft of sadness entered me for he too had now disappeared but as there was no anxiety among my relations I took it that he had been spirited away to join the Free French.

By the large landing window I paused, endeavouring to see the rest of the stairs in its dim light. The house was utterly silent and my own soft footfalls sounded unnaturally loud so that any minute I expected someone to call out asking who was there.

The kitchen too was silent, there being no Catherine the Second to rustle curiously as she had on that occasion when I found

Robert sleeping there, but there was life in the stove and I crouched down beside it.

Presently I heard the patrol. Stamp, stamp, stamp. I watched the silhouetted forms pass and heard their steps fade away until there was silence once more, but now I found it eerie, expecting something horrible to happen at any moment yet having no idea what shape it might take. I recollected Yvette Levin saying she had feared ghosts in the bushes and now I found myself suffering from the same irrational anxiety. I thought I heard a creak and immediately imagined the wood bending as the swaying form moved to and fro.

I stood up, shut the stove and tried to take a grip upon my galloping thoughts. If Gerhardt had a ghost it haunted a house in another country, not this one. Then I remembered Martin and half hoped his spirit had indeed come. The creak sounded again and the hope turned to fear. I flew to the light switch but still the power was off.

My heart was pounding as I commenced the return to my bedroom, afraid even to take the first step and open the kitchen door. When I did I looked up at the landing window, seeking its light, and saw the grey shape in front of it. As my scream of mortal terror seemed to shake the house, the shape appeared about to come towards me but a second piercing cry sent it scurrying away, back up the stairs, as confusion broke out above.

I could hear my father asking what the devil was going on and my grandmother calling anxiously from the top floor. Edouard was shouting that his light was ill and crying for my mother. Just as I began to mount the stairs to calm the situation the power came on and the house was flooded with light. I could not see the shape which had caused my terror, but I heard it. Seconds before I started up the stairs it whispered apologetically to my father and, although I could not make out the words, I had an impression of an accent which I could not then identify.

'I'm sorry, I thought I saw a ghost,' I explained as I reached the first floor landing and found my mother emerging from Edouard's room to join my father who was peering over the banister to ascertain who was there.

I expected irritable derision but instead my parents exchanged looks before suggesting wearily that we all go back to bed. A few seconds later the house was once more dark and silent.

I had not seen a ghost, but a man. Spirits did not whisper to the owners of the houses they haunted in *English* accents. I sat up in bed, my knees under my chin, the bedclothes huddled around me for warmth, my hot-water bottle too cold to serve any purpose.

My parents were sheltering an Englishman who moved about the house in the dead of night. A downed airman? A spy? An assassin? I remembered now the sudden influx of students, lately much reduced, and how on one occasion I had heard whispering in the dining room and I realised my mother and father were not just helping a single Englishman whose circumstances suddenly required it. They were planning, conspiring, resisting.

I recalled now how my father had said so urgently, 'He must not come here. I will not have Germans in this house.' Dear God, I thought, there they were setting up a resistance cell and there was I about to bring home the enemy. Perhaps it also explained why they had not tried harder to prevent my friendship with Klaus; they must have feared to make themselves conspicuous by causing a fuss among the Germans.

Certainly I saw now the reason they had been so surprisingly sympathetic after I had saved Kurt Kleist, for isolated stabbings must be a true resistant's nightmare. They could cause a flood of reprisals at just the wrong moment, delaying plans which depended on normal curfews and predictable movements.

I found a faint consolation in reflecting that their resistance work could also explain why they had become so cold. It ensured I stayed out of the house as often as possible, allowing them to do whatever it was they were doing without any awkward questions from me. Edouard was too young to become suspicious, but I wondered how much Jeanne knew and hated to think that she might be in danger.

Eventually my thoughts concentrated around a single question. Did what was happening threaten Klaus directly? Was he, or for that matter, Kurt, in personal danger? I resolved that the price of my silence would be reassurance on that point, knowing that I did not need to put my family at any risk at all, that a threat would be enough to stop them in their tracks. I had to hope they would believe me because otherwise my dilemma would be more than I could bear.

In the morning I took a different view. It was pointless to extract an assurance that I had no means of enforcing and Klaus or Kurt would not be in less danger of resistance attacks if the cell moved elsewhere. Indeed, if I tried to insist on their preservation it might have a counterproductive effect.

Instead I went along with the myth that I had briefly imagined a ghost but was now certain I had seen nothing at all. Unsurprisingly I noticed uneasy glances in my direction from time to time as my parents wondered just how substantial a form I had seen. They must have been terrified I might tell Klaus who certainly would not be fooled by any talk of ghosts. I did not tell him for exactly that reason and in any case he appeared to be almost entirely preoccupied with other matters in the last quarter of 1943, especially after Italy declared war on Germany in October.

Klaus talked less about the military or political situation than about the Italian friends he had known before the war, wondering what had become of them and their families and again railing at the futility of killing. I told him that one day it would be over and he could again visit Italy and England in a friendly spirit.

I believed that I knew what his life would be like, long after I had ceased to be part of it. He and Ellie would pick up the threads of their previous existence: travel, literature, history, a large circle of academic friends, a happy family. I wondered if he would ever come to France again and if he did whether he would be strong enough not to try to see me.

As Christmas approached I suggested we get away to celebrate both the festive season and his birthday but he said he had no leave due and that, with resistance intensifying, it would not be safe. I accepted his decision with a bad grace but was again aware of some underlying anxiety in him.

Carols were coming from the wireless and I was wondering how best to deal with presents for a sister who did not acknowledge I existed when there was a loud knocking at the door and I went out to find Kurt, who asked me to come with him to the Kommandantur. Surprised, I said that Klaus had told me he was not free that evening and that curfew was due in an hour, but on Kurt's insistence I went.

I was taken to Klaus's office through an abnormal amount of bustle. Everywhere people seemed to be on the move, engaged in some urgent activity, moving with purpose, expecting events. Soldiers hurried along corridors, officers emerged from doorways with papers in their hands to confer in huddles. Hardly anyone walked; it was all haste and importance.

'What's happening?' I asked Kurt but he did not reply, steering me forward with the same suppressed urgency.

In his own office Klaus motioned me to a chair, then ignored me for more than ten minutes while he gave a steady stream of orders. 'Back soon, tell you all then,' he said over his shoulder as he disappeared at speed through the door.

I sat in that office for three hours, my anxiety steadily increasing. Somehow I knew that tonight was the culmination of all the underlying tension there had been in Klaus for so many months. At first I took him at his word and, expecting him soon, prowled aimlessly round his office, picking up the photographs on his desk, deliberately tormenting myself with images of his family. There was one I had not seen before, a very old, fading portrait of four small boys and their parents.

I held it under the desk lamp to see it better. Klaus must have been about five and but for the obvious difference in their ages the three elder boys might have been triplets. I remembered Klaus saying that the von Ströbel features were strong amongst the males of the clan.

Behind the boys Peter and Lotte stood stiffly in the formal pose which characterised photography in the first decade of the twentieth century. I had seen exactly the same family formations captured in the large array of photographs in my grandparents' quarters.

One detail held me. Klaus sat, smiling, looking straight into the lens, sitting between Gerhardt and Willi, but his hands were not placed formally on his knees, as was the case with the other boys. Instead one was placed on Gerhardt's knee, covering the small hand which already rested there. I looked at the youngest boy, at his trusting face, his slightly unfocused gaze and wondered for the first time if Klaus had been more badly affected by his brother's suicide than Willi or Angelika had been. He had been next to Gerhardt in age, would have played with him more than the older boys.

I looked again at Klaus's protective hand on his brother's knee, the gesture clearly saying, 'It's all right, the man under that cover is just taking photographs. It doesn't hurt.'

I felt tears sting my eyes and I put the portrait back, becoming conscious that time was passing without any sign of the imminent return Klaus had promised. I looked into the outer office, which was busy but Kurtless, so I settled once more in my chair, enticing Macfidget on to my lap where he went through his kneading routine with so little sign of settling that I ruefully put him on the floor, telling him in German that I couldn't stand the pain, laughing at my idiocy in talking German to a cat just because that was the native language of his owner.

I thought only rarely of Yvette but the presence of Macfidget reminded me of her now, as he also reminded me of the lost innocence of the girl who had struggled to carry him through Paris, in the pouring rain, imprisoned in a pillowcase. I realised that I did not want to be that girl again, that for all its pain and complications I preferred adulthood.

When I had waited more than an hour I went again to the outer office and asked in German if the Colonel was expected back. One of the officers looked at me as if I had interrupted very important business with a hopelessly trivial enquiry, said, 'Soon, Fraülein' and bent his head once more over his papers.

After another hour the same officer brought me passably decent coffee and again said 'Soon', when I put the same question. By now I was fretting, having heard shots from the street and shouting elsewhere in the building. The roar of motor vehicles coming and going added to the sense of confusion but I could see nothing from the window.

A different kind of noise caused me to start but it was only a sudden downpour of rain hurling itself against the window. It fell fast and furiously, adding to the atmosphere of din and drama. What on earth was happening in Paris and why was I here in the Kommandantur? I toyed with the idea of storming into the outer office and demanding imperiously to know what was going on, but just as I was on the point of doing so, Klaus returned and with a cursory apology sat down behind his desk and began talking into the telephone. I understood enough to know he was reporting mission accomplished to a general.

While he was speaking I looked at him, taking in the dark patches under his eyes, the wetness of his rain-soaked uniform, his mildly dishevelled hair, the beginnings of shadow along his jaws.

By the time he was finishing the conversation I was standing beside him with his spare jacket and unbuttoning the one he was wearing while he held the telephone receiver higher to allow me to do so. He shrugged out of the wet top but waved away the spare, sitting in his shirtsleeves, resting his head against my waist.

Then he said, 'You had better sit down, my darling, because I owe you an explanation which may take some time and might also cause you some distress.'

Alarmed, I returned to my chair, my fears not lessened by the urgency in his voice when he began by telling me that whatever happened he would always love me and I must remember that.

'Your countrymen were a pretty feeble lot when we came here', was his surprising opening. 'We couldn't believe how glad some of them were to see us but, of course, as life has got harder so that has changed. For about a year now there has been some organised resistance and it has got a lot more intensive and a lot more effective.

'Earlier this year, before your illness, they gave me the job of tracking down and rooting out résistants. It was that mission which has prolonged my tour of duty here. It was long, hard and delicate but tonight we have made a large number of arrests across Paris, raiding houses and apartments after curfew when we knew everyone would be at home. We have found a number of English airmen, if they really are airmen, and a much greater number of Frenchmen demonstrably involved in assisting them.'

I became very still. 'You went to my house, didn't you?'

'Ah! So you did know what was going on there. Yes, your house was on the list and my men will have made arrests.'

I stared at him in disbelief. 'And that is why you brought me here?'

'Yes. I didn't want you arrested and I didn't want you there at all if I had miscalculated. You see, if I am right we will not have found any airman there tonight, he will be further down the line.'

'But what will happen to my parents?'

'It depends whether they have been careless and left any evidence of their activity lying around. It is fervently to be hoped they have not. In the absence of evidence or anyone hiding there they should be all right unless some French patriot finds he is not so brave and tells us all.'

'The Gestapo?'

'No. This was an army operation.'

I closed my eyes against the horror. Klaus had always been the enemy but I had been too blindly in love to recognise it. 'You could have warned us.'

'I could not. Your parents would have simply warned everyone else. All I could do was try to schedule the raid for a time when I believed nobody compromising was there. But there was a moment when I really did make an attempt to warn them off and the fools just carried on. At least they stopped for a little while and then started again.'

I knew at once when it had happened, remembering the scene in my bedroom doorway and the fear Klaus had caused them when he had spoken in English to my father.

'What did you say?'

'If you remember, your father was bellowing at me to leave and I simply told him that if he did not speak more civilly I should search the place on my way out.'

'What would you have found?' I put the question so softly I was not sure he would have heard.

'Nothing that I know of. It was a general warning that I understood they were up to something. I spoke in English to emphasise that I knew they were working with the enemy but it had the added advantage of not alarming you.'

'The incident alarmed me.'

'I'm sorry, sorry for all of it but you must go home. Your grandparents are looking after Edouard and Jeanne. Try to reassure them. Your father is a thorough man and a cautious one and I do not believe we will have found anything.'

'You can't be certain of that.' I found I was shaking, terrifed for my parents, dimly afraid of the man I loved, loving him still and hating myself for doing so.

Something else was tugging at my mind. 'You said my grandparents were looking after Jeanne and Edouard. What about Annette?'

Then I flew at him in fury, shouting, my hands beating his chest, tears pouring down my face.

'You've taken her too, haven't you? It isn't enough that some bastard somewhere killed Martin, you have to take Annette and my parents as well. You've been using me and I was just too stupid to see it, you went to the Café Flore to spy and took me as cover, you used my illness as an excuse to see what you could find in our house but I can destroy you, Klaus von Ströbel. I'll tell the General how you specially planned the raid so as not to incriminate my family and he'll shoot you for collaboration.'

He took hold of my hands and clasped them together, gently but firmly, placing me back in the chair from under which Macfidget looked out in alarm at the noisy scene. Then he knelt down in front of me and looked into my eyes.

'Liebchen, try to think a little. I haven't done any of those things. I could go to the Café Flore any time and indeed I did, well before I met you, because I liked to irritate the frosty-faced devils. You were not in the least bit necessary as cover. If I had wanted to use your illness as an excuse to come and spy on your house I needn't have threatened to search it – I could have actually done so. Instead I tried to warn your parents as I have already explained and after a while they decided to risk ignoring what I had said, but the very fact that I did say it will have made them careful which is why I believe we won't have found anything. As for having me shot as a collaborator, you have much stronger ammunition which you could have used at any time.'

I turned my head away, 'You still used me.'

He did not answer and when I turned back to him I was surprised to see a hint of tears in his eyes.

'No, my darling, that is the worst aspect of all of this. It was not I who used you. I never have and when you can think clearly you will realise that. It was your family who spied on you. I don't think they set out to do so but in the end that is what they did and for quite some time. Catherine, can't you see that they thought us the most perfect camouflage?'

seventeen

Apollo

I looked at him, my mind rebelling against his words, even as I understood that I had reasoned myself to a similar conclusion after I had seen the Englishman on the stairs.

'I wasn't here at the beginning of the Occupation,' Klaus told me. As soon as he saw I was calmer he had got up and was now sitting on the desk as he faced me, looking down with a strained face and pitying eyes. 'But my predecessor had taken a close interest in the Sorbonne because if there is going to be trouble the universities are always the first place to look, so even then we had an eye on your father, particularly as he made no bones about his bitter contempt for the Vichy arrangements and, of course, taught English. Still, there wasn't any resistance to speak of at that stage and the Sorbonne looked ready to disintegrate but Pierre Dessin had been noticed and we kept tabs on him. Then he began teaching at that Convent of yours and things started to happen there which came to our notice. That is why I went to see the Mother Superior – and of course saw you – that day you were having a lesson outside among the roses.

'He was more careful after that and meant little more to us than a name on a file for quite a long time. I was puzzled at first that he didn't react more fiercely when I started seeing so much of you – after all, you were only seventeen and there was a younger sister to whom you were setting the most appalling example, if I may put it bluntly. Had I a daughter of such an age in so compromising a situation, I would have been a bit more active, particularly as you had only just started work and were a long way from independent. I am aware that makes me the prince of all hypocrites, but there it is.'

I can still see his expression as he said those uncomfortable words.

'True, he came to see me and begged me to consider your youth and leave you alone and I told him what was then quite true – that nothing was happening, at least not the sort of thing of which he was so fearful. After the farmhouse affair I quite expected him to send you away but he did not and I began to ask myself why.

'One answer was that he was still up to something and didn't want to draw too much attention to himself. He even seemed reluctant to complain when your sister was attacked in the church. Something just wasn't right and we watched a bit more carefully. That was when we noticed Annette. Whenever you left the Distribution Centre Annette followed until she saw which way you were going – straight home, to the Kommandantur, to Bette or wherever. Clearly they needed to know if you were going to be out of the way.

'I am afraid that as time went on, especially this year when resistance has been more than a gleam in a patriotic eye, they tried to manipulate you by being cold and beastly so that you sought me out more. They thought a household containing the girlfriend of the man in charge of the hunt – oh yes, they would have known – would not attract too much suspicion. Then when you were ill they must have felt as bad as I did. Their only crime was resistance and we ourselves created the situation they exploited so you need not resent what they did.'

I did resent it. It seemed everyone had known what was going on but me and if Klaus was right then my parents had at once actively promoted my friendship with him and shunned me for pursuing it.

'They wouldn't have seen it that way,' insisted Klaus when I voiced the thought. 'You were hell bent on a course of action they hated and they saw a way to use it to advance a cause they would have died for.'

If we try to stop her, he will stop us. Which is more important? I remembered how I had overheard my father shouting those words and my mother quietly replying, 'My daughter.' As usual she had lost and my father's priorities had been imposed – patriotic duty had been more important than the welfare of his erring daughter.

I was confused and frightened. One minute I was grateful to Klaus for the warning he had given my parents, for the protection he had tried to offer, the next knowing that I would never want to see him again if harm came to any of my family. I was tormented by mental pictures of what might be happening to them but I knew that if they returned safe and well I would confront them with the truth, almost hating them as I did so.

Kurt Kleist came in and he and Klaus spoke rapidly. I was capable of understanding most of it but was too swallowed up by grief to bother. I felt Klaus guiding me out of the chair, saying something about no one at the Kommandantur getting much sleep that night and that he had much to do. A German I had never met before drove me home where Jeanne flew into my arms.

My grandparents, who were both downstairs in the kitchen, told me Edouard was asleep but that Jeanne had seen my parents and Annette taken away and was close to hysteria. Indeed she now began to beg me to go to Klaus and get everyone released. It took a while to calm her and persuade her that I had already done all I could, that this operation was far too big for only Klaus to be involved and that what would determine our family's fate was not influence but evidence. My grandparents were able to give me the assurance I craved: no one had been found in the house and nothing had been taken away. The Germans had, however, spent a very long time in Martin's room and I guessed this was where the English normally hid.

When at last Jeanne had been persuaded to go to bed and my grandmother was seeing her settled, Grand-père gave me another important assurance. Before opening the door in response to thunderous knocking and ringing my father had time to issue an urgent warning to the others: 'If they take us they will question us separately. Do not make up any answers to any question which floors you or we will all contradict each other. Just say you don't know.'

'Thank God there was no one here but us. One night earlier and your father would be facing a firing squad.'

I thought he could thank Klaus as well but someone somewhere would probably now face the firing squad instead. Klaus had transferred, not removed, the danger and a Frenchman would die, perhaps God forbid with his wife and family, because Catherine Dessin had won the heart of a German officer. Klaus had talked of judgement but it seemed once more that others suffered, not he and I.

My grandfather told me there had been four people over the course of the last six months who had briefly hidden in the house, all English, and, yes, the students were a mix of the genuine and resistants, the former providing cover for the latter without realising it. Other than clandestinely listening to the BBC, there was no further activity in which the Germans might be thought to have an interest. There did not have to be, I thought in angry fear, there was already enough to hang the household.

I asked him if he knew that Klaus had once tried to warn my parents off and he said they were never certain whether threatening to search the house was simply a vindictive statement to silence my father or whether it had some hidden meaning. Eventually they inclined to the former because nothing had followed.

My grandmother had rejoined us before I put the most important question of all.

'They wanted me to go on seeing Klaus, didn't they? They thought it was a convenient camouflage for what was going on here and they hoped I might drop the odd bit of useful information to help them in their schemes? That was why you all withdrew from me, wasn't it? All that is except you, Grand-père. It wasn't to get me to give him up, it was so that I would have only him to go to.'

'That is nonsense,' replied my grandmother with asperity. 'Of course we wanted you to give him up, but as you were determined to go on making a fool of yourself you can hardly blame us if we decided to take advantage on behalf of France.'

It was more or less the same argument Klaus himself had put forward and I could not oppose it with logic but I hated them nonetheless. On behalf of France, indeed. Did such grandiloquence make spite any better?

'It was your choice, Catherine,' said my grandfather quietly. 'We did what we could to stop you, but you would go your own way. You cannot blame your parents.'

The only one I blamed as I tossed and turned in bed for what remained of the night was myself, my mind tormented with the question of who had been next down the line and would now be paying the price of Klaus's determination that no stranger should be found at our house. Above all I now accepted that to which I had so long been blind. Klaus was the enemy, an active, efficient, committed enemy and not just a soldier who had happened to wander into France while waiting for the war to end. It was impossible for me to see him again.

Annette was the first to return, wordlessly tired, dishevelled, shocked. Although my mother arrived a few hours later my father did not come back for two days, days in which the rest of us clung together, endlessly discussing what might be going on, torturing ourselves with hope and fear. When at last he did return it was to sleep for twenty-four hours. The greatest gift we received that Christmas was our safety and I knew I had Klaus to thank yet he was still the enemy. On the first day of the New Year he was forty-four but I sent no birthday wishes to the Kommandantur.

My resolution held and he in turn made no attempt to contact me but I missed him horribly and after six weeks I cycled to Saint-Germain-des-Prés, ostensibly for air and exercise, in reality to revisit the scene of so much of our time together, especially that small secluded place which we had come to regard as ours.

I propped my bicycle against a hedge and parted the branches that hid our old trysting place, preparing to be unhappy at its emptiness, ready to cry and somehow to derive comfort from the tears. I was in the very act of screwing up my face for this purpose when I realised that I was not alone, that our precious private place was not empty.

A bohemian character sat before an easel, sketching. His long hair flowed greasily down his back but his ragged beard was clean and the eyes which now looked at me were young and sharp. My face returned to its normal contours and for a few seconds we regarded each other with uncertainty on my side and mild curiosity on his.

'Good afternoon,' he said gravely. 'I am Apollo.'

'Er . . . Good afternoon, I am Catherine.'

'I know. He is not here.'

'Who?'

'The one you seek.'

I repressed a giggle and thought as I no longer had privacy to cry I might as well divert myself for a while with the pretensions of Apollo, who I was quite certain was in reality called Marcel or Gaston, especially as he looked so serious.

'But he was here. Only last week he was standing where you stand now.'

'The one I seek?'

'The German. The one you love.'

I was suddenly sober, my heart leaping painfully, no longer wanting to mock.

'Klaus was here?'

'The man I have often seen you with was here, so if he is Klaus, then, yes, Klaus was here. He was kind enough to admire my art.'

I took the hint and moved to look over his shoulder at what he had called his art but which I expected to be an indifferent or possibly unintelligible sketch, full of obscure meaning, comprehensible to none but the author. I drew in my breath, unsurprised that Klaus should have admired such skill, as I peered at the single flower he had drawn.

'But there are no flowers here,' I said, bewildered, looking round at the evergreen bushes and bare branches of winter trees.

'This rose is in my heart, in my soul. I shall draw it until it is perfect and then I shall die.'

I was trying to think what might be an appropriate response to such an unlikely scenario when he added, 'Klaus', pronouncing it as I had with a careful German accent, 'Klaus thought it should have an insect inside it.'

I was silent, remembering, seeing again the group of uniformed girls with their shabby shoes, the laughing German officers on the Convent steps and that small insect, long since dead, its life of no account to anyone but us.

'Did he say why?' My voice was a watery whisper.

'Yes. I wish he had not for at first I thought he was speaking from the soul and saw the insect as a terrible ugliness deep within beauty. I was quite moved until he told me there should be an insect to make the ladies jump with fright.'

'He must have been trying to amuse you.'

'Men who would amuse do not look as if they would rather cry.'

I struggled unsuccessfully to look neutral, as if hearing an anecdote in which I had but a polite interest, then I looked down into those sharp eyes.

'Go to him,' he said.

'I can't. Not any more. He is the enemy.'

'Who says? Hitler? De Gaulle? Churchill? Why listen to them rather than your own heart? Go to him, Catherine.'

He tore off the sketch from the large pad and handed it to me.

'Alas I am a long way from drawing my perfect rose. I gave Klaus one as well. You may compare the two and see if I have made but the tiniest step towards perfection.'

'Thank you. Er . . . but I must pay you.'

'Too kind,' muttered the bohemian, as I put half a week's wages in a conveniently empty mixing pot. I looked back at him through the branches before retrieving my bicycle but he was already intent on the first strokes of his new rose.

That evening I sent a note to Klaus's hotel. It read simply: *I too have seen Apollo.* Long after curfew had descended on the dark Parisian streets an answering note was pushed through our front door. *Café Flore, Thursday, usual time.*

'We are a pair of fools,' was his unromantic greeting when I kept the appointment. 'But I do not know for how much longer I could have held out, even though I have been working myself to exhaustion.'

'I wonder what Apollo's real name is?'

Klaus's mouth twitched. 'I don't know. It did not seem the moment to ask to see his papers.'

I wondered how I had managed without his humour all those weeks. At home bad temper was rife, partly in reaction to the aftermath of the arrests but also, I realised with sadness, because the immediate purpose of my parents' lives had been taken from them. Their efforts at resistance had been brought to a stop and, fretting, impotent, resentful, they were obliged to leave such work to others. When I said I was going back to Klaus they reacted with scorn rather than disappointment and I half expected to be turned out of the house.

'Do you suppose he really believes all that nonsense about drawing a rose to perfection and then dying?'

'I hope not,' said Klaus. 'How much did *you* put in that mixing pot?'

I saw his meaning and laughed but then pressed Klaus on more serious matters. Patiently he understood that I needed to know the worst if we were to make a new start and he took me, without prevarication or apology, through events from the German side. There had been mass arrests and some executions, as I already knew, but no Englishmen had been found along the line of escape with which my parents had been involved. Others were less lucky and, while those they had sheltered were taken to prisoner-of-war camps, they met a harsher fate.

Some were found to be sheltering not enemy airmen but Jews who had been destined for Drancy. He faltered as he told me this and I knew he was remembering Gerhardt and regretting that aspect of the operation. Others had been careless enough to leave notes and plans where they could easily be found. From Klaus's point of view it had been a highly successful piece of work and one on which he was much congratulated.

'I am afraid the Gestapo are a bit jealous and they tried hard to get one of my men in consequence, a junior officer whom the Resistance had tried to blackmail when they found out he had certain proclivities. Unfortunately for them he had his priorities in order and, though he was scared silly by it, came and told me. I ordered him to pretend to give in and to let me know what they wanted and who and where. He did so, God bless him, over many months and it was that which started the whole process so he is the one they should all be thanking.

'I recommended promotion and a medal but the Gestapo actually tried to have him sent to a concentration camp because of what he is. Unbelievably, they nearly succeeded.'

I looked at Klaus, puzzled. 'What is he?'

'I told you. He has certain proclivities.' Seeing my incomprehension he swiftly added, 'He used to go to Montmartre and behave immorally.'

I knew there was something wrong with this explanation. German soldiers had been going to Montmartre throughout the war and, as far as I knew, did not risk being sent to concentration camps but I let it go, being vastly more interested in the fate of résistants than in that of the enemy.

It seemed that, after all, Klaus's attempts to make sure we were raided when our house was empty of clandestine guests had not resulted in someone else facing punishment in my parents' stead and for that I was deeply, humbly grateful. As for the rest, the German soldier would have been blackmailed by the Resistance and led them in turn into a trap regardless of whether I was going out with Klaus. Nothing had really changed, I thought, but, when I relived those two days when we waited for my father's return, a small voice whispered, *Judas*.

For now, I was happy just to be back in his arms, to rejoice in our lovemaking, to feel his embrace, share his humour, be calmed by his kindness. I knew it would not last, that the war was turning, that the events which might liberate France would rob me for ever. Unforgivably I found myself hoping we might not be liberated for a long time. I crushed the thought and forced myself to pray that Germany would be defeated sooner rather than later. Meanwhile I would make the most of my time with Klaus.

Even that was not so easy as he grew busier with the burgeoning Resistance but one day in March he asked me to call at the Kommandantur and I was taken to a different office where he rose half laughing, half apologetic, to greet me. I gasped, taking in the change in his uniform. The usual dark green and silver collar patches had gone and in their place were bright red ones blossoming with gold braid leaves.

'Herr General Klaus von Ströbel at your service.'

Even as I congratulated him a small shaft of unease darted into me. His elevation somehow deepened his status as enemy, especially as I guessed it to be a direct result of the raids he had organised before Christmas but, worse, I sensed it might presage a new posting, that he would be sent away from Paris.

'I have some champagne.' He produced a bottle from under his desk and began to open it.

All Paris was near starvation and we were to drink champagne. Indeed it would be the first time since the Occupation began that I could remember doing so. He saw my expression and stopped in the act of easing off the cork, which flew out anyway, spraying him with foam. We began to laugh and the moment of tension passed.

I raised my glass. 'To the new General.'

He raised his. 'To Apollo, long overdue thanks.'

I asked him if he was young for a general and he said no, not these days, but that he was still surprised and very flattered. Then he called in Kurt to join the celebration and ordered him to drink on duty. There was more laughter and when the time came for me to go to my icy home I realised that I wanted to stay there, among the enemy, for ever.

On my way back a young German stopped me to ask for directions. I enjoyed the surprise on his face when I complied in his own language and, as I watched him hurry away, I recalled the early days of Occupation when we had agonised over how we should respond to such requests from the enemy. To this day most Parisians found them disconcerting and Bette certainly always claimed ignorance even if the directions sought were for the Eiffel Tower or Notre-Dame. I wondered what my life would have been during the last four years had I not met Klaus. Would I now be refusing such mundane petitions for help?

At the last moment I decided not to go home, but to call on Bette. As I made my way there, I passed a queue for rations and saw an old woman with a yellow star being thrust to the front. My fellow Parisians, hungry to the point of starvation, were making way for the persecuted while I, Catherine Dessin, daughter of the resistant Professor Dessin, lately of the Sorbonne, had been drinking champagne with the persecutors.

I was still in the wine's warm glow when I arrived at Bette's. She looked at me quizzically.

'Klaus has been made a general.'

Bette went on looking at me. At length she said, 'How can you?

There is fighting everywhere. They are killing prisoners, Frenchmen are dying, they are shooting Maquisards by the hundred and all you can do is drink to a bloody German general. Shame on you, Catherine Dessin.'

'That General once saved Yvette Levin.'

'For five minutes. Where is she now?'

I turned on my heel. 'See you after the war, Bette.'

I had reached the entrance of the block when she called after me and I might have gone back had I not by then opened the door and seen Cécile and Bernadette on the doorstep. I knew Bette would not be angry for long and was unsurprised when she arrived at Le Printemps the following day.

'It's just that my father is spending most of his time patching up injured resistance workers and bringing home the most awful stories. I shouldn't have taken it out on you,' Bette explained regretfully.

'You didn't say anything which wasn't true, but I couldn't cope without you, Bette. Apart from you and the girls at work, I have only the Germans – and not many of them – and before you say I have nobody but myself to blame, I know that, but nothing, absolutely nothing, will ever make me regret Klaus.'

'That's all very well, but have you thought what will happen when they chase the Germans out of Paris and he is miles away in Germany or wherever? Who will protect you then? Do you think people will just pretend none of it ever happened? They are going to want revenge, Catherine, and I think you should start making plans to leave Paris.'

'I can't leave Klaus.'

'He will leave you.'

'Yes, I know, and I have lived with that knowledge all the time I've loved him, but the more reason to hold on to every last second we can get together.'

Bette looked at me with a mixture of pity and exasperation. 'You are about to go through one hell of a time,' she predicted. 'I hope when it's all over you really do still think he was worth it. You have defied both Church and State for him.'

I smiled at the dramatic flourish. 'Church, maybe, but Father Tessier has been kind, perhaps too kind, but not the State. The

French Government, if you remember, came to an agreement with Hitler.'

'Yes, may they all rot in hell.'

'Isn't it time you went back to your kindergarten?'

Bette looked at the clock and gasped, jumping up and hurrying out with a garbled goodbye. After she had gone I noticed she had forgotten a book she had been carrying and picked it up to see if it were something she might need immediately or if its return could be postponed until we next met. It was certainly not one she needed for teaching small children, I thought, as I recognised a heavily thumbed copy of the translation of the *Aeneid* I had read at school. Clearly Bette was staying in touch with her own education as well as dispensing a simple version of it to others.

I opened it at the fourth book and read again Dido's lament as she realised her lover was leaving her country for ever. One particular passage held my attention and I re-read it several times, my heart racing.

eighteen

Phrygian Sails

If it took the sight of the masts and sails of the men of Troy to convince Dido that the hour of her desertion was at hand, I had only to look at the chaos which pervaded the Kommandantur in the late June of 1944. Everywhere were boxes overstuffed and spilling contents, while cupboards gaped empty and the sound of shots reached us from the streets. Only three weeks earlier the Allies had landed in Normandy and all Paris was in a ferment about impending liberation.

'Take me with you,' I begged Klaus. 'There can be nothing for me here.'

'Liebchen, what would you do in Germany? I have a wife and children and can offer you nothing. Your future lies in France, in forgetting me, but not here in Paris. I promise I will see that you are far from Paris before I leave.'

'I don't want you to look after me in Germany. I just want to go with you until we are both safe.'

'Catherine, my darling Catherine.' He held me against him while I wept and went on pleading. 'This is our day of judgement that we have always known would come and we have to be brave. We cannot make it go away. War brought us together and now the same war is parting us. At this moment I do not even know what my orders will be: to return to Germany at once, to resist the invasion, to stay here even. I only know it is imperative to get you somewhere safe while I am still able to do so. If, by some miracle, we do stop the enemy advance and remain here as we are now, then you can always come back.'

'I cannot bear never to see you again.'

'It will get easier with time. I am obliged to hope that one day you will forget me altogether but I am a selfish brute and deep down I hope you will always keep a small place in your heart for me, as I will for you.

'Oh, hell,' he said suddenly and, startled, I looked at him and saw he was struggling not to break down too.

There was an apologetic cough and Kurt came into the room. Klaus put me gently from him. 'Go home, not to work. Go home and wait for me there.'

As I went, a woman who saw me come from the Kommandantur hissed words of hatred from the doorway of a shop and two children jeered 'Collaborator' from the other side of the street. I hurried home, afraid, desolate, full of the ice of impending loss.

He came at five and I ran down to meet him but by the time I had reached the bottom of the stairs he was already in the dining room talking to my father.

'Your daughter may be in terrible danger, Monsieur Dessin. We must ensure she is soon out of Paris and in a place where the vengeful will never find her. Who do you know in the country, preferably deep in the country and far away?' They were standing at either end of the table, their attitudes emanating hatred and confrontation on my father's part and authority and insistence on Klaus's.

'What a nerve,' spat my father.

'Who do you know?' persisted Klaus calmly.

'No one I would insult by asking. As you are so concerned, why not take her with you?'

'I have a wife and young children, as you know, and even were I free the road from Paris will be no sort of place for a girl of nineteen. I repeat she must go into the country where she is not known and can stay until the worst is over. She is your own daughter, dammit.'

'You should have thought of all this before enticing a girl who was barely out of school into your evil snare. Why should I help you now?'

'I am not asking you to help me. I am trying to find a way of helping your daughter.'

'Take me with you,' I whispered miserably.

'There!' said my father, triumphantly. 'She wishes to go with you. You can take your pleasure all the way to Berlin.'

Klaus was round the table in an instant and had knocked my father down with a single blow before I had even registered what had just been said. I watched my parent haul himself back to his feet breathing heavily and, purple with fury, turn to me.

'Go!' he shouted. 'Go to your room and leave me to deal with this man.'

'No, Monsieur, I will deal with *you*,' said Klaus quietly. 'We are still in charge here, if only for a little while, and I am still able to have you arrested and shot, which would be my pleasure for the way you have treated Catherine, on any grounds I care to name. However we can avoid that painful course of action by getting your daughter away in the next few days and to somewhere which satisfies me as safe. I shall, I assure you, have very high standards when it comes to safety and I am still more than capable of imposing them.'

I knew I must go. My father had suffered the indignity of being knocked down in his own house and, knowing he was about to lose the current battle, I could not oppose him at such a time but first I would have my own say in this trial of wills.

'I will go,' I said quietly. 'I have better things to do than watch grown men fighting. But why fight at all? Six years ago if you had met you would have bought each other drinks and talked about English literature and history. You would have exchanged observations on the books you had read, invited each other to the Sorbonne or Heidelberg to give lectures, swapped travel tales, recommended places to go, to see. Your wives would have got together to go shopping, to cook meals. Your children would have played in each other's houses. You would have made up parties for the opera, the theatre, picnics.

'And now? You lay aside every civilised bone in your bodies and think it clever to insult each other and fight, because some politician says so. You are both real men, born to laugh, cry, feel pain, dance in the sunshine, but you deny each other's reality, seeing instead only some rigid, wooden form called an enemy. Well, if God had wanted to divide the world into enemies we would have been born in uniforms clutching little flags and humming war songs instead of naked, helpless and wailing, dependent on love and nurture.

'I have seen the enemy and he is just another human being. I have seen him laugh, cry, yawn, stretch, itch, scratch, run, tire, fear, rejoice. I have seen him happy, sad, angry, peaceful and in that, my father, Pierre Dessin, I have made a journey in nineteen years which you have not made in your entire life, for I have seen my enemy as a man.'

I went then but as I turned to close the door behind me I saw them staring with startled expressions, my father's just then turning to amazement and Klaus's to admiration. For a while I could hear from my bedroom the distant hum of their conversation, with a voice occasionally rising, and finally the sounds of a not particularly cordial departure.

Four years before I had looked out of my bedroom window to watch the Germans preparing to settle in Paris and now from that same window I watched my lover preparing to depart. Only my hair was still the same, I reflected wryly, everything and everybody else had utterly changed.

Klaus looked up as his young officers and soldiers had once looked up but, where they had laughed, his mouth was tight and his eyes regretful. He raised his hand and waved, before getting into his car. Kurt too threw me an upward glance and a smile of farewell. Then the car moved off and I craned out of the window until it was lost to my sight as the sails of the ships of Troy had been lost to Dido's.

Much later my mother came and told me, with a disapproving mouth and sad eyes, that I was to go to my Aunt Marie, who was not strictly an aunt but a younger cousin of my father's. She lived on the edge of a small village some miles the other side of Aix-en-Provence and I would travel the following week. It was all being arranged. I wondered how my mother would react if I hugged her and told her I loved her despite all that had happened, but even as I hesitated she had gone.

I packed my faithful suitcase, the battered one I had taken to the farmhouse, and one of my mother's as well, certain I would never return, that I would make a life elsewhere, away from my family, trying to select through the ache of loss the items I must take and those I was content never to see again.

On the night before my departure, Bette came, bearing Alphonse. 'He is a symbol,' she said portentously. 'You know I could not bear to lose him for ever, so lending him to you now means we will meet again.'

'If so it will not be in Paris.' I wondered how to fit Alphonse into my luggage and was afraid Bette would think me ungrateful. Yet I cried when she said she must go, thanking her for the only constant friendship I had known from my own age group. I wondered how long it might be before I found another Bette.

In the morning I hugged my grandfather and Edouard so tightly that both protested. I asked myself how old my brother would be when I saw him next, if I would ever again see my grandfather. It was without any sense of shock or remorse that I realised I did not care how long it might be before I saw the others. I had spent much of the previous night sitting on my bed, looking around me at my room, unfamiliar now that most of my possessions were packed, once a sanctuary from the world's ills, lately a cell in a prison of my own making.

For most of my life, from as far back as I could remember until last year, Annette had been there too, first playing, crying, giggling, conspiring then advising, confiding, condescending. Now she was a stranger and the security of home and family had proved illusory.

The railway station next day was all heaving chaos, full of noise and voices which rose like those of the Tower of Babel. Jeanne had been dragooned into helping with my cases and was doing so with a bad grace and some fluster. Minutes before the train was due, when Jeanne had said she had seen a puff of steam in the distance, Kurt Kleist appeared carrying a leather holdall from which, as he drew nearer, it was possible to hear loud feline wails. It did not need the three rows of carefully punched airholes, spaced with Germanic precision, to tell me what was inside.

'The General says he would be grateful if you could take Macfidget,' said Kurt in German. 'He would almost certainly not survive if we tried to take him with us and if we leave him behind he may meet a terrible end. The General says cats are being eaten.'

As soon as Kurt had come up to us Jeanne had moved off, not wanting to be seen in the company of Germans. She was standing at some distance, but near enough to see the heaving bag at which she was now staring with incredulity.

I gave a wry smile. 'At least Klaus has not returned him to me in a pillowcase.'

Kurt smiled back. 'No. The General also says he will write, but he would like meanwhile to know that you are safe and therefore you should ring this number if you can. Also if you need help after he has left Paris, you should contact any of these three people. They know you may be in touch.'

I looked at the names and addresses, all of Frenchmen living in Paris. I glanced sharply at Kurt.

'The General says he took some risks,' continued Kurt with a deadpan expression, 'but did not like to tell you in case you were alarmed, especially as you had told him he was not to do anything dangerous. He said these gentlemen have been spared the Levin treatment through his good offices and you would understand what that meant.'

'And so do you know what it means, Kurt, dear Kurt.' I flung my arms round him as the train came in and Jeanne turned her back in disgust. 'Look after him for me and come safely through the war yourself.'

He helped me board the crowded train with the suitcases and holdall, making sure I found a seat. As the train drew out of the station he waved, walking beside the slowly moving carriage, and I reflected that it neatly summed up my life that my departure from Paris should be marked by the fond farewell of a German officer and the retreating back of my sister.

As passengers got off at every stop the train grew less crowded until only an elderly, poor-looking woman and I were left in the carriage. She spoke to me in a patois which I found difficult to interpret, but it was not hard to guess that she had noticed my tears. I told her that I was fleeing Paris because I had been in love with a German officer and that I could not imagine my life without him. She clucked sympathetically and I wondered how much she knew of life under the Germans, if she understood the hatred which seemed to rise from the very pavements of Paris or if she had spent the war on some country farm, inconvenienced but not persecuted with curfews, hostage taking, executions and the perpetual presence of the conqueror.

Yet I found it soothing to confide in her, even admitting to Klaus's married status. When she told me I must look forward, I said that if I could turn the clock back I would, but only so that I could go through every minute of being in love with Klaus again. She did look at me a little strangely then, muttering about age and wisdom, but her rough sympathy was still a comfort to me during the remainder of the journey.

Macfidget howled almost throughout. Once my companion was foolish enough to put a finger in one of the airholes to reassure him and withdrew it covered in blood. She wrapped up the limb in a none too clean handkerchief with the resignation of one who is used to being attacked by animals.

It was dark when I arrived at my destination and, with the help of another passenger, had unloaded my luggage on to the platform. I waved to the woman as the train pulled out and then looked about me for Aunt Marie, wondering how coldly she would greet her errant young relative until a voice cried, 'Catherine! Catherine!' and I turned to find myself smothered in an enthusiastic embrace.

After we had disengaged I looked at her, seeing a dark-haired woman of thirty-five or so, with an air of sense and kindness and above all of humour. As we regarded each other uncertainly Macfidget gave a long-drawn-out wail, protesting at his incarceration.

'A cat!' Aunt Marie looked startled. 'How exciting.'

It was then I knew that whatever might lie ahead of me in the years to come the next phase of my life would not be lacking in love or warmth. I was being taken to a strange house but I believed it would be home in a sense that I had not experienced for a long time and I was not disappointed.

My father's cousin lived on the outskirts of a small village, in a modest but pretty house with a garden which was much bigger than such a dwelling warranted. Over the coming months I was to appreciate that garden for it represented my only physical freedom as Aunt Marie insisted from the start that I must not be seen by any curious villager, that although my arrival at Aix might have attracted some attention we had reached her home under cover of night and people would forget.

Aunt Marie was well respected in the village, where she taught in the tiny school and played the organ at church and if anyone came looking for me she would assert her authority, but we took no risks and I went neither to Mass nor to work, paying my way as best I could by helping in the house and garden. We agreed that if challenged she would say I was a sick cousin who was so unwell that I could not leave the house. Such an excuse might placate, she believed, even if it failed to deceive.

As Allied forces entered Provence her precautions proved effective. Later, the news from Paris proved our fears well grounded. Collaborators were put on trial or shot out of hand, while women who had consorted with Germans were paraded through the city with their heads shaved. I felt my long, golden hair as I heard this and tried to imagine myself being thus punished, understanding why Klaus had been so insistent that I should go away, horrified afresh at the vengeance that had led my father to oppose him. I saw Aunt Marie looking at my hair, my greatest glory, and knew that she too was imagining it all cut off, thinking of me dragged before a jeering, spitting crowd.

'How could they?' I asked, not needing to explain that I referred to my family. What would Edouard have made of it all?

'They might well have prevented it. Your father was, after all, in the Resistance.' Aunt Marie did not even try to make the reply sound convincing.

'I loved them.'

'And they love you, but you hurt them dreadfully with what you did and when people are hurt they can react in funny ways, sometimes seeming to hate when they are only crying inside. When all this is over you will gradually learn to love each other again.'

I shook my head. The abyss which yawned between me and most of my family was too wide and too deep. I hoped again that I might see Edouard and my grandfather soon, but knew that I could happily live the rest of my life without seeing the others. As for Paris itself, which was now frenzied with an orgy of vengeance, only its connection with memories of Klaus gave it any charm. One day I would go again to Saint-Germain-des-Prés, to the place of our trysting, where a dirty, mad artist, a prey to none of the conventions, had brought us together after our only voluntary separation.

'Is Paris burning?' Hitler demanded, wanting to raze that city as completely as Troy in a final act of spite. Cécile had once told me it could never happen and I recalled that conversation in the playground of the Convent when we had wondered if a modern city could just disappear like the one in the *Aeneid*. *Caelum ruit, Troia fuit.*

My personal Troy had collapsed, its walls breached by hatred and fear, but Paris stood, saved by the moderation and reason of the German commanding the last stages of the retreat and surrender. I was sure that by then Klaus had already left for I had heard nothing from him in the weeks I had been with Aunt Marie. I could only hope he knew that I was safe for I had been unable to contact anyone by telephone, the lines unusable in all the confusion. I had sent a letter to him at the Kommandantur and another simultaneously to his hotel but I had no means of knowing if either had reached him before his departure or indeed exactly when that departure had taken place.

Daily I looked for his own letter, remembering how Kurt had told me that Klaus would write. When it did not come I wondered if Aunt Marie had intercepted it, mistakenly believing she must preserve me from any further contact with him, either because he was the enemy or married or both. Perhaps she had even promised my parents she would do so. I asked her outright and she said no, there had been no letter, nor would she ever take it upon herself to keep such a secret from me. I had to work things out for myself and she would help me to do so when I was ready but meanwhile there was no purpose in stratagems which would only cause me distress.

I wondered how far Klaus was from Germany, from home, from Ellie's arms. 'Just be safe,' I whispered, 'just be safe. If we never see each other again, let me know that you are safe.'

'Let him be safe,' I prayed. 'Let him suffer no judgement for my sins. It was my fault not his. Thou rememberest the farmhouse and how it was all my idea. Let not Ellie and his children suffer but bring him safe unto them.

'Oh, and grant that his wife may never find out,' I added.

Often did I try to placate a potentially angry Deity, endeavouring to bargain future good behaviour in exchange for Klaus being spared the consequences of the past. Let any punishment be mine alone, I begged, over and over again.

Yet, though I prayed in terms of punishment and sin, I knew I fooled not Heaven but myself, for the most important element was missing from my earnest petitions, the pre-requisite to prayer itself – repentance. I could not say I was sorry because it would have been, massively, a lie. I had loved, still loved and was certain I would always love a man who had taken vows of fidelity to another. That he was also an enemy of France did not matter, I was certain, in the eyes of the God who had created him. That he served the regime which had killed his own brother might, I supposed, be held to his account in any Divine reckoning, but when I remembered the risks he had taken I dismissed that too.

Sometimes, when I walked among the flowers which blazed in the summer sunshine, I believed my prayers answered. I began to hope that somewhere Klaus also walked safe in a peaceful garden under a kindly sky. It was from one such moment that I was returning when I saw Aunt Marie coming from the house, her face ashen. She hesitated and I knew what she was going to tell me. I turned and ran from her, from the words I could not bear to hear, from finality, from the destruction of that small hope which had always grown green and which told me that one day Klaus and I would be together. Now it turned from green to brown, withered and died.

Aunt Marie caught up with me and held me, telling me to have courage, that she had bad news from Paris, that my parents had heard on the wireless reports of the deaths of several prominent members of the forces recently occupying the city. One of them stated that General Klaus von Ströbel had been killed in an Allied strafing attack.

The icy pain of loss was seared by the fire of the images that danced before my eyes as I tried to picture that final agony. I looked at Aunt Marie and thought she must be relieved, they all must be because now I was parted from him for ever and could bring them no more anxiety, no more shame. Klaus was dead and only I, in all France, would mourn him.

nineteen

Luckier than Dido

My pity was all for Klaus, for any pain or fear he had suffered at the end, for the unlikelihood that so many he had helped would mourn him, that some would rejoice in his death, that he could not look forward to life, that he could no longer enjoy the beauty of the summer flowers in those long hot days in which he would have once rejoiced. For a long time I could only imagine his death, not knowing if it had been instantaneous or painfully drawn out.

I thought of the Frenchmen he had saved, just names to me on the short list Kurt had handed over, and seethed with indignation at what I believed would be their indifference. As for my family, I was sure they rejoiced loudly. I hated actively and deeply the British pilot who had slain him and then had doubtless gone back to drink with his fellows and enjoy a sound night's sleep, careless of whom he had killed.

Eventually I thought of Ellie and their children, of his mother who now had but one surviving son, if indeed Willi still lived, of Willi himself and Angelika. My spirit shared their grief and I knew that I would rather he had gone back to Ellie and never thought of me again than that he should be with neither of us. I became too engrossed in my misery to have patience with anything else, wanted to talk about nothing but Klaus, to think of nothing but him.

Aunt Marie tried to coax, reason and eventually to bully me back to competence but I would have none of it. I could not eat without suddenly crying for Klaus and I slept only at dawn, exhausted by grief.

Much later – much, much later – I was to learn that as he left

Paris, Klaus twice looked back towards the city. 'Dear God, what have I done?' he asked Kurt on the first of these occasions and 'Whatever will become of her?' on the second. I was then to draw a lasting comfort from that knowledge: he had looked back to me rather than forward to Germany and Ellie.

He had taken a letter from his inside pocket and told Kurt that it was for me, as yet unfinished, and that if anything should happen to him he must make sure I received it. I winced at the thought of such a document despatched to Ellie along with his other effects and was sure that a similar dread had occurred to Klaus.

The retreat was bombarded from the air and sniped at by resistants. Klaus, who had been drafted into the army after two decades spent in universities and civil administration, and who had undergone a swift officer training, now found himself on his most demanding active service since he was eighteen and commanding men in a highly confused situation. He never finished his letter.

The day before his death his staff car overturned trying to avoid a strafing attack, but all the occupants crawled out uninjured if shaken. Others were less fortunate and the medical personnel were stretched to the limit. With a grim face, Klaus visited field hospitals where nurses and medics bustled about amid the groans, shrieks, prayers and curses of the dying.

Kurt heard rather than saw the aeroplane diving towards them, guns blazing. At the last minute Klaus, who was shouting orders to the occupants of another vehicle, turned and looked up just as a horrified Kurt saw the vehicle in front explode in a ball of flame and the impact of flying metal hurl his superior from the car. He leapt out himself, trying to reach his dying General, who was moving feebly where he now lay at a distressingly unlikely distance from the car.

'The letter. Take the letter,' whispered Klaus. 'Tell Ellie and the children I love them.'

Kurt bellowed for a medical orderly.

'Too late,' murmured Klaus. 'Godspeed back to Germany, K.K.'

As Kurt looked at him in disbelief he said only one more thing.

'Forgive me, Catherine.'

Kurt took the letter, soaked in blood, wondering if he should still send it now that most of it was illegible, blotted out by the red flow of Klaus's terrible injuries. It was a decision he was to postpone for a long, long while, for this time it was he who was not alert to the aeroplane, regaining consciousness first in a field hospital and then in a real one, where Kurt woke to find himself a prisoner of war with only half a leg.

None of this did I know in that summer of 1944. In my dreams Klaus emerged whole from the smoke and din of the battlefield hell, running in slow motion, arms outstretched. In my nightmares he faded from my vision and I ran into the smoke after him to find it all flames. I never doubted he was dead, never deluded myself about mistakes or confused identities.

In the darkest hours of my life I had no word from any of my family but my grandfather, who wrote to tell me to be brave rather than to express regret at my loss but also that he missed me and thought Edouard did too. He enclosed a drawing, by my small brother, of an endearingly ill-proportioned horse.

Bette wrote at length, recalling Klaus's kindness and humour and hoping that Kurt had survived. With a jolt I realised that I had scarcely given a thought to Kurt and, thinking of him walking beside my departing train while my sister turned from me, I wept from a fresh source of grief.

To my surprise Sister Thérèse also wrote to me, telling me that I was in her prayers and saying it had taken her a long time to work out who had inspired that magnificent essay on the Fronde. Father Tessier, she told me, was saying a Mass for the repose of General von Ströbel's soul on a private occasion.

I reflected that as Klaus was both an adulterer and a heretic it would certainly have to be private and was almost equally certainly being done without the Bishop's permission. I wondered what Father Tessier knew of Klaus to lead him to such a course of action and sensed that the risks he had taken must have been rather more extensive than I had imagined. For the first time in many months I prayed for the soul of the hanged Gerhardt from whose legacy such risks had flowed.

Yet Klaus himself had talked unforgivingly of judgement and it was in those uncompromising terms that his death haunted me. He alone had paid for the sin of both. As once I had taken the grubby Christmas gift tag from its hiding place and hugged myself in hope so now, in despair, I read a collection of pathetically small notes over and over again, trying to draw near to Klaus through his handwriting, the only tangible thing I had left.

To Catherine, with compliments, Klaus von Ströbel.
The Kommandantur when you finish work.
Café Flore, Thursday, usual time.
Sorry, my Darling, am sending this by Kurt. Work calls.
All my love, Klaus.

This last had been attached to my nineteenth birthday present, scent and silk stockings which, when I wore them, proclaimed my status as a German officer's girlfriend more surely than if I had carried a placard.

Once, when I was putting the notes away with the resolution, doomed to almost instant failure, of not taking them out again for a day, I sensed Klaus very near, as if his spirit were trying to comfort me. I knew that, if he could, he would tell me to pick up the pieces of my life and seek out the sunshine.

Aunt Marie took up the same refrain. 'Klaus would never have wanted you to grieve like this. He would have wanted you to be happy not to pine away your youth.'

'I am not unhappy for myself. I cannot bear what happened to him.'

It was quite true. Since hearing of his death I had given no heed to my own situation, to my life in hiding with a maiden aunt, to the estrangement from my family, to the absence of employment and friends.

When he came to me one night, slowly running from the smoke and flames, reaching out, he seemed to be mouthing not 'Catherine' but 'Dido'. I woke and as I had once stood stock-still in a Parisian street, my hand over my stomach, icy fear in my heart, so now I lay, with the ache of hope, searching for movement. There was none, but as I became more fully awake, my brain raced with calculations. Had I been less preoccupied with grief I would have noticed much earlier. Three months at least, maybe four. I switched on the light and examined my profile in the mirror over my dressing table. Perhaps.

I said nothing because I was not yet sure and I did not want to tempt a fate which had shown no disposition to be kind to me in the past, but hope made me braver and at least willing to believe that there might be happiness waiting for me somewhere in the future. Aunt Marie noted my recovering spirits with approval and I felt a twinge of guilt that the news which would make me whole again would be less welcome to her. Incredibly my imagination took me no further than that, showed me not the faintest glimpse of the furore which was about to break out around me.

As I could not leave the house to see a doctor I had to possess my soul in patience as best as I could until some incontestable proof of my condition presented itself. At length I felt the child within me move and knew that Klaus had left me the most precious gift of all, that a living reminder of our love would comfort me all my days.

If only I had thought just a little more carefully about how my situation would seem to others, about how it would have seemed to me had it happened to someone else, I might have handled the uproar better. As it was I told Aunt Marie without the slightest preparation for difficult news. We were sitting companionably after supper when I asked her if she had ever read the *Aeneid*.

'Of course, along with every other schoolgirl. I seem to remember doing Aeneas's visit to the Underworld for bac. It was not a great success for our pious hero when he visited the dead. On the whole it is better to stick to the usual arrangement whereby they visit *us* even if it is a bit disconcerting at the time.'

I smiled. 'Do you remember Dido and how she raged when Aeneas left her?'

'Yes, poor soul, him and his wretched *pietas*.'

I began to quote the words I knew by heart, the lines on which my eyes had dwelt when Bette left her schoolgirl copy of the *Aeneid* behind at Le Printemps.

If only, before you had gone, I
had conceived your child,
had some little Aeneas to play in my halls,

whose face should remind me of yours,
though you were lost to me, then
I should not seem to myself so lost and unhappy.

Looking at Aunt Marie, I saw she had already turned white, even before I concluded, 'Well, I am luckier than Dido.'

To my distress and bewilderment she began to cry. 'How could he? Oh, surely not that! How could he?'

'But, Aunt Marie, I am *happy*. Don't you see? As long as I have his child, Klaus will never be wholly dead to me.'

It seemed an eternity while my relative struggled for control.

'Catherine, my poor Catherine, you are lost. They told me you grew up overnight when that man came back to Paris from Germany, but you are just a child, a baby. You have no idea. If Klaus von Ströbel were not already dead I should kill him myself.'

'You mustn't blame him. It was the last thing *he* wanted, but I read those lines of Virgil a few months before he left and I knew what *I* wanted. I made sure it happened, Aunt Marie. Bette told me how, without realising why I wanted to know.'

She put her head in her hands but when she next spoke it was with her usual even tones and some of her old kindliness.

'Catherine, we must plan this out properly before telling your parents. Of course there can be no question of your returning to Paris. It is in any case far too soon and therefore dangerous for you. There is also Jeanne. Your mother would never let her see her sister with an illegitimate child and Edouard is old enough to ask questions.'

Illegitimate. I was bringing a branded child into the world. For the first time I had a glimpse of the hurdles ahead not just for me, but for my son. I never doubted it would be a son, a little Aeneas, a little Klaus, because the von Ströbel features ran strongly through the male line. Illegitimate. A German officer's bastard.

'You must stay here, where nobody cares to know about you and question your presence. Then we can arrange the adoption.'

The words hit me like a physical blow. Only now did I consider that everyone would expect me to follow the usual course: go away somewhere quiet, give birth, hand over the child into the care of strangers, never see it again, never know what happened to it and then quietly reappear with a story of illness and recovery. I struggled desperately in my memory for a single instance of a girl I knew, however indirectly, bringing up her illegitimate child and was chilled by failure. I had broken many taboos over the last two years, but the convention with which I now battled was the strongest of all. I reminded myself that I would soon be twenty, that I must stand my ground.

'There will be no adoption. This is my child and Klaus's. I will raise it myself.'

'Catherine, think, for goodness' sake, think. How can you raise a child on your own? Your parents will never take you back. How could you support it?'

'I will do what widows and deserted wives do: work.'

'And who will look after the child?'

'I will take in typing or washing and ironing. I can give German lessons. It can all be done from home.'

'All of which will bring you pocket money and no more. It is the sort of work women do for pin-money, not for keeping children.'

'Nevertheless I will not give him up.'

'You have no choice. I am sorry, Catherine. As you cannot marry the father you must give this child to those who will in turn give it a proper family upbringing. Indeed, how could you do any other for the child's sake? What would you tell it? Are you going to pretend he had a real daddy, married to mummy but that daddy died? What happens if he or she finds out the truth? Think, child, think. You would be bringing up a German officer's illegitimate child.'

'I shall tell him the truth. Plenty of children will grow up without fathers thanks to this insane war.'

'Catherine, you have nothing to offer this child except poverty, shame and struggle. Klaus would not have wished that on any child of his. He would tell you what I am telling you now.'

'Aunt Marie, I know you and all the family think I was just a silly girl who had her head turned by a married man far away from home and perhaps there is some truth in that, but it really wasn't just a dalliance. Klaus could have had other women, sophisticated worldly women, any time he wanted, but he didn't.

Nor did he just want me in the way you all believe. It took time and a massive tragedy to lead to that. We *loved* each other.'

'The history is not important but the future of your child is.'

We were still arguing when I rose to go to bed. I was too exhausted to sleep and tried to reach out to the spirit of Klaus but I was alone and knew that would be how I must face the future. 'I will not give him up,' I whispered to my pillow. 'I will never give him up.'

Aunt Marie kept up the pressure for a few days and often I escaped to the shrubbery to weep, afraid the strain would hurt my unborn child, but I would not give in and when she finally accepted that her counsel was not going to prevail, she wrote to my parents. She must have told them everything for my father telephoned, unable to contain his fury. That his daughter should be about to give birth to an illegitimate child was, he would once have thought, the worst thing which could happen to a father, but to hear that it was of her own quite deliberate making and that she saw fit to boast about it was a fall from grace beyond his wildest nightmares. As for the lunacy about keeping it, I must be mad and he was tempted to have me certified as such.

He would personally see to the adoption, he shouted, and if I resisted he would ask the courts to overrule me. I bore it all until he called Klaus a Nazi swine and then I gently replaced the receiver on its rest.

I wondered what my mother had made of the situation, if she longed to comfort her daughter, if she could bring herself to accept that Klaus's baby would be her first grandchild or if she shared my father's disgust and now believed she had only two daughters worthy of the name. Did she weep either openly or in secret and if so for whom? For me? For the innocent child? Or for herself, who had lost a daughter to shame and the life of an outcast?

The threat of court proceedings terrified me, especially as I was certain any judge would see the issue from Aunt Marie's perspective. I knew I had only a limited time in which to make arrangements and I wrote immediately to Bette with an audacious proposition, suggesting that we might find somewhere to live together and that I would support my child by taking in work and meanwhile keep house for Bette until I could piece together a more permanent arrangement. Unfortunately it would have to be somewhere other than Paris and very secret.

Bette wrote back kindly but said it was just not possible, being fraught with all manner of practical difficulty. However she would see if anyone else might help. Although I had not seriously expected her to agree, I still felt deserted while knowing myself to be unreasonable. I wrote to all three of the people on the list Klaus had given me and each replied sympathetically, regretting Klaus's death, averring that he had saved their lives but reluctantly concluding that adoption was the only way forward and that it was what Klaus would have wanted. All three also sent money.

Money. At first I resented it, feeling insulted, believing those who sent it saw it as just a substitute for real help, a salving of the conscience. I tore up the list and threw it away but I kept the money and offered none of it to Aunt Marie for my keep, slowly coming to see it as a gateway to freedom. Shamelessly I wrote to Bette asking her for a loan and she replied at once with a generous offering, doubtless grateful to receive a request with which she could so easily deal.

I considered applying to my grandfather, but feared he might tell my father who would guess my intentions and speedily thwart me. I thought of Father Tessier, but priests were always poor. Still, the Frenchmen had been generous and I had enough for my immediate purpose which was to leave Aunt Marie clandestinely, settle in a city other than Paris, in the opposite direction to the Allied forces which were now moving, heavily resisted, through France towards Germany. In such a place I would be anonymous in the cheapest lodgings I could find and give birth. Afterwards I would move again before anyone could challenge my right to keep my own child. Even I knew it was a harebrained scheme but it gave me hope which I was sure the courts would not.

On the night I had set for leaving I fed Macfidget and bade him goodbye, collected my already packed case and left a note for Aunt Marie who was rehearsing a children's choir in the village hall. Outside I placed my case on the saddle of my bicycle, which I began to push gently and unhurriedly, looking up at the brightly twinkling stars, remembering so many night walks with Klaus under those same planets. They would shed their light for millennia to come on soldiers and lovers, on happiness and tragedy, on all man's petty schemes and would not change because Catherine Dessin had loved and Klaus von Ströbel had died. I was insignificant in a great universe and would surely be able to stay hidden for long enough to outwit the equally unimportant Pierre Dessin. Those stars shone down on Germany at this very moment, on Ellie and her children, on Willi, Angelika and their mother, the same stars as my own family could see in Paris. Why did we fight, we mortals under the same Heaven?

It was my plan to travel on foot for some days, not to use a station where Aunt Marie might search for me. By night I would sleep in the fields and then when my pursuers were confused I would seek out transport to whichever city it might be travelling. I had some bread and thought I would find a stream somewhere for water.

I got no further than the corner of the road outside our house before Aunt Marie herself came running round it, having left a musical score at home. I pushed the case off my bike and in a panic tried to mount the vehicle and pedal furiously off into my uncertain future. Aunt Marie caught me and we struggled briefly until my concern for my unborn child grew stronger than my need for immediate escape.

'Catherine, Catherine, what nonsense is this?'

'I won't give him up,' I sobbed. 'I will escape you all. I swear it.'

'Well, not tonight. Come home with me now.'

'No.' I looked her straight in the eyes. 'You will tell my father and then he will go to the courts at once.'

'I promise to tell no one at all until you and I have talked.'

I gave her my word that I would wait until she had returned from the choir, but she came running back, her eyes wide, evidently not sure she should have trusted me, nearly overcome with relief when she found me in a chair with Macfidget on my lap.

Panting from the exertion she watched me wearily and incredulously from the opposite chair while I explained my plans. I concluded with the same refrain. 'I will not give him up. He is mine. Mine and Klaus's.'

'You call that a plan? It's just about the dottiest story I have heard in years and I teach infants. Still, one thing is clear – you are more likely to come to harm by going off on your own than if you stay here. So as you will not remain on our terms, I suppose we must just accept yours and fervently hope that you will come to a more rational view of your own accord at some later stage.'

I could hardly believe my ears, nor was I convinced.

'What about my father?'

'My dear, the court threat was to frighten you into doing the right thing. The outcome would not be anything like as certain as you appear to think. You are twenty not sixteen. You are not destitute, homeless or likely to be an unfit mother and, anyway, apart from all that can you really see your father making a parade of the infamy in his family?'

So the stormcloud I had so feared was nothing more than a small white puff. I wondered that I should have been so gullible.

'Catherine, were Klaus here I am sure he would tell you that it is better to fight than to run away. Can you imagine what would be happening now had I not appeared so opportunely round the corner? Every gendarme in the district would be looking out for a pregnant girl with a case and a bicycle and I would be frantically calling on half the village to help. Secrecy would be at an end and everyone would know who you are and why you are here.

'You would not have got far, but supposing you had eluded us for a night, how would you have slept in a field at this time of year and what damage might you have done to the child by even trying? In case you haven't noticed there is still a war on and you can't just travel about the country on a whim. Finally, what on earth were you going to do for money?'

On the last point only was I able to reassure her, but her reaction was of anger not relief. 'Asking for money from strangers! You had better let me have this list and I will send it all back.'

'I no longer have the list. I tore it up in disgust and anyway I didn't ask them for cash. They just sent it as a sop to their consciences when they refused the real help I had sought from them. So much for Klaus saving their lives. Perhaps he should have sent them a bundle of money instead.'

'Don't be bitter, Catherine. They were doing what they thought best for you, what we all think is best for you and more importantly best for the innocent child who has been caught up in all this mess and whom you are hell bent on denying a proper home and family. If you had decided to go away, none of us could have stopped you, but you should have planned it all properly.'

I knew she was right, that I had been no more sensible than when I had crawled out of a window after curfew in a party frock or when I had carried a struggling, terrified cat through Paris in a pillowcase. This time it was not a cat but a child I had put at risk. I wondered if my elders were right after all when they said that I was not yet ready to take on the role of parent.

'I was frightened and desperate.'

'And stubborn and stupid.'

She had never yet spoken to me so harshly and, looking at her, I realised that she was badly shaken. Mercilessly I tried to turn her anxiety to my advantage.

'Aunt Marie, I am truly grateful for all you have done for me and I really mean that, but I will not stay here only to be told every day that I have made the wrong decision.'

'Very well, I won't try to persuade you any more, but you have no idea what you are doing.'

Certainly I had not known what I was doing when I decided to sleep in the open, I thought, as I huddled under the blankets to keep out the cold, but I had won more comprehensively than I would have imagined possible only hours ago and for that alone the farcical, humiliating episode had been worth it just as the incidents of first the curfew breach and then Macfidget had been worth it for bringing Klaus and me together. Yet I knew I had been stupid and was alarmed when I reflected how little I had grown up after all and that in a few months' time I would be a mother.

Aunt Marie was as good as her word and wrote next day to my father to say that I was unmoveable and that it was now time to accept my decision. What else she said I do not know, but I received a furious letter from my father a couple of weeks later, disowning both me and my child. She also told me that I had no need to rely on the charity of strangers or even Bette because Klaus had left money for me with my grandfather.

'Of course it is nothing like enough to help you bring up a child, but he didn't know about the baby.'

Aunt Marie told me that Klaus had turned up at my parents' house the day after my own departure and insisted on leaving money for me, pointing out that if I was to hide I would not be able to work and that when the time came for me to do so I might find it hard persuading anyone to employ me. Hatred would live on in France for a long time, he predicted grimly, and I must have the means of survival especially if I needed to live independently.

There had been a fierce row, with my father shouting that Klaus obviously believed he had bought his daughter, whereupon Klaus pushed past him and went upstairs to my grandfather where a more rational, if frosty, conversation ensued. The old man accepted the money with reluctance and promised it should be kept for me, aware that I might need a small measure of independence and that I would not be able to rely on my father to provide it.

'It would have taken you more than two years at Le Printemps to earn what he gave you,' Aunt Marie said as she concluded her description of the scene.

I did not need to ask why Klaus had not given the money to me directly rather than through my family. The previous night's episode was explanation enough. For all that he had depended on me, he knew I was not yet ready for some of life's bigger decisions. I tried to be grown up now and said that Aunt Marie must accept payment for my keep. She refused, claiming my work in the house and garden was sufficient. I must keep Klaus's nest egg for when I had his child.

Now that she had accepted my decision Aunt Marie began to ask questions about Klaus, as if needing to know the nature of the man whose child would soon be born in her house. What had he done for the Frenchmen who had sent me money and, more importantly, why had he done it? When I told her about Gerhardt she held me tight and I felt the child within me move as if in protest. She tutted over the episode with the curfew, laughed at my description of carrying Macfidget, smiled sadly when I told her of Apollo.

'I could wish you had never met Apollo, but from what you tell me you wouldn't have held out for much longer and nor would your Klaus. Catherine, we will always see this man as the insect which ate the heart out of our beautiful rose and I know that will hurt you, but if it is any consolation I now believe that he really did love you and that is what we all find so hard to accept.'

With that she turned to more practical matters, saying she would arrange for a doctor to call discreetly and that she knew a midwife who would help. Between us we worked out that the baby must be due at the end of January and, as Christmas approached, we unpicked old jerseys and reknitted them into baby clothes. I detected still an underlying tension in Aunt Marie and I knew she found it hard not to ask if I would reconsider my decision about adoption but soon a fresh source of strife erupted, resulting in a bitter argument on Christmas Day when she casually asked if I had given any thought to names.

'I shall call him Klaus-Pierre.'

When she saw I was serious Aunt Marie begged me to have more sense. I would be branding the child with his German parentage and making it more difficult to settle down anonymously and put the past behind me. As for combining Klaus with Pierre my father would take it as a deliberate insult and the estrangement from my family would only be prolonged.

'I want him to be proud of his parentage, not ashamed of it. He is Klaus's son and shall bear his name and as he is my son too I want him to carry a name from my own family.'

'Well, choose another one from the family.'

'Grand-père is also called Pierre so that only leaves Martin and I cannot believe that would please anyone.'

'There is your other grandfather.'

'I do not like the name Robert.'

'You could at least separate the names and let him choose later.'

'No. Klaus-Pierre. He is German and French and must grow up knowing it.'

Aunt Marie grew angry but tried to lighten the atmosphere by saying she hoped it was a girl and when I riposted that I would call her Klausine-Margot our festive celebrations dissolved into acrimony. I was, she said, irresponsible, headstrong and cruel and Klaus must be turning in his grave.

I had tried not to think about Klaus's grave, the burial party digging pits by the score, the small white cross, the rest of the column moving on, their thoughts on their own survival, heedless of the dead. Had Kurt marched on or had he died with Klaus? I hoped that, after the war, Klaus's family would have him reburied near his home, but had no idea if that was possible. One day I would find his grave and take his son to visit it.

I wondered what sort of Christmas, her first as a widow, Ellie was having. The younger children, used to their father's long absences, would scarcely realise what had happened but Johanna would be facing the reality that her father would never share Christmas with them again, never watch in amusement as presents were torn open with eager anticipation, never decorate a tree, never preside over the festive meal. I hoped the British pilot was dead.

I knew so vehement a reaction to be both wrong and illogical, but it possessed me all the same and I vowed that the one characteristic of Klaus's I would not allow in our son would be love of the English. From the sum of such individual instances did nations come to hate each other and I had always railed against the futility of war but, when I thought of the airman, I was not sad but savage and no amount of reason could crush the vengeance in my heart.

I would have liked Klaus-Pierre to be born on the first day of the year as was his father but the day passed uneventfully and Aunt Marie said it would do no good to the child to be born early and that first babies usually came later rather than sooner. Her words caused me a small chill for I did not think there would be other babies. This would be the first and the last. I wanted no man but Klaus and even were I ever to change my mind I did not think I would find one willing to take on what the world would see as a fallen woman and her illegitimate child. It had been one of the arguments Aunt Marie had used when trying to persuade me to give up my baby, though her phraseology had been more tactful.

It now occurred to me that I knew little about the mechanics of giving birth, that all my knowledge came from Bette at an age when her own information would have been incomplete, but I had an idea that it was quite painful and might be slow or quick. I thought only in terms of the actual birth and was unprepared for the long labour which began to pound my body in the early afternoon of 13 February. Had Aunt Marie not assured me this had happened to her friends and was all perfectly normal I would have believed the baby was stuck and we were both dying.

I could feel Klaus very near, tender, encouraging and that was all that kept up my courage through the pain of birth which was itself prolonged and difficult and during which I felt my body was on fire. I screamed and screamed again, clutching Aunt Marie, heedless of the midwife's instructions to push. I called out for Klaus and my mind showed him once more running out of the smoke and flames, reaching for me.

In another house, in a far-off city, children's screams echoed my own, as bombs screeched and exploded throwing huge sheets of flame into the air, filling the night with terror and death. Their mother had made them hide in the cellar because she dared not go out to find a shelter and was holding them to her, praying, praying, praying, thinking of another child, the youngest, who had been left with her grandmother deep in the countryside. Perhaps the woman cried out to her husband, many months dead, and thought she saw him run from the smoke and flames towards her.

I screamed again and the midwife said, 'Be brave, it will soon be over.'

Did the mother also say that to her children? Did she promise them the bombardment that had rained down for so long would suddenly cease? Did she know they would die? Did she, at that moment, when another bomb fell on Dresden and the onomatopoeic giggle of a small child was silenced for ever, call out to the one I felt so near as at last his child was born, covered in blood and screaming in protest?

twenty

Klaus-Pierre

As Klaus had always said, the von Ströbel features ran strong in the males of the line. As I looked down at the child in my arms I thought of Dido's words: 'Some little Aeneas to play in my halls, whose face should remind me of yours. . .' Now indeed I knew I was not lost, that as long as my son was well and happy so would I be.

Aunt Marie had called in a priest she knew, not the local one, to baptise my baby, agreeing with the same reluctance that Bette had shown to act as godmother. The ceremony was performed over a large copper bowl which she used normally to display flowers. Amused, I heard the priest try to pronounce Klaus as I did while Aunt Marie had already overcome this difficulty by nicknaming my child Aeneas.

Hiding the presence of a child was proving more difficult than hiding an errant cousin as we needed to obtain milk and appropriate foods while the war raged on, moving inexorably towards Germany. I do not know what sort of story Aunt Marie told, but no vengeful patriots arrived at our door.

I did begin to notice how some people would linger a little as they passed our gate and throw curious glances as if to catch sight of something about which they were uncertain, but I always parked Klaus-Pierre's pram at the back of the house and took him in at once if he cried.

I spoke to him mainly in German and once called him 'mein Liebchen, Liebchen Klausi' before realising what I was saying. It was one of the few occasions on which I had blinked back tears lately, for on the whole I was happy and therefore puzzled when I saw Aunt Marie was still worried.

No member of my family wrote to congratulate me on Klaus-Pierre's birth, not even my grandfather, but I cared little. If they did not wish to know my son it was their loss not his. Bette wrote in restrained terms and one of the Frenchmen, a Monsieur Blanc, from Klaus's list rang Aunt Marie two months after the birth to make sure I was safe and well. My cousin returned from that conversation deeply pensive.

'This Klaus of yours must have been a brave man,' she commented wonderingly. 'Presently I will tell you all Monsieur Blanc has just told me but it looks as if your friend took the most awful risks. Apparently he would have been quite happy to strangle any resistance worker with his bare hands if such a person posed any threat to Germans, but at the same time made a positive practice of warning people who were about to be rounded up and sent to Drancy. Odd.'

'Perhaps it is not so odd to know the difference between war and murder,' I countered. 'I myself made the same distinction once in a Métro station but nevertheless I am glad I didn't know what he was doing because I would have been terrified for him. Sometimes I wonder if I let him down, if I should have been braver so that he could have told me, could have confided. He must have felt terribly alone when he was taking those risks.'

My cousin looked down at a sleeping Klaus-Pierre. 'He too will need to be brave,' she said and my heart jolted with sudden fear and a cold premonition of the time of trial ahead.

The war was many months over and Klaus-Pierre trying to crawl when I received the first indication of what lay in store for my innocent child. Two workmen were carrying out repairs to the gutters on Aunt Marie's house and I was in the tiny boxroom which we used as Klaus-Pierre's nursery, trying to settle him for his afternoon nap, transferring him from my arms to his cot, waiting for him to perform his usual trick of pretending to sleep while I held him and then crying as soon as I laid him down.

As he obliged on this occasion I heard one of the workmen say, 'That must be the German brat.'

'Yeah, bet his dad won't be too keen to know him. They say the girl is about fifteen.'

With more indignation than judgement I threw open the window.

'Thank you. I am twenty-one and his father is dead.'

With satisfaction I watched him nearly fall off his ladder, just preventing such an accident by grabbing the window-sill. I shut the window firmly and with unnecessary force, reflecting that the story would shortly be all round the village, doubtless confirming the view of many a scandalised Frenchwoman that Aunt Marie's young relative was a brazen hussy.

The German brat. The words echoed in my head, foretelling a world in which my son would carry a mark on his forehead more shameful than that of Cain. It was, however, time for me to meet that world and to give up the hermit's existence I had led since coming to Aunt Marie's. Discarding her reservations that it might be too soon I went to Mass on the Sunday with Klaus-Pierre in my arms.

The congregation and I surveyed each other covertly, on their side with embarrassed, curious glances, eyes turning away as soon as they met mine, and on my part with a frank assessment of the ravages of war and the extent of kindliness on each countenance. The women were dowdy but not as thin as many I had seen in Paris, while the men were surly, some scarred, one disabled. The priest gabbled the Mass as if he could not wait for it to be over and the faithful scurried away. None cooed over the only baby present. A few spoke briefly to Aunt Marie, their eyes flicking nervously in my direction.

It needed more time, Aunt Marie consoled me, but I was miserably unconvinced. In a few months Klaus-Pierre would be walking and not long after that he would be looking for playmates. I even wondered if I should return to Paris where there would be other girls in my situation, where I would be too small a fish in too large a bowl for people to gaze at, where I had a grandfather and people who owed their lives to Klaus to help me.

Aunt Marie disagreed. 'Your grandfather is housebound and as for Monsieur Blanc and his like, I do not see what they can do, having no reason to suppose they have children of Klaus-Pierre's age. Anyway feelings still run high in Paris. You are better off here for a while yet.'

As ever my cousin's advice was sound but I wept for my son whose first birthday was celebrated by just Aunt Marie and myself, with a belated and dutiful rather than loving card from Bette a few days later. He was as isolated as his father had been among Nazis, as I had been among patriots. How long would it be before he noticed, before it puzzled him? For the first time I understood why I had been so earnestly urged to have him adopted.

I contemplated a more mature version of my plan to run away to another city and begin again.

'So long as he is called Klaus everyone will know his parentage,' reasoned Aunt Marie without any hint of 'I told you so.'

I decided to face down the spite and began to take Klaus-Pierre to the small shop, to church, to the tiny recreation field with its swings and slide. Once when he toddled up to a small girl, her mother called her away and Klaus-Pierre stood still, staring after her in bewilderment. On another occasion when he had wandered a small distance from me an elderly lady bent down and asked him his name.

'Clow air.'

As I came up she raised enquiring eyebrows and I heard myself say, 'Pierre.'

'*Clow* air,' he insisted indignantly.

The old lady smiled at him fondly. 'What is he saying?'

'Klaus-Pierre.'

Her smile faded. 'Oh.' At least she had the grace to pretend not to be in a hurry as she left us.

In the shop a child of five or so pointed at Klaus-Pierre and asked his mother in a loud voice, 'Is that the German brat?'

'Shush,' she hissed, with a glance at me, while my child stared at hers, uncomprehending, sensing hostility but with no means of understanding its cause.

By the time he was two the only words Klaus-Pierre had exchanged with his peers were snatches of talk before the adults intervened to withdraw the other children. He had played with none of them for more than a few minutes, had no friends, could not share his toys. Aunt Marie argued bitterly with the priest about the absence of Christian compassion towards an innocent child and said he should preach on the subject. He countered that it was all he could do to reconcile his parishioners to my presence at the Communion rail and that they would not want to have to explain to their children why Klaus-Pierre had such a funny name and no daddy.

Aunt Marie gave up playing the organ and insisted we travel seven miles each week to another church in her ancient car. As our reception there was no more cordial it was beyond me why we bothered.

'German brat! German brat!' The refrain was always a signal that Klaus-Pierre had run off, when my back was briefly turned, to approach a group of children. He never seemed to learn, but would always rush up to them with great energy and bright, hopeful eyes.

Once an older child called 'Nazi bastard!' and was bitterly berated by his mother not for hatred but for bad language.

As Klaus-Pierre approached his third birthday I knew it was no longer any use just trying to face down the spite and hatred, the censure and the disdain. We must move or his development would be permanently damaged. I resolved that for a while he would be called just Pierre. In those darkest of days I even thought of adoption.

'What should I do?' I asked Klaus's spirit in agony. 'Whatever should I do?'

This was indeed judgement, I thought, judgement with a vengeance, that I should daily, hourly have to watch my bright, playful, innocent child paying the price for the sin of his parents.

I watched his small face, set in fierce concentration, as he tried to balance six bricks of varying sizes on top of each other. So far he had not gone beyond four and never failed to cry or stamp with frustration when the pile came tumbling down. Now I held my own breath as the fifth brick stayed in place, albeit precariously balanced, and Klaus-Pierre carefully laid the final one on top of it. The pile held and he turned to me shouting with excitement. As I congratulated him the tower wobbled and fell in a disorderly heap, scattering bricks across the carpet and on to the floorboards.

I watched him absorb the failure, waiting for the tear storm. Instead he surveyed the ruins and made a small grimace before turning to his top. My hand which had been reaching out to comfort him froze in midair, for the grimace was an exact replica of Klaus's Flore face, saying more clearly than words, 'Oh well, that's that then.'

He paused in surprise as my face crumpled, then began an inept spinning of his top.

'You are *Klaus*-Pierre,' I whispered. 'And I will never give you up.'

In the spring of 1948 a family from England came to spend two months in the village and moved in next door to my aunt. The wife, who was French, had married an English airman shortly before war broke out and had not returned to France. Now she came to see her mother, bringing her three children aged four, three and one. Despite the size of our garden the noise of children playing next door was painfully audible to Klaus-Pierre and he did what I had not realised was within his capabilities for, when I went indoors on an errand, he climbed the front gates of both houses and rushed to join the others.

The next fifteen minutes were a nightmare of fear and anguish as I could not find him. Aunt Marie and I raced about the garden, peering in bushes calling 'Klausi! Come on, we have some nice cake.' 'Aren't you clever to hide so well? Where are you?' 'Come on, our little Aeneas, it will soon be dark.'

This last was from Aunt Marie at three o'clock in the afternoon. I began to build terrible pictures in my mind of what might have happened, becoming afraid that my son had been abducted by vengeful French patriots who would kill him in revenge for what the Germans had done to their families.

'Nonsense,' said Aunt Marie firmly. 'No one is going to murder Klaus-Pierre.'

'So where is he?' I cried in torment. 'Where is he?'

'Well, the gate isn't open so he must be here, somewhere,' reasoned Aunt Marie and, the same thought occurring to us both, we ran out into the narrow road.

'He couldn't have got over it,' I said in disbelief.

Aunt Marie was already walking along to the next gate. 'He could if he wanted something badly enough.'

In the front garden of the house next door, whose owner had not exchanged a single word with me in the whole time I had lived with Aunt Marie, my child played with two others. For a while I just watched, unwilling to do anything which might disturb that scene. Then a man emerged from the house and, joining them, bent down and helped Klaus-Pierre put his feet in the right place on the tricycle pedals. As he straightened up he saw us and walked to the gate to greet us in passable French. I left Aunt Marie to make the conversation, afraid that if I spoke he would ask who I was and send Klaus-Pierre away.

'You will be Catherine,' he said, turning to me suddenly. 'My wife says you must be a very brave lady indeed.'

Her mother would have said something quite different, I thought, but relief washed through me. They knew and were not rejecting Klaus-Pierre. It was only afterwards that I realised I had talked to an English airman without it crossing my mind to hate him.

The next eight weeks brought me the first sustained period of happiness I had experienced since Klaus-Pierre had been old enough to want friends. The children raced in and out of the two houses, played hide and seek, caused much noise and chaos, occasionally arguing. I noted that Klaus-Pierre often sought to include the one-year-old, sometimes impractically, and recalled the photograph of Klaus with his hand protectively on Gerhardt's knee. It was not only Klaus's physical features he had inherited, I thought, as I prayed the happiness would last.

The children were called Alice, Nick and Julienne but I was more interested in the other companions they brought to play: Louis, Christianne, Helene, Marcel, Jean, and another Pierre. On these would depend a normal life for Klaus-Pierre when the English children had returned to London.

There were plans to take the children to Paris to meet up with their mother's other relatives and, knowing that I had a large family in Paris, she offered to take Klaus-Pierre but I forbade him to go. Yet it had the effect of turning my mind to that city once more and I was eager for news when Bette came to visit towards the end of the year.

Cécile was married and Bernadette engaged, Bette told me, but none of the Levins had returned after the war. She had seen Annette once or twice in the street but other than that had met no member of my family in more than three years.

'The Convent is still there and Father Tessier . . .' She broke off in amazement as the sound of chanting from the front gate filled the room.

'German brat! Nazi, Nazi, Nazi!'

I rushed outside and the children ran off, but it took me a few minutes to locate Klaus-Pierre who had crept behind a bush to cry, his sad little snuffles the only clue to his whereabouts.

Bette uttered a fierce expletive and ran to the gate but I called her back.

'How long has that been going on?' she demanded incredulously.

'Ever since he was old enough to notice except for a few months earlier this year when he seemed to be accepted at last. He can't understand why everything has changed again.'

'Haven't you complained to their parents?' Bette's voice shook with outrage.

'Yes, but I suppose to them Klaus-Pierre is not a real child.'

'Savages!'

'Klaus used to say we were all savages,' I remembered. 'And that man had made no real progress in all the millennia he had been on earth. I'm beginning to believe it too. In Germany it was Jews and here it is the innocent child of a German officer.'

'You have to get away. People are beginning to calm down after the war and to look to the future not the past. Make a new start somewhere else. You would even be better off in Paris. If only you hadn't called him *Klaus*-Pierre.'

'Bette, I tell you now it is four years since he died and I love him more each day.'

'He's dead, Catherine. Your child is very much alive and you have to put him first. Call him something else for a while and then you can always revert to Klaus-Pierre later.'

'No.'

'The same old stubborn Catherine. Well, if ever you decide to return to Paris let me know.'

As it happened there were three occasions in 1949 when I might have visited Paris again, but on only one of these did I actually do so. In March Annette married Emile after a stormy on–off relationship following his return from the war which he had spent with the Free French. Although Aunt Marie was invited to the ceremony I was not, the first big family gathering since my departure pointedly excluding me. I felt only mildly hurt and realised with sadness that I had ceased to miss them and that I no longer yearned even for Edouard.

Initially we agreed that I would travel to Paris with Aunt Marie and visit Bette but at the last moment Klaus-Pierre contracted chickenpox and so my cousin went alone, returning four days later to report that all my siblings were well with Edouard having grown into a sturdy lad and Jeanne a very presentable young woman at twenty. My grandmother was still amazingly well for her age but my grandfather was too frail to attend the wedding. He alone sent his love.

In June my grandfather died and I insisted on going to the funeral with Klaus-Pierre. Aunt Marie tried to persuade me to leave the child behind but I would have none of it.

'Who's that?' piped up Klaus-Pierre, pointing at my mother as we arrived at the church and I walked slowly towards my parents, seeing them for the first time in five years, noting my father's loss of hair, my mother's deepened lines.

'Your granny,' I told him. 'Don't point. It's rude.'

He broke away from my hand and raced up the path to the church steps. 'Granny! Granny!'

My mother said, gently, but very firmly, 'No, sorry I am not your granny,' and turned to speak to my father.

I came to a halt, halfway along the path, staring at them, at each in turn, as my son ran back calling, 'That's not Granny. Which one is Granny? Hurry, Mummy, we must find Granny.'

He spoke in French and they would have understood every word but none showed any mercy. My own grandmother was still too preoccupied with the grief of her loss but the others just looked back at me, uncomfortable, embarrassed possibly, but utterly unrelenting. Even Edouard, I realised, struck by an almost physical pain, even Edouard had become cruel.

Klaus-Pierre sensed something was wrong and became very still, no longer searching for Granny. In church we sat at the back and at the graveside I stood with Aunt Marie, looking round at the mourners, recognising Emile and Robert, also the country cousins to whom we used to cycle for fresh food. They kept their eyes lowered and I did not for one moment believe it was just in reverence.

We left immediately the interment was over, Klaus-Pierre pretending not to cry. At the church gate Father Tessier caught up with me and asked me to visit him before I left Paris. At the presbytery he had biscuits waiting for Klaus-Pierre and when I explained I had left him with Aunt Marie he wrapped them in a napkin for me to take away.

'I know it's easy to say, but time will heal this, Catherine.'

'I've been hearing that for far too long, Father. Klaus has been dead for five years.'

'I suppose they cannot get over the Germans killing Martin.'

'The British killed Klaus but last year it was an Englishman who made life bearable at last for Klaus-Pierre. I've hated in my time, fiercely and unreasonably, Father, but there is no point to it. You saw what my family did today, to an innocent child. Why should I believe time is going to make any difference? Klaus-Pierre's childhood will pass and then there will be no time to put it right for him.'

'Catherine, your father could never accept what was happening. You are the most beautiful of his daughters, indeed the most beautiful in generations of Dessins, not pretty or attractive but truly beautiful, something very rare and precious. Your parents had to watch you throw all that away on a middle-aged German who could offer you no future, to stand helplessly by while you wrecked your reputation and annihilated your chances of happiness. You turned your back on them, on every principle you had ever been taught, on everything which was right and proper.'

'So Klaus-Pierre pays?'

He did not answer that but sat for a while saying nothing. When he did at last speak it was not about Klaus-Pierre but Klaus.

'I asked you here today to tell you that I owe a great deal to Klaus von Ströbel and that I pray for his soul almost every day. What he did to you was deeply wrong but what he did for others was well beyond the call of duty. You see, my brother-in-law is Jewish and when things began to get very bad here we decided he and his family would be better off with some relatives in the country who could hide him if necessary, but of course Jews couldn't travel.

'Then I remembered that once someone had told me something in the confessional which might suggest von Ströbel could be sympathetic. As you know, or perhaps you do not, priests are not only bound never to reveal what they hear in the course of confessions, but they are not really supposed to act on such knowledge either. I did. I went to see von Ströbel and asked for a travel warrant for my sister's family. I told him bluntly that my brother-in-law was Jewish and he asked why I thought he might help. Then he said, "Oh! You're the one she told at confession. You're here because you know about Gerhardt."

'Of course I played dumb and he laughed, telling me that he supposed it could be a trap and that he would have to think about it. Within a week the documents came through.

'He did that for others too. He was hugely brave, Catherine, and what I really wanted to tell you is that he lives on, not just in Klaus-Pierre and his children in Germany but, in a different way, in the descendants of those he saved. My sister will have grandchildren thanks to your Klaus von Ströbel but it could have been so different. It could have been Drancy and Auschwitz.'

'Do my parents know this?'

'They know he helped a lot of people. Of course they do not know why I went to see him in the first place.'

'Yet they won't forgive.' I heard the bitterness in my own voice as I remembered Klaus-Pierre's face when my mother turned from him.

'If he had saved half the world he would still have been the man who ruined their daughter.'

'I loved him, Father.'

'It was unlawful love, my child. He was given to another.'

To that there had never been any answer. What he had told me about Klaus confirmed what I already knew from Monsieur Blanc and the other Frenchmen. I remembered Klaus's description of his time in the trenches and how he had won medals because he had wanted to die and then I knew that here in France, under my very eyes, he had again courted death, as surely as had his mentally defective brother, and had again miraculously survived.

'He would never help anyone if he thought he or she posed any threat to Germany because he loved his country deeply,' Father Tessier continued. 'He was a bad enemy but he hated that cruel regime with venom and to those who fell quite needlessly foul of it he was a friend. Catherine, once he asked me if it was possible, in the sight of God, for a man to love two women and I told him no, not if he was bound to one of them, but I want you to know he asked that question.'

I smiled weakly. 'I don't need convincing, Father. I have always known ours was a true love whatever the gossips may have said.'

The priest also smiled though his eyes were anxious. 'I pray, Catherine, that your time of trial may soon be over. Now to practical matters . . . When did you last go to confession?'

I was so deep in thought when I left Father Tessier's that I almost missed Bette who suddenly hailed me from the other side of the road. As she ran across to where I stood my mind went back many years and I saw again a schoolgirl in white blouse and navy blue skirt running to meet me and I saw myself greeting her, artless and carefree.

'We can walk all night,' said Bette. 'No curfew these days.'

'Then let's walk to the Kommandantur.'

Her face fell. 'It isn't that any more.'

'Of course not but I want to see it again.' I assumed that big hotels like the Majestic and the Meurice had reverted to their old functions once the invader had gone, unless of course they had been damaged in the fighting.

As she came with me reluctantly I said, 'I wonder what happened to them all, Kurt Kleist and that awful Heini? The chap by the window of Le Printemps?'

'Who?'

I described the incident and for a while she was thoughtful. 'Maybe you were right and I should have hated a bit less.'

I looked at her, surprised. Then I said, 'And the man with the watch?'

I recalled how I had sat in the outer office on the night we broke the curfew and watched a man's hand writing, a man whose face I never saw. I wondered if that hand was still alive, if it was even now lifting, writing, gesturing, washing or if it was dead, for ever still, rotted to crumbling bone.

Then I forgot the Germans as I told Bette what had happened at that day's funeral. 'It's over,' I said. 'I have no family and it isn't just Paris I never want to see again – I don't want to set eyes on them either.'

As I uttered these words I felt the stupid tears hot on my cheeks yet it was not for my parents I wept but for Klaus, for we had come in sight of the Kommandantur, which was not the Kommandantur, and he would not be coming from it, smiling, to melt in my arms. He would never smile again, not at anything: he was lost to me forever.

'Oh, God,' whispered Bette. 'After all this long while. We were wrong then, those of us who thought you mad. It really was the love of a lifetime. I'm so sorry, Catherine.'

Despite my sudden outburst of grief her typically dramatic flourish amused me. 'He would have gone back to Ellie anyway, but I could have borne that if I knew he was happy somewhere now. Don't be sorry, Bette. We *were* mad, but if it were 1942 now I would be mad all over again.'

'Fine,' replied Bette, recovering quickly. 'But it is now 1949 and you owe it to Klaus-Pierre to be sane. Things can't go on as they were when I was staying with you.'

I told her that my child's lot had changed for the better, that taunting him had gone out of fashion, but that it still broke out spasmodically and I had decided to move before he was old enough to have to go to school. Aunt Marie was making enquiries of some friends and I might go to Versailles or Cahors. Bette approved and made a point of seeing us off next day. As the train pulled out of the station I remembered how Kurt had walked beside my carriage as it left Paris five years ago. This time I swore a secret, solemn oath never to return.

That oath was the reason why I did not go to Paris in the

234

November of that year when Bette got married in one of the biggest society weddings since the war. Wild Bette of the bad reputation secured for a husband Jean-Marie de Berault du Plessis whose family had played a huge role in public life since before the Revolution and for the last quarter of a century had dominated the diplomatic service. Jean-Marie himself was a fledgeling diplomat and four months after the wedding was posted to Germany. I wondered how Bette would cope and if she would learn to like the natives.

twenty-one

Letters

By the summer of 1950 I had made little progress towards leaving Aunt Marie and was beginning to think I should stop trying to make so many arrangements in advance, but instead simply depart and trust to luck. After all, it would not be much of a risk when I knew I could return to my cousin at any time. There was much less tormenting of Klaus-Pierre these days but that was largely because he had developed a wariness of other children and often hid behind me if we passed one in the street. With the passage of time, adults were becoming kinder and I think one or two may even have been ashamed of their past brutality but it was too late. My child could not start school against such a background.

I was coming in from the garden, my arms full of freshly cut roses, when Aunt Marie emerged from the house in a hurry on her way to some village activity. She was nearly at the gate when she turned to call out that there was a letter for me on the hall table.

I recognised Bette's handwriting and the Berlin postmark, but it was the size of the letter which told me that this was not her usual missive, sent dutifully on my or Klaus-Pierre's birthday and which would invariably be short and stilted, or even one of her better efforts when she would fill two sides of a large sheet of paper. Bette hated letter writing and now that she was married into a family that never had to count its costs she used the telephone immoderately.

As I picked up the packet and felt its weight in my hand I was conscious both of alarm and excitement. Bette clearly had news to impart and Bette was in Germany. I forced myself to be patient while I settled Klaus-Pierre down to listen to a children's programme on the wireless. Usually I heard it with him but today I explained I had a very important letter to read so he must be a big boy and enjoy the story on his own. As I slipped upstairs he was humming along to the signature tune of the programme.

My hands shook as I opened the letter.

Dear Catherine,

I know you will be surprised by the size of this letter but I have so much news to tell you and because some is good and some is bad, I thought it better to write it all down now than to wait until I am back in France and can see you or telephone. You haven't given me a new address so I am assuming you are still at Aunt Marie's, in which case I hope poor little Klaus-Pierre is all right and as happy as he can be in such circumstances. Also hope you are all well and that the summer is fine.

Bette's impatience to get down to the real business fairly screamed through these not particularly tactful opening lines.

We have been in Germany for three months and are now in Berlin where Jean-Marie is on a special three-week familiarisation with the set-up here. Although you will probably hate me for saying it, it does my heart good to see the terrible state the place is in. Even some of the grandest Germans are slogging away at manual labour just to feed their families. Jean-Marie is always reminding me that we are on a diplomatic mission but so what? The wretches do look pretty forlorn – just like we used to – and seem to spend all their time picking up the rubble of their ruined city. Serves them right.

Sorry, I know that probably hurts, but presumably your Klaus's family are far away in the country and don't suffer any of this.

Anyway let's start with the big news. I've seen Kurt Kleist. He is well and sends you his love but he was terribly injured in the same attack which killed Klaus and has lost one leg altogether and the second below the knee. That was how I met him, having gone to the east side of Berlin to see a place they've got there which gets people who lost limbs in the war active again. He is amazingly cheerful under the circumstances and is making good progress.

He is in touch with the von Ströbels occasionally. Klaus's mother, Willi and whatshername the daughter are well but, please prepare for what may shock you, Ellie and two of Klaus's children died in the Dresden bombing. Oh, my dear, if only he had lived! He would have been free to marry you. I know that sounds callous and I tried not to think it when Kurt told me but I guess he read my thoughts and then I told him about Klaus-Pierre. He was very shocked.

The youngest child was with the rest of them at Klaus's mother's when it happened. Apparently she had been ill with some childhood ailment and couldn't travel with the others to Dresden when they went to see Ellie's own mother who was dying. They stayed on at the house in Dresden for a few weeks to deal with all the formalities and clear out her mother's belongings. I do feel for Klaus's mother. The war cost her two sons, a daughter-in-law and two grandchildren. I am beginning to agree with you that it's all a pretty futile way of settling international differences.

Kurt himself is looking a bit older (Don't we all? I found a grey hair the other day. Dash it all, Catherine, I'm only twenty-six!) but otherwise he is just the same and as soon as I saw him I recognised him. I am afraid he had a bit more difficulty placing me. So I miaowed a bit and made some inane comment about pillowcases and then he started laughing and asked if Mr Wriggle still lived. I reminded him grandly that the animal was called Macfidget and he said his English was never good enough to work out the name, despite Klaus's patient explanation.

Catherine, I must now come to a very difficult bit. Kurt told me exactly what happened on the road from Paris. Klaus looked back twice, worrying about you, and he was writing you a letter which was only half-finished when the plane got him. Kurt has that letter to this day because Klaus asked him to make sure you got it if anything happened to him.

*Of course, it was Kurt who came to the station to see you
off and so he knew you had left Paris and Klaus had given
him your new address, but it was in his bags which got lost
in all the mêlée. However, he knew your address in Paris off
by heart so he wrote to you asking if you wanted him to
send on the letter, expecting his own letter to be forwarded
to you.*

*I am so sorry to have to tell you this, but your parents
opened the letter, read it and sent it back to Kurt telling him
to make no further contact with you. I am sure they thought
they were doing the right thing.*

*Kurt thought for a bit, wondering what to do with
Klaus's letter and then remembered that you had often
spoken of a grandfather who was kind to you so he tried
again, writing to your father's house, but of course he did
not know your grandfather's name, whether it was your
mother's or father's parent. He tried his luck with M. Dessin
senior, but back came the letter with an even more furious
note from your father and he gave up for a while, resolving
to track you down once he regained some mobility and
could travel himself to France. He had some notion of
approaching the Convent or the priest.*

*He knew nothing about your child and assumed that
when all the dust of war had settled you would make a
fresh start and eventually marry a Frenchman. He said with
your looks you had absolutely no chance of remaining
single. He did go on a bit about how beautiful you are –
enough to give me an inferiority complex.*

*Catherine, this is the really, really terrible bit. By now you
will be wondering why I have not sent you Klaus's letter
myself. He died almost immediately, so please don't think he
suffered, but in those last few seconds he asked you to
forgive him and reminded Kurt to take the letter. Obviously
he had been very badly injured and – I am so sorry – the
letter was soaked in blood and a lot of it is illegible. Of
course I haven't read it, but I did see it and certainly no one
could send you such a thing without warning. You will find
Kurt's address at the end of this letter if you want him to*

send it on. I am sure he would love to hear from you
anyway.

I do wish I could be with you as you are reading all this.
Be brave, Catherine. One last thing – Kurt says Klaus loved
you deeply and passionately, that it was never just a case of
a soldier far from home taking advantage of a pretty girl.
Kurt is sure that, had he lived, Klaus the widower would
have come back to France for you after the war.

Love and hugs,
Bette

In the room below Klaus-Pierre giggled with amusement and
delight. Upstairs where I sat on the side of my bed, still trying to
absorb what I had read, no longer shaking but still, very still, I
sensed the presence of his father filling the room with love and
reassurance, as I began to read again from the beginning and then
again and yet again.

I sat on that same bed three weeks later and read the words
Klaus had written to me as he was about to die, my tears splashing
on the stiff, brown-stained letter, my eyes straining to read words
blotted out by his blood.

I loved you with every fibre of my being . . . wronged you
greatly . . . your future is with your family . . . forgive me,
my darling Catherine . . . always remember Saint-Germain-
des-Prés. I like to think, in my selfish heart, that you will go
there occasionally and think of me as I will go there often in
spirit and think of you . . . when you begin to forget do not
resist, it is better that way . . . let no one ever tell you I was
just using you. I promise you with any oath you care to
exact that I adored you to distraction . . . your wonderful
hair . . . that marvellously puzzled look you used to have . . .
destroyed your youth . . . Gerhardt . . . unpardonable but I
could not help myself . . . as wildly distracted as any
lovelorn boy in the first flush of love . . . how can I ever live
without seeing you again . . . We must have been mad,
wonderfully, painfully, gloriously, shockingly mad . . . no
regrets and I hope you do not . . . my only grief what I

have done to you ... my only shame your loneliness ...
even now I want to turn round and run back to you, to
hold you in my arms ... must both be brave ... shall find
it as difficult as you but we have done too much that is
wrong and must now do our duty to those we love and
who love us. My greatest punishment is our separation ...
again, forgive me, ... perhaps one day when we are old and
grey we will meet again and laugh at ourselves ... resign me
now, do not waste your time pining, face the future now,
now, now.
Dear God, how I have loved you, mein Liebchen, Liebchen
Catherine.

I knew that but for his death I would never have received this
letter, that he would have destroyed it and written to me in much
more sober, responsible terms. This was the Klaus of that wild
Scottish dance in the sunshine, one I saw only occasionally
beneath the burdens of his grief and duty, this was the Klaus who
had loved me, a younger, wilder Klaus not Herr General von
Ströbel, Iron Cross first class and *pour le mérite*.

Aunt Marie took care of Klaus-Pierre that night, bathing him,
reading a story, giving him his supper. I sat on my bed, reading,
re-reading, deciphering suddenly an extra word here or there,
hearing Klaus's voice through the words he had written.

'Your future is with your family.' I remembered the funeral and
a small boy scorned; my father opposing Klaus's plan to move me
far from Paris, willing instead for me to face the head-shaving and
the jeers; the hours of loneliness in a home where I was frozen out
of love; the way I had been encouraged to see Klaus while they
went about their resistance activities.

'No,' I said aloud, but I forced myself to think of how they had
all loved me before I started consorting with a married German
officer, of my conversations with my father as we walked to the
Convent, of my parents as towers of strength when I was so
unjustly expelled, of Catherine the Second and small, giggly
Edouard. I remembered the whispered confidences with Annette
after we had switched out our light, how we peered laughing and

afraid out of our window when the Germans arrived and I thought of Martin, now just a distant memory.

'No,' I said again. 'It was an illusion. It did not stand up to the real test. They loved me only on their terms, when I did what they wanted me to do. They do not love me as I really am.'

The words hung in the air, the final dismissal of my family from my future, more conclusive even than the oath I had taken never to see Paris again.

Eventually I read Kurt's covering letter, learning more than Bette had told me about the retreat from Paris. He wrote in German, saying his French was too poor for letter writing and he remembered that by the time Klaus left Paris I spoke his language rather well. Obviously Bette had not told him that I spoke to my son nearly always in German.

It was clear, from the shock and sorrow he expressed, that Bette had told him all about the persecution my child had endured. He also told me exactly where Klaus had died, so I would now know where to look for his grave, although naturally Kurt made no such suggestion. Ludicrously he asked me to forgive Klaus the wrong he had done, assuring me that he had really loved me. Did he seriously think I had the smallest grudge against Klaus?

Kurt was a limbless, defeated foe, struggling to come to terms with his condition in another country but as I read his letter I sensed a strength and wisdom which left me strangely comforted. It was many years since I had relied on Germans for courage and comfort but now I recalled Kurt's steadiness and loyalty.

Something of that thought must have stayed in my mind for when I saw the woman entering our front gate and walking towards the house a few weeks later I knew at once who she was, without any reason for such knowledge or certainty. People often came to see Aunt Marie about the children she taught or some village activity and they were nearly always women of about this one's age but perhaps less smartly dressed, less self-assured. She did not look in the least like Klaus, but then Klaus had said she was completely different from the others. I went downstairs just as Aunt Marie opened the door to our visitor and heard Klaus-Pierre being enthusiastically greeted by Angelika von Ströbel.

When she saw me she held out her hand and came straight to

the point. 'You poor soul. We had no idea, of course. Dear God, what an unholy mess Klaus managed to create!'

Aunt Marie, her voice faint, asked her to come in and sit down and then went dazedly to the kitchen to make coffee. Angelika's French was almost as good as her brother's and I reflected, irrelevantly as if to gain time for more important thought, that Peter and Lotte von Ströbel had made a good job of their children's education. In order to include Aunt Marie in what might be said I decided not to speak in German and I was surprised when Klaus-Pierre confidently addressed Angelika in his father's language.

He was, of course, bilingual, but had never spoken German to anyone except me and certainly always used French whenever we had visitors, yet he seemed to have no hesitation in answering in German when she spoke to him in French.

'Kurt wrote to Willi,' she said by way of explanation, but I had already guessed, realised that I had been half expecting something like this, that though they might have learned about the existence of a mistress with indifferent surprise, they would not be Klaus's relations if they could ignore the plight of a five-year-old child, their own flesh and blood, who was isolated and scorned in a hostile French village.

'It was all a bit of a shock for Mutti,' she told us calmly as she took the coffee from Aunt Marie and leaned back in her chair, elegant legs crossed. 'It seemed so unlike Klaus. He was always so responsible and sensible and he just adored Ellie and the kids. I never really knew Lothar, my eldest brother, but Mutti said she would have been much less surprised had it been he.

'We had a hell of a war. Mutti lost two sons, two grandchildren and both daughters-in-law, because Willi's wife died of natural causes just before the end, so we all live together in Mutti's wonderful big house. Willi is still a schoolmaster and little Lotte, Klaus's youngest, is being brought up alongside his children so we have six youngsters in the house ranging from seven to nineteen. It's chaos sometimes.'

Angelika paused awkwardly, the first loss of assurance I had seen. 'I think I had better just say it without any prevarication and if you want to throw me out and tell me I've an almighty nerve then so be it. For all I know you may hate us, but I've come to France to say that if you would like to join the chaos you and Klaus-Pierre would have a home there for as long as you wanted it. I promise you it would not just be duty. We would love him to bits.'

From the moment I had seen her enter our gate I had known she had come to rescue Klaus-Pierre and I had begged God for the strength to let him go, to accept our parting as part of the judgement my actions had invited, uncertain even as I prayed that I meant the words, but what I was now being offered I had hardly dared to hope for even in my most optimistic moments. I knew I must owe it all to Kurt, who must have persuaded them that despite the unpromising circumstances I was respectable, a practising Catholic, a professor's daughter, modest not brazen, innocent not wanton, a suitable addition to a family bringing up six children.

Above all he must have convinced them that Klaus had really loved me, that had he survived Ellie, he would have presented me to them as his bride, that he had not just been engaged in some casual affair and that he would have wanted me to be part of his family. For Angelika to have made the offer immediately without bothering to assess me for herself was a tribute to Kurt's success.

Yet such an arrangement was hardly conventional. 'Your mother . . .'

'Is looking forward to seeing her grandson. The elderly are not always as shocked by these things as we expect them to be, having seen it all before.'

'Ellie . . .'

'If Ellie were still alive then obviously we would have had to make other arrangements. The real difficulty of course will be what to tell little Lotte. She was very young when Ellie died and has no real memory of her and none at all of Klaus, but it will still be awkward. She is not yet ten and there will be limits to how much she will understand. The older children will just have to know the truth but we must work out exactly what to tell the little ones for the time being.'

'What about . . . morality?' I spoke in little more than a whisper.

'What you and Klaus did was exactly what we will teach the children they should never do, so, yes, you are setting an appalling example, but Willi and Mutti feel as strongly as I do that it would be far more immoral to abandon a child.'

I was grateful for the frankness but I was by no means convinced their view would be universal.

'What about the neighbours?'

'My dear, it isn't France. We've just lost a second war and the country is broke. Husbands and sons haven't come back, there are ruins everywhere and people are just too busy picking themselves up and starting again to bother with hatred. Anyway the village is a long way off because we are much more isolated than you are here. Furthermore, we hate ourselves. We all knew someone who was Jewish, someone who disappeared and ever since those camps were liberated everybody has known chapter and verse what happened to the poor devils and we have to live with it. So you won't find much moral condemnation in Germany.'

'You must go.' For the first time Aunt Marie spoke. 'Catherine, if you do not go, I shall turn you out on to the streets to beg.'

I saw Angelika looking at my long fair hair, still golden, still luxuriant, still as it had been when I fell in love with Klaus von Ströbel. 'No,' I said. 'They didn't shave it off. Klaus saw to that.'

'I know. Kurt told me. I didn't mean to stare but he also told me how Klaus raved about it.'

'They would have cut it off if I had stayed, because I loved your brother. They said it was an act of treachery.'

'I suppose it was, even if not in the way they meant. It was certainly treachery on Klaus's part towards Ellie and on yours towards your family, but then all love is an act of treachery,' said that surprising woman and I suddenly remembered how Klaus had guffawed when I had asked if his little sister was domesticated. 'It is treachery to oneself. You give up control over your own happiness, your time, your emotions, your body, your future, your life itself and entrust it to another, betraying your very being, your ownness, your soul. That's what I call treachery.'

She got up from her chair and turned to more practical matters. 'Will you be bringing the cat?'

twenty-two

Heimat

Angelika stayed three days while we discussed practicalities. When she had gone Aunt Marie and I looked at each other mentally mopping our brows.

'Well, I hope they are not all quite so formidable, my little cousin.'

'Klaus-Pierre liked her,' I said happily. 'Did you notice how he always spoke to her in German?'

'Yes, I'll miss him dreadfully, but at last I am confident of his future.'

'So am I. He will miss you too and also Macfidget I suppose. He loves that cat.'

'You must take Macfidget,' said Aunt Marie. 'At least this time we will be able to get proper carrying equipment.'

I looked at the smoky creature, sleeping peacefully in an armchair. 'He must be getting on now. It's more than eight years since we took him from the Levins' apartment.'

'My dear, you and that cat came for six months and stayed six years. I want the house to myself again. He goes with you.'

I realised that behind the humour was truth, that Aunt Marie was one of those women who genuinely preferred to live alone, without husband, children or pets and the complications they brought. She had built such a paradise for herself and I had rudely invaded it and could have gone on doing so for as long as I needed. I hugged her briefly, blinking back the tears.

I wrote to my parents telling them I was going to live with the von Ströbels and that I knew how they had intercepted Kurt's letters, that whatever had been their motive in doing so it had cost

Klaus-Pierre years of unnecessary suffering and that neither of us would ever return to Paris. It was a deeply bitter letter of which I was half ashamed and I was unsurprised when there was no reply. I know now, and I think I knew then, that I should at least have thanked them for the good they had tried to do and expressed some regret for the misery I had brought them, but I was too angry on my son's behalf to do so.

When the day came for me to leave a chauffeur-driven car arrived at the door, just at the time the children were coming out of school, and I knew that Angelika had arranged it deliberately so that they might see Klaus-Pierre departing in style and briefly envy the victim of their taunts. At the station I found myself installed in a first-class carriage and started to wonder which nation had lost the war.

The vet had given me sedatives for Macfidget. Klaus-Pierre also slept but at the border I woke him. 'Klaus-Pierre,' I shook him awake as I reached in my bag for our papers. 'Look, Germany! Heimat.'

He looked drowsily about him, made Klaus's Flore face and fell asleep again.

Despite the cosy words I was not without misgivings, knowing that I was crossing a wider and deeper Rubicon than I had in 1942, that there was a finality about the step I now took, that I was effectively deciding to bring my son up as a German and entrusting myself to a land of strangers. In the von Ströbels I had the utmost confidence but Klaus-Pierre's future would not unfold only within the confines of their home and family.

My doubts grew as the train pulled into a station and I heard, for the first time since 1944, male voices calling to each other in German. One was bad-tempered and suddenly I remembered the soldier in Les Trois Quartiers who had shouted at the sobbing woman who feared for her elderly mother. I thought of the arrogant daily procession along the Champs-Elysées, of the notices of executions, of two Gestapo men chasing a forlorn boy, of the mimed horrors Gerhardt had seen at Dachau, of an empty, looted apartment in which the only living thing spared had been a cat.

As the train moved off I glimpsed a sign in Gothic lettering and fought down panic. What on earth was I doing? Klaus and Kurt had been different but there had been so many others and now I was taking my son to live among such people. Yet Aunt Marie had thought it right.

'Here you have tried to bring Klaus-Pierre up as a von Ströbel among Dessins and you have seen the result. Do not try there to bring him up as a Dessin among von Ströbels. Let the child feel he belongs. Let him be one of them as completely as he can be.'

I recalled those words now, uttered earnestly, urgently, as she had hugged Klaus-Pierre goodbye, but although I knew the advice to be sound I was still afraid.

The train juddered to another halt and, looking out of the window, I saw the carriage was still alongside the platform and watched a family greeting someone who must have alighted when we first stopped. Two small boys hurled themselves at a middle-aged man while an older child struggled with a case far too big and heavy for him. A smiling woman watched them with fond amusement. As the man detached himself from the children and insisted on carrying the case he looked back at the train and, our eyes meeting, we smiled at one another.

I leaned back in my seat, calmed and reassured. They were like any French family. The parents would alternately rejoice in and worry over their children as did parents everywhere, the children would catch chickenpox and measles, play and argue, pass from innocence to curiosity and from curiosity to knowledge of the world about them. So would millions of other children in Germany, France, England, Russia, Africa, China. In 1933 when Hitler had come to power the father I had just seen would have been a young man about to make his way in an uncertain world.

It took several days, delayed trains, changes at busy stations where it was difficult to manage all my luggage in the absence of available porters and food that made me wonder if war had come again before we were on the last lap of the journey through the countryside of northern Germany. Macfidget was showing signs of recovering from the last of his sedatives and Klaus-Pierre was fractious with boredom from seemingly endless travelling when we finally arrived at our destination. It had seemed a journey of unrelieved grey: children on platforms wore grey shorts and jerseys and men grey raincoats; the skies were dull; everywhere were dark, unlit, bomb-damaged buildings; the countryside looked as if the very fields were demoralised and discouraged, crops straggled in the rain.

Willi was waiting on the platform with two small girls whom he introduced as Lotte and Elsa. At the sight of children Klaus-Pierre hid behind me, peeping uncertainly at his half-sister, while I tried not to stare at Willi, realising with a renewed sense of loss that this was how an older Klaus would have looked.

By the time we had loaded the car and I was steeling myself for another long trip with a yowling Macfidget the children were chatting away happily in German. Willi and I spoke in French that they might be less likely to understand when I asked if everyone was still happy with the arrangement.

He nodded. 'I believe I have seen you before, Catherine.'

'You have. You and Klaus were looking at the Eiffel Tower.'

'Ah! How discreet you both were.'

'We had to be. Whatever would you have said?'

'I should have told my little brother not to be such a bloody fool,' Willi replied uncompromisingly, but there was no malice in his voice.

'I wish people would stop blaming him so much. It takes two.'

'He should have thought for two, given your age. How on earth old were you when it all started?'

'Seventeen, but he didn't mean to "start" anything. It was when he came back to Paris after Gerhardt's death and had no one he could trust that we drew so close. I was eighteen then. We were both isolated from those around us, but whereas I had only myself to blame his loneliness was driven by circumstances. Yet he talked of judgement and how we could not escape it. Klaus-Pierre was my doing. His father was always so careful.'

'Not careful enough, it seems. Seventeen! What on earth possessed him? My mother believes it's because we didn't have any youth ourselves. We went from school desks to fight, Klaus and I. Certainly Klaus always enjoyed mixing with the youngsters he taught, finding them less irritating than some of our generation were prone to do and he got immense satisfaction out of stretching their minds, out of enthusing them for his beloved

Scottish history or whatever. After that, life in the army must have been hell when the only contact he would have had with the young would have been giving orders and seeing them obeyed. But none of that adds up to what happened.'

'I think at first he was, as you say, in search of young company. Indeed in those early days I used to wonder if he saw me just as a daughter and I would alternate between finding that reassuring and feeling disappointed. I suppose you could say he was a sort of Uncle Klaus and if we had met in different circumstances then that is probably what he would have been – a family friend. Looking back now, I think I may have been looking for someone to be the sort of father I didn't have, someone uncensorious, humorous, always kind, invariably admiring, undemanding. Then Klaus came back to Paris after Gerhardt's death and wanted something different and suddenly we couldn't live without each other.'

'Even so, my brother must have known the danger. I still have difficulty believing that he could have been so selfish. It just wasn't like Klaus.'

'My parents would give you a similar lament, saying it just wasn't like Catherine. If I hadn't met Klaus and he hadn't met me we should not have acted out of character, but we did meet and we did fall in love and we did act out of character and I don't regret it and, if that rather incautious letter is anything to go by, nor did he.'

Willi's expression momentarily aped my father's when I was in one of my less pliant moods, then he sighed. 'It is all in the past. Let's leave it there until one day we have to explain to the children. It may look different then.'

When I thought of the children I began to laugh and had to think up a reason quickly when Willi asked to share the joke. I could hardly tell him that one of my childhood fantasies was about to come true as I prepared to help look after a grieving widower with six children.

Instead I told him about the past, about how I had come to forget that Germans like Klaus and Kurt were the enemy, about my shock when Klaus had my parents and sister arrested, about how the light, warmth and bustle of the Kommandantur had sometimes seemed more appealing than my emotionally frozen

250

home, about my refusal to typecast people according to which side of the war they were on.

'Kurt told us that Klaus said you once made a very fine speech to that effect. He returned from a violent argument with your father and told Kurt that you had, so to speak, jumped on your soapbox and declaimed in what he described as "the pacifist interest". He said it was quite magnificent and even your father had been impressed.'

I smiled. 'I'm not a pacifist but those two had so much in common that I was nearly mad with frustration at the enmity between them and, anyway, Klaus had just punched my father.'

'I would have thought in the circumstances that it might have been the other way round.'

'No. My father may have been in the right but he was cruel to me whereas Klaus, who many would say had wronged me hugely, was always kind.'

'How confusing,' murmured Willi in the tone of one who cannot think of an appropriate response. Nevertheless it seemed a fair summary.

For a while we were silent as the chatter from the back of the car grew louder and Macfidget protested at the continuation of his bumpy confinement. Then Willi said, 'Here we are. Ströbelweise.'

Ströbelfields. I looked around me in surprise as we made a lengthy drive through a large estate of rolling meadows, fields and woods, before seeing the dark outline of a house in the distance, by which time I would not have been surprised if it had turned out to be a *Schloss*.

'I thought Klaus said you had got rid of most of your land after the Great War.'

'We had to sell off a huge amount but we hung on to this. Our ancestors owned about three times what you now see. My grandfather also kept a vast staff but these days we do most things for ourselves. My father was ruthlessly practical and told us we could choose between pride and survival, then Klaus was clever enough to foresee another war and a lot of our money was invested in Switzerland. We don't starve and Angelika is a pretty shrewd manager.'

I remembered Aunt Marie's urgent pleading and I began to

laugh, not in triumph but relief. *You have nothing to offer this child except poverty, shame and struggle.*

Klaus-Pierre only showed the most momentary confusion when we arrived, exhausted and nervous, to find Mutti on the doorstep waiting to greet us. She was the tall, erect Lotte von Ströbel of Klaus's family photograph, only half a century older.

'Who's that?' he asked.

'Your Granny.' Too late, I realised I was repeating a scene from the past in which my tiny son had been cruelly repulsed and I half expected him to hide behind me in fear. There *was* just a fractional hesitation and then he was running towards her and Mutti was saying, 'My, what a big boy my grandson is.'

They gave me Klaus's room, the one he had grown up in, the one he would have shared with Ellie when they visited and, as I looked at his possessions, his photographs, the relics of his childhood, I knew his family was acknowledging that I was taking Ellie's place, was acknowledging my ownership of Klaus.

Over the next few days as Klaus-Pierre and the other children played noisily I picked up each thing in the room that was his and held it close, smelling him still in the old, tattered dressing gown, smiling wistfully at the childish scrawl which was his name in the front of schoolbooks. I flicked through the lessons, trying to imagine him learning them, puzzling over them, developing his formidable brain. I ran an old train engine along the wood surrounding the carpet, I wept into a pair of rolled-up socks, but I knew the time had come to let go. *When you begin to forget do not resist, it is better that way.*

I remembered still but from a greater distance. I saw him as a man with a man's contradictions; strong and brave when nothing but his life was at risk, weak and perhaps afraid when he faced being without me; in control of a city but not in control of his own feelings and desires; protective yet exposing me to horror; farsighted but anchored in the needs of the day; kindness itself but daily endangering my future; determined in so much but hopelessly irresolute in love. I remembered him singing, churning out impurity in the purest of voices while, in his darkest hour, he forgot I was there, hearing in my mind, as though the strains were echoing around me still, the notes of that soldier's song.

My idol had feet of clay but I knew that many, whose lives were models of rectitude and who would regard an affair with an innocent young girl with scandalised horror, would not have shown a tenth of his courage and compassion in defying that brutal regime. He was as other men but I was certain I wanted no other, could not believe any might measure up to the stature of Klaus von Ströbel.

Eventually, my grief sated, I went outside to the large black shape standing some twenty metres from the kitchen. The door of the barn was heavy as I pushed it open through cobwebs and breathed the must and closeness. It seemed the von Ströbels had not been able to face using the building again. I looked up at the rafters.

'Go in peace,' I whispered, not to the spirit of Gerhardt, but to that of Klaus and I knew he heard me, that he saw I was safe and happy at last and that I had brought his son home. For both of us the judgement was over and somewhere, in a place I could not see, he made his Flore face and turned from me to rest in peace with Ellie.

epilogue

Berlin 1961

That is my story, one with neither hero nor heroine, but which I must soon tell Klaus-Pierre, because it is his story too and he is now sixteen, the age I was when I first met Klaus von Ströbel, and I am thirty-six. I am catching Klaus up and he has never become the old man I once tried to picture.

Of course my son has known for many years why he bears a different surname from the children with whom he has grown up, that his father and I could not marry, that Lotte's mother was Klaus's lawful wife, that neither of his parents emerges from the tale with much credit. Now that Lotte has married and Elsa is away in Switzerland, studying at Berne, Klaus-Pierre is the last of his generation still living at Ströbelfields, but even that is about to change because next month he goes to school in England. I am uncertain, feeling it is too soon, but Willi insists.

'It is what Klaus would have wanted,' he told me. 'If human beings are to live at peace they must grow up together, become men together, understand each other from the early years of their lives.'

I agree only because Klaus-Pierre seems very enthusiastic about the idea but I know that I must now tell him everything because his story is not one only of love but also of hatred.

I recognise now that I blamed my family too much, that if Klaus was an abnormally brave man so was my father whose resistance activities were aimed at the very regime with which Klaus was taking such risks. My mother may have been weak when dealing with her husband, but both were trying to do what was right. Consumed with hatred, they concentrated on my so-called treachery in loving an enemy and all but forgot the much greater issue of his married status. Even at this distance it seems an odd order of priorities. I was young and silly and longing to be in love. Had their brains not been addled with hate they must surely have handled it better.

I regret I was not older, but not because I wish the past undone. Had I been only a little older I could have supported Klaus better and he might have confided in me what he was doing to help Jews in Paris and been less lonely in that terrifying endeavour. I hate to think how he must have borne such dread and risk alone, but I realise that, even if I did not play as full a part as I might have done had I known all, I was still his comfort, his support, his rock and, by so being, I played some small role in helping the persecuted, which must be my claim to forgiveness from those I wronged.

For one act, however, there is no forgiveness. I will never forget nor excuse what my family did to Klaus-Pierre.

I look at Kurt and he knows I have been remembering. He smiles sadly.

'When I was posted to Paris, I just couldn't believe my luck. Regiments were being sent to Russia and North Africa and Heaven knows where and I got Paris. It was the jewel in our crown, chaps were always coming there for sightseeing and there was no fighting, just a quiet city to administer. And now . . .' he looks down at the ruins of his limbs.

I place my hand on the shattered remains of his one leg. 'Dear Kurt. You were always so kind to me.'

'I would never have dared to be anything else. Herr General von Ströbel would have sent me to the Russian Front.'

'Oh, no he wouldn't. You were the nephew of top brass – he told me so.'

Kurt smiles again. 'Still, it was a tough war.'

I am about to ask why when Willi interrupts to say we had really better be moving and he pushes the wheelchair into motion. Kurt gives a small groan for which he immediately apologises and I ask him in alarm what is the matter.

'Nothing. I am just a little stiff from being carried in that blanket. Now I know what poor old Macfidget felt like when he was finally let out of the pillowcase.'

'We must have looked pretty silly.'

'Nothing like as silly as I did when Klaus made me carry that caterwauling brute into the Kommandantur. You should have heard the jeers of my colleagues. It was months before they would let me forget it. The Colonel of course just came behind at a great distance as if the smell and the noise were nothing to do with him. I felt like resigning my commission on the spot.'

I laugh, remembering Kurt as he was then. His hair is beginning to grey now and it is much thinner but his kindness and humour are as they ever were. I see the way the crow's feet crinkle round his eyes when he in turn laughs.

Something stirs in me, very faintly, something reminiscent of another time when I yearned to smooth away a man's anxiety lines. I look at him sharply.

'Why did you say it was a tough war? In Paris you had everything. You ate well, you drank well, you were warm, you didn't have to fight.'

He looks at me, hesitating, and I know, with wonder, what he is going to say. 'Yes, but I spent two whole years as miserable as the grave because I was in love with my commanding officer's girlfriend.'

We are all silent and Willi makes some excuse to move ahead of us, leaving me to manage the wheelchair.

I think of how Kurt walked beside the moving train when I was leaving Paris. Had I not been so preoccupied with the grief of my own love I might have wondered before why he had done so.

'Did Klaus know?'

He looks up at me from the wheelchair. 'I had thought not, but when I went back and reported to him that you were safe on your journey to Aix and how you had hugged me on the platform he looked at me and said, "Congratulations. You've been waiting all war for that." It was the first time I had heard him laugh for a long while. Then he said, "Come back for her after the war. I want her for my own but I will never leave Ellie and France will be a seething cauldron of hatred. Get her away, if you can, but don't tell me because I would be jealous enough to kill you." He said it again when we were leaving Paris: "Come back for her".

'He loved you, Catherine.' Kurt adds, 'And so did I. Of course I wanted to come back for you but this happened and I could have been of no use.' He indicates his wrecked legs. 'Anyway I knew you had eyes only for Klaus, even though you would know he was dead.'

I look at him and I realise that I might just be able to love again for the first time since Klaus von Ströbel.

We both look back at the girls who are watching the activity from their window. I wonder what the future will hold for them. Will they resist the Russians or just put up with them? Will they hate them or will one of those girls fall helplessly, passionately, treacherously in love with an enemy? I look keenly at the one with the long fair hair. Whatever happens they are facing a harsh winter: they are on the wrong side of the wall.